FOREWARNED

FOREWARNED

A Daphne Ann Post Novel

By

Tracey S. Phillips

GENRE: Paranormal Thriller

This is a work of fiction. All of the names, characters, organizations, places and events portrayed in the novel are either products of the author's imagination or are used fictitiously. While some of the locations are real, the author has added fictional touches to further the story. Any resemblance to real or actual events. Locales, or persons, living or dead, is entirely coincidental.

ISBN: 979-8-9908191-1-5 (paperback)

ISBN: 979-8-9908191-2-2 (audiobook)

Cover Design by Tatiana Vila at Vila Designs

Lake House illustration by Dylan A. Phillips

Lakeweed illustrations by Tracey S. Phillips and edited on Canva.

All illustrations copyright © by Tracey S. Phillips

First edition; August 2025

TABLE OF CONTENTS

Dedicated to my grandmother Lucina
because she was the first to tell me a real ghost story.

"Monsters are real, and ghosts are real too.
They live inside us, and sometimes, they win."
—Stephen King

CHAPTER 1

A MONOTONE SONG

Carlson, Indiana; June 4, 1976: Daphne Ann Post

"Who's gonna see the lake first?" My mom sang the monotone song ending on a mystery note with a minor third. It conjured the kind of anticipation and excitement I felt watching scary movies. And this time it triggered a new dark melody. I heard it in the sinister thrum of the car's engine and in the wind roaring through the windows.

Nothing seemed to have changed along East Lake Shore Drive. The winding narrow road that led to Nana's cottage in Carlson, Indiana was treelined on the lakeside, farmland on the other. Lush greenery and sprouting corn grew beneath cloud-specked Indiana sky as far as the eye could see. On the breeze, faint smells of cornflowers, manure from nearby farmland, and lakeweed.

Wind from the open car window blew my short haircut, styled like the Olympic ice skater Dorothy Hammill, in every direction. I searched between the trees for the telltale reflection of the sun on the lake. I wanted something happy to cheer me up. Today was my fifteenth birthday.

"Who's gonna see the lake first?" my mom repeated.

"It's right there, Marianne." I'd been calling my mom by her first name since she divorced my dad last year.

"I saw it!" announced my younger brother Brandon. "I saw the lake first!" Brandon was nine and a half. He was born when I was five, and from the moment he could walk, Marianne and Dad expected me to help look after him. Most days it took all three of us to keep track of him.

"Why are you still calling me that, Daphne?" Marianne asked.

I shrugged. The only way I knew how to deal with my rage about the recent divorce was to disassociate from her. To pretend she was just a friend. To call her Marianne.

Despite knowing I'd be expected to babysit my brother and two younger cousins, I usually felt excited about our yearly summer trip. But this year, I resented Marianne for pulling me away. I wanted to celebrate my birthday with Dad. I wanted to start driver's ed. I wanted to be with my friends.

Who was I kidding? I didn't have any friends. Not after Ruth turned everyone against me.

Icy dread laced with a sense of danger crept up my arms. Not my typical reaction to approaching the lake for the summer. I loved to water-ski, and I was good at it. I loved to lie on the dock and listen to the water lap against the pillars. I loved the musty, mildewy smell of the cottage. I loved searching for fossils and beads in the clear shallow water.

This chill skittering from my elbows to my hairline evoked a sense of déjà vu. It reminded me of the day my best friend Ruth stopped being my friend.

It's all your fault, Ruth had said. I'd believed it. My stomach flipped and I wanted to throw up. Ruth made me feel so guilty.

Marianne said, "When we get there, I need help unloading the car before you can play with your cousins." She glanced in the rearview mirror at Brandon in the back seat. After the divorce, my mom changed her look and started dating again. Today she wore a paisley lace-up top and bell-bottom jeans. Her new shag haircut showed off bright green eyes and long hoop earrings accentuated her high cheekbones.

I looked nothing like my mother.

Between the trees the lake glittered as if sprinkled with shards of broken glass. Lavish summer homes with three- and four-car garages lined the shore. Some, newly remodeled, towered above the rest with third-story additions. Others behind the trees were unpretentious cabins, blending in with the forested shore. An adjacent golf course with green carpet-covered hills smelled like fresh-mowed grass.

Trespassing on the golf course was forbidden. I imagined what it would be like to run on the soft grassy hills in bare feet. I wanted to sit in the gazebo high on the hill on the far side of the fairway. Though I'd never been there, I imagined it had a wonderful view of the lake.

As we drew closer to our cottage, the prickles had fled my arms to reside in my scalp. I tried to ignore the sensation and the feeling of dread. The last time I had feelings like this, my friend Ruth almost died. It happened when I touched her. She had welcomed me into her house, and she'd hugged me. The warning had become so clear in my mind—like the developing image of a Polaroid picture—that I had to tell Ruth. I pleaded with her and tried to stop her from skating on the ice.

Now I wished I'd never said anything. Because maybe then it never would have happened. Maybe if I hadn't told Ruth, we would still be friends. My cheeks heated with shame and embarrassment, and I turned my face to the open window.

Weirdo. Freak. It was all my fault.

The road wound down a steep hill. At the bottom on the left, our sky-blue Victorian cottage, with its peaked roof and scroll details, was the oldest home on the lake. White window trim popped against the pale blue siding and dark gray shingles. Mowed grass full of pink clover and rows of orange and yellow lilies blooming along the sidewalk led to the familiar screened porch. Gabled windows and a spire on the crest of the roof gave it charm like no other house on the lake.

Duke, our half golden retriever, half collie mutt, knew this road as well as we did. He stuck his long nose out the back window of the Volkswagen bus and the wind blew back his floppy ears. When he snorted into the wind, Brandon cried out, "Gross. Duke blew snot all over my face." He wiped his face on his shirt sleeve.

"Look, your cousins are already here." Marianne pulled into the carport, where Auntie Beth and my cousins were unloading their station wagon.

We piled out of the VW bus, and Duke led the way.

"I'm going to play with Sammy," Brandon said.

"No, you're not. You need to help unload the car first," Marianne said.

Brandon opened a white-painted wrought iron gate leading to the yard and ran to Sammy. The two boys body-slammed each other in a frenetic hug, Brandon's wild blond hair contrasting with Sammy's neat brown military cut. They chattered and ran toward the lake with Duke at their heels.

"Brandon, what did I say?" Marianne called.

"Happy fifteenth birthday, Daphne." Auntie Beth pulled a suitcase from the back seat and set it on the driveway. A brown-leather barrette held back her long red hair. She wore a light-orange flower-print T-shirt and overalls. She gave me a warm hug.

"Thanks," I said. She reminded me that I'd rather be with my dad.

"You've grown six inches since I saw you." Auntie Beth was exaggerating but not by much. I'd grown taller than Marianne this spring. Now I could see the top of my aunt's head too.

"She's growing up before our eyes." Marianne sparkled with something like pride. I chose to ignore it.

My aunt picked up a laundry basket full of bedding and headed toward the house. "Aubenaubee Lodge is open, so come on inside." Years ago, Nana had named the house after Aubenaubee Creek that ran beside it and into the lake.

"Happy birthday." Margot, who was twelve, brushed a lock of straight, walnut-brown hair away from her face. "It never feels like summer until we get here." Her awkward, open-mouth smile revealed a flash of silver from the metal in her mouth.

"You got braces!" I said, "let me see."

Margot showed them off with a grin more like a grimace. "They hurt and I have headgear."

"Look what I got." I tossed my head and pointed to two new, gold-post earrings. Marianne had finally let me pierce my ears.

"I know everyone does it, but I don't want mine pierced." Margot held a small gray-blue suitcase. "Did you bring your Breyer horses? Misty of Chincoteague and her foal?"

"Yeah. The two you like best." I smiled.

"Dad got me a new Breyer horse. She's a bay with a long mane and tail. I can't wait to show you." Margot was on the cusp of putting childish games away, but for some reason she wasn't quite ready to.

Marianne opened the tailgate of the VW bus and handed me my suitcase. "The house is unlocked. Take your things up to your room and come help with the rest, please. I've no doubt the boys aren't coming back."

"Okay." I longed to see the familiar cottage. It reminded me of happier days when my parents still loved each other. Days filled with summer sports and sunshine. Lately, the only activity that gave me joy was playing the piano. "Did Nana tune the piano this spring?"

"I asked Nana about it," Marianne said. "That old console has seen better days. The technician said it needs too much work."

My hopes to improve the Chopin *Étude* crumbled. "How will I practice?"

"There will be other things to do, Daph. You'll be so busy you won't even miss it."

"You don't know anything!" I pushed open the wrought iron gate and slammed it. This summer was quickly becoming the worst ever. It was Marianne's fault. *No Dad, no friends, and now, no piano.* Life sucked.

I passed the little house attached to the back of the carport on the way to our big Victorian cottage and looked over my left shoulder. The neighbor's house was still dark. The summer renters hadn't arrived yet. But from the black windows, in the quiet stillness, I heard whispered warnings, and I knew, I just knew, someone in that house would die this summer.

WHEN YOU'RE NOT A JET

Daphne:

The cottage smelled like summer, mildew, and memories. Margot and I took to our familiar bedroom at the top of the stairs, my bed closest to the door and Margot's next to the closet. Though I'd never say so to my younger cousin, I hated that creepy cedar closet. When I brought my suitcases upstairs, goosebumps rose on my arms again.

I kept repeating to myself, "There's nothing to be afraid of. There's nothing to be afraid of."

I had to peek into the closet to be sure no one hid inside. I had to reassure myself that no ghosts would jump out at me. Because it always seemed like someone—a soldier—*was* there. Though I never saw him, I'd been afraid of that closet since I was little.

I peered at the smelly dark clothes hanging there. Mold and faded perfume mixed with the fruity cedar fragrance and tickled my nose. Dirty curtains and musty-smelling pillows lay in a pile atop an old trunk on the floor of the closet. Opaque zippered clothing bags hung from hangers and contained men's suits and smoking jackets—I'd opened them last summer. In the corner, an old set of curtain rods leaned into one another, sharing their misery and rejection. I rattled the rusty lock on the mildewed trunk and a parade of invisible ants marched up my spine, daring me to be afraid.

I sprung the trunk lid open in one swift movement and it clattered

against the curtain rods. The sudden noise set my heart racing as I glanced down at folded blankets and moth-eaten linen. I quickly closed the trunk and straightened everything. In my mind, I saw a man in a faded green uniform with badges on the upper left of his jacket. A folded rectangular hat on his head. Gold stripes on his cuffs. I imagined he was sadly watching years pass.

I shut the door. Stiff hinges resisted as if fighting back, so I threw my hip into it, securely closing it.

The prickles on my arms subsided.

"Checking the closet again? You do that every year." Margot set her hairbrush and headgear out on the dresser.

"So. I don't like it." I unzipped my suitcase. When I saw the book of Chopin *Études* on top, a wave of sadness came over me. As soon as I unpacked, I'd play something. I needed to see for myself what shape the piano was in. More than anything, I longed to play music. To escape through Chopin or Ravel, or Debussy.

Stairs creaked outside the room, and I peered out. Following Auntie Beth, Marianne carried the laundry basket full of bedding through the library across the hall to the sleeping porch.

Auntie Beth went into her bedroom at the bend in the hallway. "House cleaners came last week," she said. "They told Mother there were mice in the sleeping porch again." The name sleeping porch came from the old days when homes like this had no air conditioning. People made their beds outside to cool off on the very hot summer nights. "The mice chewed up bags of snack food in the dresser drawers. I think the boys left them there."

"I thought we cleaned up before we left." Marianne brought sheets into my room.

Downstairs the one and only phone rang. Marianne flew down the carpeted stairs, passing beneath a taxidermized stag head. Curious, I followed, unable to keep my gaze from the stag's glass eyes. We didn't often get phone calls here.

The yellow phone was ringing on a small table behind the swinging door between the kitchen and the living room. Marianne swung the door to the kitchen closed and lifted the receiver.

"Hello, Aubenaubee Lodge." Marianne stretched the phone cord and leaned against the sofa. "Hello, Mother. The house is fine. We just got here and we're unloading the cars now. Yes, Beth told me about the mice in the sleeping porch. When are you coming?"

In the living room near Marianne, I pulled the chain on a dusty lamp perched on top of the painted console piano. It illuminated traces of past summers—cigarette burns, rings from sweaty drink glasses, and melted wax. I sat on the cracked leather piano bench. Grasping the rusty knobs, I jiggled open the rollaway key cover. Dirty white keys were chipped and split. The white ivory had peeled off the bass G key, exposing bare wood. Another burn mark scarred the highest C, as if someone forgot their cigarette while singing a tune.

I dragged my fingers across the keys without playing a sound. When I finally pressed down A440, the A above middle C, my fingers flew along an ugly, discordant chromatic scale.

Marianne waved at me. "Can you stop? I can't hear Mother."

I wanted to ask Nana to send a piano tuner out. She and Dad were the only family members who understood my deep connection with music. Nana loved her community theater productions and musicals and, though she didn't sing anymore, she'd once starred in a Broadway show.

Auntie Beth rounded the corner from the stairway and opened the extra wide double doors and secured them with heavy iron doorstops. A breeze blew in from the flagstone patio near the lakeshore, clearing out the musty, mildewy smells. "Is Mother worried about the damage from the mice? Tell her it's hardly noticeable."

Marianne relayed the message as Auntie Beth busied herself with opening windows. She left through the kitchen door.

While Marianne talked, my fingers made the motions of playing E major scale without actually pushing the keys down. I longed to play a sonata or an étude and imagined the pure melodies cheering me up and chasing the whispered warnings from my mind.

Nana's voice droned from the phone like the teacher on the Charlie Brown specials. Unintelligible and scolding. Nana had helped finance Dad's deli, The Asparagus Sandwich, in Indianapolis. She'd given him money and expected to be paid back. When the divorce was finalized, she also helped Marianne buy another house. It was a lot of money, and Marianne couldn't afford much now that she was single. The way my mom shopped with coupons and looked for sale specials, I worried that someday she wouldn't have any money left.

"—loaned him. He will pay you back, Mother." Tension poured off Marianne like vapor from dry ice. "Before you hang up, Daphne wants to know about the piano. Can we have it tuned?" Marianne made eye contact with me and shook her head.

"Oh. You bought a new piano? I'll let her know."

I threw up my hands in a cheer. "Yes!" This changed everything.

"They're shipping it next week," Marianne told me as she hung up.

I played a happy chord progression that fell flat. Notes that should have been cheerful and uplifting made sour discordant sounds.

Beneath the sturdy maple tree, hordes of gnats swarmed in the warm rays where Margot and I settled in for a morning of play. There was nothing better to do until the piano arrived. *One week?* Waiting was torture. Margot laid towels over the damp grass between the neighbor's house and the Victorian cottage. I spread out the horses and toys and waved gnats away from my face and mouth.

I gazed across the lake while Margot dressed the toy horses in blankets and saddles.

Last night we celebrated my birthday. If I could describe the day with music, it would have been like Chopin's "Revolutionary Étude" with those long descending minor arpeggios and big thunderous chords. I really wished Dad could have been here. It was the first birthday I'd ever celebrated without him. Around dinnertime, he'd called. I didn't tell him how much I missed him or how sad I was. I hadn't told anyone.

After dinner, the family sang "Happy Birthday." I opened a few more presents from Margot and Auntie Beth. Marianne finally came through and gave me the bikini I'd tried on while shopping with Dad. It made me feel so grown up. I don't know how she knew which one, but it was perfect.

Margot pushed away a long lock of hair that fell across her thick glasses and focused on fastening the saddle on her Breyer horse. She picked up a short length of string and began tying it in a double loop. Since a very young age, she'd been riding and competing in horse shows. "Can you put Misty's halter on?"

"I don't know how." I'd ridden horses a few times at a dude ranch in Wyoming, but never learned anything about the tack.

"Like this." Margot demonstrated, but my mind was elsewhere. My gaze locked on the calm surface of the lake beyond the buoys.

I tried tying a halter on Misty of Chincoteague as Margot had shown me. "Is your dad coming this weekend?"

"I don't know." Margot pranced Beauty in the grass.

"How can you not know? If my dad was coming, I'd be so excited." I plucked a clover from the yard. "He's coming to visit later this month."

"How often do you get to see him?"

"Every weekend. Except . . . now that we're in Carlson for the summer, I won't see him for a while. He's too busy with his deli." The Asparagus Sandwich took most of his time these days. I mindlessly trotted Misty over a stick in the grass. "You're so lucky."

Margot looked up. Her glasses fogged near the bridge of her nose. "Why?"

"Your dad comes home every night to hug you and tell you stories." I longed for those days.

Margot turned toward the lake and seemed lost in thought. "It's not like that. It's not what you think."

"What do you mean? Your dad loves you and Sammy. He still loves your mom. They don't fight all the time like my parents do." I only knew that I never liked Uncle Chuck. Whenever he hugged me, I got the creeps.

"You don't know, do you? Sometimes I wish he wouldn't come home at all."

I tried to recall something, any reason why Margot should feel that way. Could it be that I didn't know Margot at all? And we were practically sisters.

The last time I saw Uncle Chuck, it was Easter at Nana's house. He'd taken Marianne outside to have a talk with her. He pointed his finger, making accusations at her. She was red-faced and crying. Auntie Beth just stood there. Silent. She didn't defend her sister from him, and that struck a minor chord in my heart.

The entire day replayed in my mind like an episode of *All in the Family*. Only Uncle Chuck never apologized at the end of the day as Archie Bunker would have. And Marianne went home in tears. Uncle Chuck never would have behaved that way if Dad had been there. Dad would have stood up to him. He would have stood up for his wife.

After Margot played silently for a few minutes, I asked, "Did something happen?" I wasn't sure if I wanted the answer.

Margot focused on her horses. "Forget it. Forget I said anything." She pushed her glasses up on her nose and lowered her gaze to her Breyer horse. She adjusted the bridle and saddle, then pretended to groom her with a small brush.

Movement in the neighbor's yard caught my eye. Just over the stone wall that abutted the neighbor's yard, two boys were carrying a pair of water skis and vests toward the lake. The blond boy looked close to my age and the other was a taller, darker, more mature version of the blond one. The younger boy, with a smile as big and bright as the sun, wore wire-rimmed aviator sunglasses. The older one shook his tousled shoulder-length brown hair.

The two boys walked so confidently, with their broad shoulders set and heads held high. They moved like dancers on stage. Physical. Athletic. I wanted to meet them. They looked like movie stars. Like the cool kids in the musicals Nana took me to see last year. The music from *West Side Story*—"When you're a Jet"—drifted through my mind. I wanted to follow them wherever they went.

They turned their gazes toward us, and the younger boy nodded a hello. A weird sense of déjà vu coursed through me, as if I'd seen him before.

The dark-haired one said, "Babies. Look at them."

Mortification warmed my cheeks. Did they think I was a little kid?

The boys continued walking to their dock and removed the cover on their speedboat.

"What are you looking at?" Margot held out the saddle for Misty. "Can you put this on?"

A sense of doom like a dark storm cloud spread across the lawn. I didn't want to play anymore.

CHAPTER 3

I'M GOING TO BE AN ACTRESS

June 6, 1976: Lara Vaughan

"We need to stock up the fridge. I'm not driving back and forth to The Pig every time you run out of Honeycomb cereal." Mother hated grocery shopping. She rarely cooked as it was.

Lara thought menial tasks like shopping for food and vacuuming only reminded her mother that after marrying Father she'd traded in her dream of becoming a lawyer for being the wife of a prosecutor. Her mother's family had money, lots of it. But she'd married for love. Lara almost choked whenever she heard that story. It usually ended with her mother saying she should have gone back to school. Followed her dream. Because being a housewife, raising three kids and answering Father's beck and call like some fifties sitcom wife had made her bitter.

"I can drive," Lara said.

Mother peered at her through the rearview mirror. "Good. I have a busy schedule this summer."

This summer was already going wrong. Lounging against the car door of her mother's Lincoln Continental, Lara Vaughan straightened her legs on the roomy back seat and tuned out the staticky oldies radio station. Mother insisted they all spend the summer in Carlson, Indiana because Phillip, Lara's older brother, got a job at Carlson Academy. Camp counselor or something. And Mother had friends who summered there. She could spend her days playing bridge and tennis and who knows what-all with a gimlet in one hand and an Eve cigarette in the other.

Lara had no one to confide in but Phillip. She missed him since he went to college. He used to call every weekend and tell her all the fun things he was doing there. She envied him for his parties and independence and longed for the days when she could finally be on her own.

"Bacon for BLTs, Wonder Bread, Coke, Colby cheese, Doritos . . ." In the front seat, Lara's younger brother Lewis was rattling off all the food he wanted from The Pig.

She gazed out the car window and thought someday she'd move away from all the cornfields and hicks in this backward state.

Someday I'll escape.

Since she was twelve, Lara wanted to be a fashion model for one of the big magazines. She subscribed to *Glamour, Vogue, Mademoiselle,* and *Teen.* Finally last summer, for her sweet sixteen, Lara's parents took her to New York to get a modeling portfolio.

They had stayed in a Manhattan high-rise with Father's friend, an heiress—the daughter of some millionaire—and her lover. Lara had a photo shoot with a photographer from *Elle* magazine. She'd posed in a doorway as a girl-next-door type with bright pink lipstick, then lounging on a chaise as a sultry vixen, in a low-cut black beaded number. In Lara's favorite photos she wore a burgundy hat tilted over one blue eye.

She could be whoever they wanted. Hadn't she proven that?

She wanted to move to California, or New York, or Paris. She wanted to be a model or an actress and imagined her name on a movie poster.

Besides, Mother's money secured Lara's future. The *Elle* photographer said she was too old for the runways. Maybe she'd get a job modeling for some clothing catalog. Or—if she couldn't become a fashion model—she wanted to go to California and become an actress. When they read *Desire Under the Elms* in English, Mr. Trotter chose Lara to read Abbie's lines out loud.

I was good as Abbie. She could see herself in a blockbuster movie, a bigger star than Jodie Foster or Sissy Spacek. *God knows I'm prettier than both of them.*

In New York, Mother and the heiress smoked their cigarettes and pot when they thought no one was looking. They mixed cocktails for breakfast and sipped champagne in the afternoon. The heiress's lover poured champagne for Lara too. Lara fondly remembered him, and the giddy feeling of the champagne.

Lara watched out the window as they passed small houses in the small town of Carlson. Next year when she graduated from high school, she'd get away from Hickville. It couldn't come soon enough. She didn't want what Mother wanted—to go to Sarah Lawrence or Vassar for her obligatory degree. She didn't have patience for four years of school. For what? To learn how to be the wife of a wealthy man?

Like Mother? God!

If she'd grown up anyplace but godforsaken Indiana, she'd already be famous. She planned to go to the West Coast where she'd meet a rich young producer. Then she'd become an actress and host parties for the rich and famous, have luncheons with Hollywood actresses and politicians' wives.

In the front seat, her younger brother Lewis rolled down his window. The stench of manure forced Lara to cover her mouth and nose. She inhaled the perfume from her wrist, Opium by Yves Saint Laurent.

"Close that, Lewis," Mother said. "My hair." Mother's perfect hair. She'd used half a can of Aqua Net to make it stiff as a paper doll's.

"Sorry, Mother. The smell." Lewis slowly rolled the window up with his nose to the wind.

"It will go away." Mother could ignore the most obnoxious intrusion.

Lewis turned to look at Lara and she scowled at him, mocking their mother in silent protest. She mouthed the words *it will go away.*

Lewis smiled. "Father's looking for a job for me this summer."

"Since when?" Mother said, keeping her gaze on the road. Lara wondered too. Lewis was only fifteen.

"I told him I want to be a lawyer someday. He's asking around the courthouse if anyone needs an assistant."

No wonder Father favored him, Lara thought. So compliant. So predictable. Jealousy seeped out as she glared at the back of his head.

"That's silly," Mother said. "You're spending the summer in Carlson. You can golf and water-ski. You don't need a job. You're not one of those people."

"Those people, Mother?" Lara asked. "Like Phillip? He's working."

"He's in college." Mother scratched the back of her neck.

Neither of their parents supported Phillips's choice. He'd won a hockey scholarship and wanted to ice-skate for the rest of his life. Lara didn't get it either.

"What difference does that make?" Lara asked. But she knew. Phillip had refused to fall in line with Father's wishes. Once Phillip had gone away to college on a sports scholarship, Father refused to support him. Phillip was following his dream. Lara respected him for that.

"Phillip is on his own."

Lara twirled her long blond hair. "Isn't that the truth."

"That's not the point, Lara," Mother said, catching Lara's eye in the rearview mirror as she pulled into the grocery store parking lot.

"Why can't I stay in Indianapolis with Father this summer?" Lewis asked.

"Why can't I stay in Indianapolis with Father," Lara said to mimic her younger brother.

"Shut up, Lara. You're just jealous because Father likes me."

"He likes me too!" Lara reached over the headrest and pulled Lewis's hair.

"He loves you both. Now stop it." Mother parked the car.

"Lara pulled my hair."

"Don't whine, Lewis. It's not becoming."

Baby. And now Lara was stuck with him for the whole summer.

CHAPTER 4

WHISPERED WARNING

Daphne

Overnight, the thunderstorm lit up our dark bedroom. I lay awake listening to the trills and escalation of raindrops on the roof above. As always, the storm came from west to east, crossing the lake before it reached Aubenaubee Lodge.

I remembered rainy days with the family—Dad was always there—sitting in the living room and watching the weather fronts blow toward us from across the lake. The rain whipped waves into a frenzy. Water splashed up over the dock and onto the lawn, rocking boats in the lifts and carrying blow-up floaties to Timbuktu. Dad would tell us it was just a storm. *Just a storm.*

A light knock on the bedroom door startled me. I just reached the crystal door handle from my bed, and it opened with a squeak. "Are your windows closed?" Auntie Beth whispered.

"Yes." Light from the hallway lit a narrow strip across both beds. Curled in a ball under her blankets, Margot slept heavily.

"Just checking. Go back to sleep." My aunt closed the door and left me in utter darkness.

I sat up and listened to the rain *tickety-tac* on the windows. A flash of lightning illuminated the tree. Leafy tendrils swept the air like a long witch's broom. As soon as the blackness of night returned, I began to count.

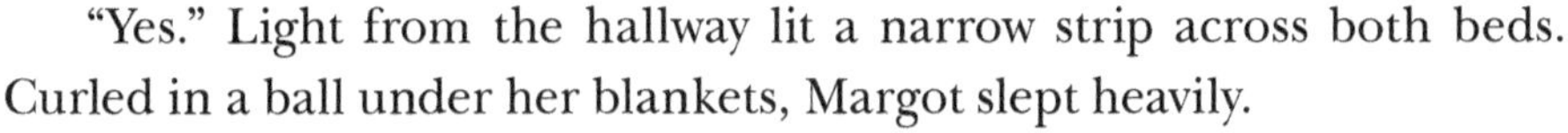

One, one thousand. Two, one thousand. Three, one thousand . . .

I got to five before the boom shook the floor and rattled the window glass. A door closed somewhere in the house. Rain pelted the glass and another flash behind the giant sycamore momentarily blinded me.

One, one thousand, two—

Thunder roared overhead. The closet door popped open. I turned my head slowly toward it, eyeing the dark interior warily.

Margot rustled her bed covers. "Daphne?"

"It's okay. I'm right here." With my gaze locked on the closet door, I climbed into bed with Margot. I curled up against her warm body and put an arm around her.

"Okay. I love you," Margot said and rolled over sleepily.

"I love you too." I needed comforting as well. With one eye still on the closet door, I pulled the blankets over my shoulders.

Another crack of lightning illuminated the tree waving wildly in the wind. I hoped I'd never have to go out on the lake in a storm like that. I imagined the waves thrashing against the boat and the spray and raindrops soaking me. Blinding me.

I closed my eyes.

One, one thousand—The explosion of thunder came quickly.

"It's just a storm." I held Margot tightly and looked at the closet. "It's just a storm."

I awoke tucked in beside Margot with the sun streaming through the windows. It reminded me that, like my parent's marriage, nothing was permanent.

After breakfast, I stripped down to my new bikini bathing suit and bare feet. I didn't think of myself as pretty. The flat triangles of the top covered what little I had for boobs. I was way behind the girls in my class. Sylvia had been wearing a bra since she was ten. I rubbed the red mosquito bites dotting my long legs, wishing they would go away, and regretted touching them as they began to itch.

With a beach towel slung over my arm, I sped down the carpeted stairs, beneath the stuffed stag head mounted above the stairs. Hating its watchful glass eyes, I zipped through the back hallway with its un-lit, shadowy corners and into the bright living room. This year I was tall enough to touch the ceiling. I dragged my fingers along the low beadboard.

The rest of the family were already out on the dock. Though being alone in the old house gave me the creeps, I went to the piano and pushed back the rollaway key cover. My music was still in the bedroom, since I figured I wouldn't get the chance to practice until the new piano arrived.

I set my towel on the chair and sat at the worn leather bench anyway. My fingers hovered over the keys as I recalled the first notes of Chopin's *Trois Études* No. 1. It began with a six-note minor phrase that was repeated twice. The third time through the phrase, it changed, ascending to a major third—giving the listener a brief moment of hope—before returning to minor and settling there.

I played the first three notes and added the fourth, B flat. That key made an unfortunate plink instead of a clear tone. As I hit the last note in the phrase, a sour sound made me pull my hand away from the keys. I made a face.

Still hopeful, I thought perhaps the rest wasn't so bad. Perhaps I could play it anyway . . . My left hand connected with the introductory F minor arpeggio. I knew the way it should sound. The noise emanating from this—*instrument*—was not the étude I knew. The piano was so out of tune that the ugly, raucous sound hurt my nearly perfect-pitch ears. I tried again, hoping for a different result, and cringed.

Longing for a tune I recognized, or something familiar to bring a little joy, I tried scales. C major became A minor, then transitioned to F major and D minor. Across the keys, notes ranged from slightly flat to very dissonant. Disheartened and disappointed, I dragged the key cover shut and went outside to join the others on the dock.

In the yard, clover, creeping Charlie, and small purple flowers punctuated the short green grass. Half-buried paving stones near the lake led to the dock. Our cottage was the only residence on this side of the lake with direct access to the water. Uphill either way, the others had steep approaches and staircases leading to the shore.

I looked over at the neighbor's house. All was quiet on their dock. There was no sign that the neighbors were home. *Just as well,* I thought. I didn't want to meet them after what they'd said.

Babies. I wasn't a baby.

The painted white dock drubbed and clunked as I walked out to join the rest. At the end, the light blue Hydrodyne boat Nana bought sat on a lift with a white plastic cover.

Marianne and Auntie Beth lay on towels with bottles of Hawaiian Tropic tanning oil and plastic glasses full of iced tea. Margot, in shorts and a T-shirt, dangled her feet in the water. Sammy stood on the ladder, dabbling his toes in the cold, spring-fed lake. Brandon sat cross-legged on the other side of the dock, toying with the cover of Uncle Chuck's prize vintage speedboat.

"Leave it alone," Marianne said. Her short shag haircut stuck out like fringe from the blue bandanna on her head. Long hoop earrings hung beside her thin neck.

"I just wanted to sit in the boat," Brandon said, backing away. His mop of hair fell into his eyes.

"Not until your Uncle Chuck gets here. You know the rules."

It was a stupid rule. "Why can't he sit in the boat?" I asked.

"Don't start, Daphne," Marianne said.

"Nobody touches Uncle Chuck's boat except Uncle Chuck," Auntie Beth and Marianne recited together.

Brandon joined Sammy in the water while Duke paced nervously, watching the boys as they swam.

I sat down between Marianne and Auntie Beth.

"Where've you been?" Margot asked.

"I was checking out the piano."

Auntie Beth asked, "What's the verdict?"

"She's not going to make it."

"That piano should be put out of its misery," my aunt said.

"You can take the week off. The new one will be here soon," Marianne said.

I grumbled. Mom's idea of a break from music didn't suit me. Didn't she know? Playing music was freeing. It was a salve against all the angst, all the turkey splat going on in my life.

For most of the morning we sunned ourselves on colorful towels arranged in a semicircle while Brandon and Sammy swam under the dock in chest-deep water. Margot read a book in the shade of the boat lift. The smell of coconut and summer caught in the breeze.

The rhythmic splash of waves hit the shore as motorboats zoomed past with goggle-eyed passengers looking to see who had come for the summer.

"Look, it's the Andersons." Auntie Beth, her long hair pulled back by a dark green headband, waved and sang a greeting toward a pontoon boat.

"I never liked Alice." Marianne waved and smiled a phony smile.

I often wondered if she liked anyone. I sat up on my elbow and adjusted my bikini triangles.

"Are the Andersons staying all summer?" Marianne asked.

"They always do," my aunt said. "We'll invite them for happy hour next week."

"Do we have to?"

"They don't have any kids," I said.

"No, but the new renters next door have kids," Auntie Beth said.

Blood rushed from my face. I hoped Auntie Beth didn't invite them over. I wanted so badly to be liked by those boys. To fit in.

"Aren't they too old?" Margot asked.

"They're too old for you, I suspect," my aunt said. "The oldest son is going to the University of Wisconsin on a sports scholarship. We know the family, Marianne. It's the Vaughans."

As I gazed at the dark windows of the neighbor's house, gooseflesh rose on my arms. I pulled the towel around me.

"Ugh." Marianne squeezed Hawaiian Tropic into her palm. "I went to school with John. He's a first-class jerk. And Adelaide is a drunk."

Sammy climbed up the ladder and out of the lake. "When are we going out in the boat?" Dripping beside his mother, his teeth chattered as he rubbed his arms.

Auntie Beth tossed him a towel. "Is it lunch time?"

"When are we going out in the boat?" Brandon echoed the question from under the dock.

"Later," Marianne said. "After lunch we'll go to the marina and put gas in the tank."

My aunt stood and folded her towel. "Who wants sandwiches?"

"I do!" Sammy said.

Marianne looked around the dock. "Brandon, get out of the water, it's time to take a break. Daphne, keep an eye on him until he comes out of there."

The two moms took their belongings and walked back to the house. Margot and Sammy followed with armfuls of blown-up water toys.

I stood and stretched my long legs. "Mom said it's time to get out, Brandon."

The cool breeze brought a chill, so I wrapped the towel tighter around my shoulders. Looking for Brandon, I peered behind Uncle Chuck's boat and under the length of dock near the shallow end. Then I lay down on the white-painted dock and hung my head off the edge to see below.

"Brandon? Mom said it's time for lunch. Let's go."

Triangular spider webs stretched between the metal piling posts under the dock. Near the ladder, an electric-blue dragonfly was caught by its wing in a spiderweb. It flapped and twisted, struggling to get free.

Holding onto the curved metal handle of the ladder, I reached for the insect. I tore the spider web with my other hand and helped it free. The dragonfly clung to my fingertip like sticky burdock, opening and closing its clear fairy wings. Tiny front legs groomed its head with inky black eyes. It seemed to look at me, tilting its head one way and the other.

When it flew to the ladder rail, landed, and took off, I called my brother again. "Brandon. Time to go inside."

Something pale floated below the surface in the four-foot-deep water. Looking closer, I determined the pale something was hair.

"Brandon? Brandon!"

My brother didn't move. He floated very still like . . . like he was dead.

I scrambled to my feet and jumped in. I didn't feel the cold as I reached for Brandon's shoulders, his clammy skin soft beneath my fingers and his body heavy. I cradled his head and lifted him out of the water. His wet hair plastered to his face.

A cold rush of panic hit me. "Brandon!"

His eyes popped open. "Gotcha!" A face-splitting grin stretched his mouth wide.

I shoved him away. "You idiot! What were you thinking?"

He swam to the ladder and climbed out, shivering, but laughing so hard that he stumbled. "You should've seen the look on your face."

"I wish you were dead."

Wrapping my towel around his shoulders, he said, "Yo' mamma." He'd learned that saying from kids at school.

"That's my towel!" I clambered up the ladder. "I'm gonna kill you."

Brandon darted away.

"No running on the dock!" I ran after him. Where the dock met the yard, half-buried stones stuck out beneath the mowed grass. I tripped and fell on my hands and knees.

Angrier than ever at my brother, who shouted with glee as he ran inside, I stood and brushed off my bruised ego and knees.

A whispered warning drifted on the afternoon wind and as it picked up, I shivered.

In the neighbor's yard, three teenage kids—the two boys I'd seen before and a tall, pretty girl—were all watching me.

CHAPTER 5

THE BOY WITH THE WEIRD FINGER

Daphne

Marianne and Auntie Beth couldn't wait to see the changes a year had made to downtown Carlson. I just wanted to get out of the house. This summer started out creepy and I couldn't shake the feeling something bad would happen.

Our VW bus emerged from the woods along the north shore of the lake, where soccer and football fields spread out wide before us. Marianne drove slowly past Carlson Academy, the boarding school campus for high school students. On the right, rows of wooden bungalows housed campers for the summer. During the off-season, the school hosted sailing, hockey, soccer, and woodcraft summer camps. The school's most famous feature was a stable with more than forty black and bay horses.

"Campers are here early this year," Marianne said, turning onto Campus Road.

Auntie Beth sat in the front seat with her elbow hanging out the open window. "Not early," she said. "The specialty camps begin this weekend. They're here for registration. Oh, look, Margot. The horses are out to pasture."

We craned our necks to see the school's prize-winning herd. The Black Horse Troop led summer parades all over Indiana, including the Indianapolis 500 race day parade. Grazing in pairs and alone, the elegant animals swished their tails and stomped their feet. Long strong legs carried a prancing pair to the wood fence. They tossed their noses, nipping at each other in play.

"Next year Dad said I can go to the horseback riding camp," Margot said.

I was instantly jealous. "Can I go, Mom? I wanted to take horseback riding lessons like forever."

"Not this year, Daph." She lowered her voice as she stopped at a stop sign. "I can't afford it."

"Why don't you ask Mother to pay for camp?" Auntie Beth asked quietly. I focused to hear their conversation over the boys joking around in the back seat. "It would be good for Brandon, and Daphne would enjoy meeting kids her own age."

Marianne shook her head. "I can't ask Mother. She's sending the kids to Orchard Park private school in the fall. She helped pay for my house and she loaned Jeremy the money to start his . . . project."

I groaned. She never gave Dad credit for his work. "It's a deli, Marianne."

"She's paying for my kids too," Auntie Beth told Marianne. "I assure you, it's not a problem. All you need to do is ask."

"I can't deal with the guilt that comes with the handouts."

Marianne's punishing decision about horseback riding camp had more to do with the divorce and nothing to do with what I wanted. Nana was generous, wasn't she? She'd given Dad money for his business, and helped Marianne buy a house. She was sending a piano to Carlson. The sense of scarcity—the finite nature of money—loomed in the back of my mind. Would we end up being poor?

Marianne said. "Just because we come from money doesn't mean we need to act like it. Look. She can pay for private school—the kids deserve a good education—but that's where I draw the line. I'm trying to make my own way,"

"How's that working out for you? How much artwork do you sell? Oh, and I see that joining the . . ." Auntie Beth glanced over her shoulder and dropped her voice to a whisper. "Joining the sexual revolution has been so good for your marriage."

My aunt's stab surprised me.

"Do you mind? The kids are listening." Marianne looked in the rear-view mirror and caught my eye.

"She's right, Marianne. It's your fault."

"Daphne—"

"What?" Everyone knew Marianne had caused the breakup.

I looked out the window at the single-story small-town homes and wondered what it was like to live in a place like this. In books like *To Kill a Mockingbird*, folks all knew each other. They stood by each other, or they ostracized you. If we lived in Carlson year-round, would people cast out Marianne because of what she'd done to Dad?

"You two need to talk," Auntie Beth said.

"Not here." Marianne stopped at a stop sign and looked over her shoulder.

I refused to meet her eye. I lived in Marianne's shadow. I heard people talk. Because of the divorce, I'd do whatever it took to avoid being cast away. Because I knew what that felt like when Ruth stopped being my friend. *"There's no room for you at this table, Freak."*

I'd do anything not to be labeled ever again.

Marianne changed the subject. "Tony works at a graphic design place in Indy. He thinks I could earn enough money doing freelance work for them to support my studio."

"I thought you wanted to paint nature and animals," Auntie Beth said.

"I will if I can."

"It sounds like giving up your dream to me."

"I have to try this. At least designing ads would get my name out there." She rounded the curve near the dormitories, where kids and families were unloading suitcases for summer camp.

In town, we passed a beat-up pickup truck parked at the gas station. Two bird-like men in dirty blue jeans and T-shirts with cutoff sleeves stood nearby. A large woman sat in an upholstered chair in the back bed. One of the cadaverous men, with a cigarette held between his lips, gripped the neck of a big bottle of brown alcohol and set it in the truck beside her. The other handed the woman a carton of cigarettes. His gaze followed our VW bus as it passed, and he ran his tongue over brown teeth.

It was impolite to stare, but I couldn't take my eyes off them. These people looked nothing like the families at the academy. It seemed likely they were struggling with money. Like Marianne and Dad, only worse.

I couldn't help wondering if Marianne was taking us down a road leading to the same driveway where those folks lived. And it scared me.

I wore the cool new sunglasses I picked out at the five and dime. In my lap, my fingers twirled the fringe on a new crocheted purse. Margot held a new toy horse with curly plastic doll's hair. Behind us, the boys tore open their one-dollar fishing poles, sure to break during the first use. Twisting my earring studs, I decided I liked looking older. I didn't want to be a kid anymore. I didn't want to be a baby.

When we returned to the cottage with our treasures in hand, I spotted a woman in a slim white tennis skirt and pink short-sleeved polo shirt standing in the neighboring driveway.

"Look, there's Adelaide Vaughan," Auntie Beth said.

Mrs. Vaughan wore white tennis shoes that didn't have a scuff on them, and her pink ankle socks had those little balls to keep them from sliding. Compared to Marianne, who wore a loose-fitting hippy-style shirt, Adelaide looked neat as a pin. She was ready for the tennis court, the country club, or lunch at a downtown restaurant.

Auntie Beth opened the sliding side door of the VW bus. "Let's say hello."

"Do we have to?" Brandon asked. I wondered the same thing.

"Yes, you have to. Be polite. It will only take a minute." My aunt walked toward the neighbor's house.

Margot elbowed me. "It never only takes only a minute."

I slunk out of the VW bus and tried to sneak away. I didn't want to meet the boys who saw me playing with Margot.

"I want to play with my new fishing pole," Sammy said.

Auntie Beth waved her hand. "Howdy, neighbor."

Mrs. Vaughan took her tennis racket from the trunk of her bronze Lincoln Continental. She turned, her keyring with a miniature tennis racket dangling from one hand. "Well, if it isn't Elizabeth Thallman. What brings you to Lake Carlson?"

"My mother owns the cottage next door," my aunt said. "We've been coming here since I was a child. In fact, we're staying until mid-August."

Curious, I hid behind the VW bus. Mrs. Vaughan's eyebrows twitched with judgment like she'd moved next door to a laundromat. Her shimmering shoulder-length blond hair defied the swift breeze coming off the lake. Manicured and elegant as a picture in a magazine, she looked as though she never had to work for anything in her life. She peered out from beneath rose-colored sunglasses at the Victorian cottage. "Looks like we'll be neighbors. We rented this place for the summer too."

While Auntie Beth and Mrs. Vaughan spoke, Marianne came up behind me. She nudged me forward with my brother and cousins.

I wanted no part of this. It felt like I was five again.

"Hello, Adelaide," Marianne said.

"Oh, Marianne. The ladies at the club told me all about your divorce."

"Really?"

"It's obvious Jeremy Post could never keep you in the lifestyle you're used to, anyway. I mean, your family comes from old money. Certainly, your mother can introduce you to someone."

"I'm not looking for a husband, Adelaide."

"Well, being a single mother doesn't exactly send the right message, does it?"

"What do you mean?"

"I'm just saying, Indianapolis is a small city. With your family's reputation, it won't be hard for you to marry up. To keep your family's reputation intact."

Marianne took a step backward. "I'm not sure what you heard, Adelaide. But let's not talk about this in front of the children, hmm?" She rubbed Brandon's shoulder and threw a pinched smile Adelaide's way.

Adelaide stretched her neck straighter. "I'm sorry, I thought everyone knew that you were—"

"This is my son Brandon." Marianne's voice pitched upward. "Sammy here is Beth's boy. Say hello, boys."

The boys mumbled a greeting.

Brandon held up the cheap fishing pole. "Can we go now?"

Auntie Beth waved them along.

As they darted away, Marianne called after them. "Let Duke out of the house, please."

"Good-looking kids," Adelaide said.

I couldn't keep my gaze from drifting to the neighbor's windows. The sounds of music and voices came from the kitchen. I hid beside Marianne, hoping none of the kids saw me.

"And who's this?" Mrs. Vaughan looked right at me.

Marianne introduced us. Margot stepped forward to shake Mrs. Vaughan's hand.

Mrs. Vaughan said, "Hold on. You girls must be about the same age as my son Lewis. Come on up to the house. I'll introduce you."

I gagged. "Oh, that's okay. I have to go . . . practice . . . the . . . piano."

"Daphne?" Marianne asked.

"Do you play?" Mrs. Vaughan asked.

"A little," I said.

"She's very good." Auntie Beth flashed me a smile.

"There's a piano in the house and we don't use it," Adelaide said. "You'll have to give us a concert."

They have a piano? I perked up. But I didn't want to perform for them like some show pony. And what if the kids made fun of me? "No, thank you. We have one too . . ." I turned to go.

Auntie Beth caught my arm. "Daphne would love to play for you."

"Come on in and meet the kids." Mrs. Vaughan beckoned us to follow.

"Come meet the Vaughans, Daphne." My aunt's tone meant business.

I dragged my feet to the Vaughans' kitchen door. Margot and I waited outside while the women went in.

When the adults were out of earshot, Margot said, "I can't believe Mrs. Vaughan said that to your mom. She's one of those ladies from the club who talks about everyone else because she has no life of her own."

"How do you know that?" I said. Marianne should have stood up for Dad when Mrs. Vaughan said those things. More importantly, she should have stood up for herself.

"My mom said so. She says all those tennis dress-wearing women sit around with gimlets. They live to gossip and spend their husband's money."

"I wouldn't say that to her face."

"No way. What's a gimlet?" Margot asked.

A tall blond boy was standing at the screen door. I peered over Margot's head. Bathed in light from behind, he looked like an angel from heaven complete with a halo. His light-blue shirt with the wide collar and chestnut-brown stripes around the armbands clung to his shoulders. I could easily imagine him playing football or soccer, but there was also something familiar. If only his hair were messier. *If only . . .*

"Hi. I'm Lewis."

Appearing behind him like some mystic being, Lewis's taller sister looked over his shoulder at us. She too had a glow about her, and I noticed Margot's mouth hung open. I elbowed her.

She raised a shy hand and flashed her braces at them. "I'm Margot."

"I'm Lara. Mother says you live next door." She stepped to Lewis's side. Straight blond hair fell to her chest. The smooth skin of her belly showed between her halter top and white hot pants.

Lewis's gaze had never left me. "I saw you outside. What's your name?"

I tried to clear my throat.

"This is Daphne," Margot said. "We're cousins."

Lewis's dark amber-brown eyes scanned my face as he reached for the door and pushed it open. His right hand was missing the tip of his ring finger. The sight stunned me for a second. I'd never seen anything like it and wondered how it happened.

"Come on in," he said.

I grabbed the door handle and inadvertently touched Lewis's fingers. The moment stretched out as if held by a fermata. I didn't—couldn't— pull away. And Lewis changed before my eyes. His skin became very pale.

His hair stood on end as if charged with static electricity. The breeze off the lake and the lapping sound of waves splashing on the shore grew to an inexplicable volume. *Fortissimo!* And somewhere hidden in the harmony, the wind whispered, *Save me!*

I jerked my hand away and the door slammed shut. The tingles started up again, traveling from my fingertips all the way up my neck. I thought of Ruth. Of her accident. Shame heated my cheeks.

Weirdo. Freak.

"You know, we can't come over right now," I said. "We have stuff to do, don't we, Margot?"

Margot's gaze flicked back and forth between us. "I guess."

Lara whispered something to Lewis and smiled. "Our brother Phillip is at the marina filling up the boat with gas. You wanna go for a ride later?"

I shook my head nervously and took Margot's arm. "No thanks." As I backed away, gossamer threads pulled at me. I wanted so badly to accept the invitation, but worried what they would think of me. I worried about embarrassing myself.

Once we were out of their sight, Margot whispered, "I don't like them."

CHAPTER 6

"BACK HOME AGAIN IN INDIANA"

June 8, 1976: Mark Walters

On the way into Carlson, Indiana, the Greyhound bus passed the A&W Root Beer stand, the central hub for teenagers back in the day. Mark Walters recalled going there with his high school friends. They ordered root beer floats and burgers and whistled at the waitresses on roller skates. In those days, Mark still had hopes and dreams. By now, all his friends had grown up and graduated from college. They'd probably moved to the big cities where there were jobs—Indianapolis, Plymouth, and South Bend.

The bus stopped near the library at half past four and Mark stepped off it with nothing in his pockets. Wearing an old pair of jeans and a work shirt, he didn't even have a dime for a pay phone. As the bus drove away, he inhaled the fishy lake smells and savored the breeze on his face. The faint odor of manure drifted on the wind from the nearby farms. Had to be the Garside's farm from the direction it came. Mark smiled because that's the direction he was headed. Home.

Except for the abundance of American flags and red, white, and blue banners in preparation for the bicentennial, downtown Carlson looked pretty much the same after seven years. Seven years that seemed like an eternity. A lifetime. He'd missed out on high school graduation and college. His basketball scholarship became a useless checkmark on the pages of his life. All because he'd beat up the wrong kid.

American flags surrounded the 76 gas station on the corner. In the parking lot, an old Ford pickup reminded him of the one his Pops used to drive. He wondered if Pops knew he was coming home today. Though their trailer was five miles out of town, he didn't mind walking. He passed the five and dime and a new bar, The Corner Tavern. The scent of fried chicken made his stomach rumble. He hadn't eaten since breakfast.

The movie theater advertised the latest summer hit: *JAWS* in bold red print with the mouth of a giant shark coming out of the water. He chuckled at the thought of teens frightened out of their wits by a big shark. A shark in the water wasn't as scary as some of the men he'd met. Mark had missed out on all the things kids look forward to. Losing a limb to a mouthful of teeth was nothing compared to losing your hope for a future.

He walked past fragrant flowerpots and a fireworks stand. This summer, the US of A was celebrating two hundred years. The bicentennial was a big deal for some. More American flags hung from front porches and mailboxes. Mark couldn't care less. He strolled past Carlson Academy, where uniformed kids were loading up their parents' cars. They looked so clean-cut in their military-type navy pants and plaid skirts. Not a bad bone in their bodies.

Their high school graduation would have been last weekend. Envy spread like a poisonous vine through Mark's chest, burning through the apathy that had come with time served. If only he didn't have a temper like Pops. If only he hadn't been robbed of his opportunities.

If only he hadn't gone to prison.

CHAPTER 7

FREAK

Daphne

Something in the air felt different. As if trouble found its way to Carlson overnight. A heaviness hung over the house, the trees and the lake. None of us wanted to lie in the sun today. Margot and I were playing a somber game of cards at the living room table when Sammy and Brandon stampeded through the wide barn door leading from the living room to the patio facing the lake.

"Brandon pushed me in the lake," Sammy said. He was fully clothed but soaked to the bone and dripping on the carpet.

Margot and I looked up from our card game. Brandon, in notably dry clothes, grinned at me. With my eyebrows raised, I mouthed the words *What did you do?* I hated it when my little brother got in trouble. It usually meant I took some flack too. After all, I was the one supposed to be watching him.

Marianne stared from an armchair, her drawing pad in her lap. "Towels are upstairs in hall cabinet. Go dry off and change."

Sammy ran upstairs dripping water all the way.

"You know better than to push someone in the water, Brandon," Marianne said. "The lake is too shallow for that kind of behavior. Sammy could've been hurt."

"It was at the deep-water end of the dock." Brandon looked at the floor and kicked my chair leg. He'd been acting out since the divorce.

Last week he dumped out Marianne's oil pastels and scattered them across the floor. He drew cartoons on every clean sheet of her expensive drawing paper.

"Still, we never push someone in. If your father were here he'd ground you for the next three days."

"Well, Dad's not here, is he?" Brandon darted out of the room.

Lately, he didn't get in trouble for anything. I don't know if it was the weird, heavy haze I felt or just the final straw. I couldn't contain it anymore. "Why isn't he grounded?"

"What?" Marianne's cheeks reddened like she'd been slapped.

"You let him get away with it!" Anger shortened my breath. I threw my cards in the pile at the center of the table.

"We're not having this conversation, Daphne."

"Why not?"

"Because it's not true."

I shoved my chair back and stood. There were so many things I wanted to say.

"Does this mean I win?" Margot asked.

I stomped up the stairs to my room and tried slamming the door. Warped from years of humidity, it didn't close. I pushed it as far as it would go, then sat with my arms crossed on the edge of the unmade bed.

Later that day, I combed the beach all the way to the point with Duke at my heels. Pushing aside willow branches and chasing off ducks, I took off my Dr. Scholl's and waded in the cold feeder streams. I collected purple butterfly shells and found a flat skipping stone in the sand. I flicked my wrist like Dad showed me and the stone disappeared into a wave and sank to the bottom.

When I'd touched Lewis Vaughan's hand—with his short, weird finger—an image of him so pale, popped into my head. His hair looked like he was touching a static electricity ball. What did the image mean? Was he a swimmer? Was he into water sports? The vibe of the whole moment seemed more dangerous than that.

But what did it mean?

It reminded me of the time I'd warned Ruth about ice-skating.

In fifth grade, Ruth and I were still friends. Our desks were right next to each other and after school and on weekends we rode bikes and had sleepovers. We were in orchestra. Ruth played cello and I played the violin—I hated the violin—and we practiced together. We stayed up late watching scary Vincent Price movies on *Sammy Terry's Midnight Theater.* We laughed so hard when it was over.

The bittersweet memories sank like stones to the bottom of my stomach. Ruth was never the same after the accident. I blamed myself.

That day, a winter storm had coated Indianapolis in two inches of ice. Everything shut down, and schools closed. We made the best of the rare snow day and decided to go ice skating. I brought an old pair of my dad's ice skates to Ruth's house. When I got there, she hugged me in the doorway and our cheeks touched. That was when I knew.

Those stinging, burning tendrils crawled up my arms and I saw poor Ruth lying on the ice at the end of her driveway. I didn't know if I was imagining things, but I didn't want her to get hurt.

"This is a bad idea," I warned Ruth, and she laughed. *"Don't be silly,"* she said.

I tried to change her mind. "But . . . I have a bad feeling about it, Ruth. Let's watch a scary movie instead."

"Stop it." Ruth took the skates from me. "What could possibly happen?"

Ruth's mother stood by with an armful of scarves and mittens for us. When I told her I was worried, Ruth's mom pshawed. "Now, go on outside. I'm heating some hot chocolate for when you're done."

Terrified, I watched Ruth lace up her skates. I followed Ruth outside to the ice-coated yard and offered her a hand. Ruth wasn't a good skater, and though the driveway was mostly flat, she struggled to stay on her feet. When she got near the road, where the driveway sloped, I couldn't stop her.

It was my fault.

Ruth started staggering and slipping at the end of the slanting driveway. She picked up speed. She couldn't keep her feet under her. When she fell and landed flat on her back, her head hit the curb. The sound—the crack her head made when it hit the frozen concrete— would be etched in my mind forever.

Ruth didn't get up and no amount of pleading helped. Ruth's mother ran outside in her slippers. She slid to a stop on her knees beside her daughter. Ruth's older brother called an ambulance, and they sent me home. That still wasn't the worst of it.

After Ruth fell, she was hospitalized with a head injury so bad she had surgery to relieve the pressure. I recalled Ruth's shaved, bruised head. She looked like a war victim. And when Ruth finally went back to school, she told everyone I caused the accident.

This one time, I walked into the lunchroom carrying my tray to the table we'd sat at since sixth grade. All the chairs were taken, and Ruth said, "There's no room. You should sit somewhere else. *Freak*."

I slunk to the empty corner table and ate by myself from then on. Kids gave me plenty of room in the hallways and laughed behind my back. As the school year went on, Ruth embellished the story, turning it into something fantastical.

Daphne's mental. She's psycho. Weirdo.

Over time, Ruth's teasing tales and lies sank deep under my flesh and resided there. I became so comfortable with the deception and false accusations that I started to believe they were true. I would do anything not to be labeled ever again.

It had been my fault. If I hadn't warned Ruth, it might have never happened.

As I headed back to our cottage, the red sky over the western shore of the lake signaled a warning that entered my bones. The laughter coming from inside the cottage wasn't my dad's. Uncle Chuck had arrived.

Once inside, I slunk down the back hall and darted upstairs. I set my collection of shells on the dresser and dried Duke with a towel. Eventually, the smell of good things to eat drew me down to the kitchen. Margot and the boys were chowing down sloppy joes at the dining room table. I went to the kitchen to make a plate.

"Nice of you to join us, Daphne." Marianne had mascara on, and she smelled like patchouli oil and Herbal Essence shampoo. She hadn't worn makeup or perfume since she was married to Dad.

I was still kinda mad at Marianne, so I couldn't even look at her.

Uncle Chuck stood near the bar with a drink in his hand. His bald head glistened under the fluorescent ceiling light. "Boy, every time I see you, Daphne, you're even taller." He stopped me in the doorway and placed a hand on my shoulder. Though I'd grown almost three inches since Easter, I shrank next to him.

His gaze slid down me like a snake moving through grass.

I faked a smile. After what Margot said, I didn't trust him. He made me uncomfortable and there was something yucky about his teeth.

Gross.

"Hi, Uncle Chuck." I took my plate to the table.

A car horn honked outside, and Marianne said, "Tony's here."

Tony. *Who was this loser?* I set my plate down and ran to the dining room window.

Auntie Beth was in the kitchen. "This should be interesting," she said.

Tony honked three more times as he parked his blue sports car on the street, a Datsun 280Z. I reached across the top of the silverware hutch and pushed a candlestick out of the way. Leaning on my elbows, I cranked the window open all the way for a good view.

"Who is this guy?" Uncle Chuck asked.

Tony popped the trunk of his little car and took out a cardboard box. He had black hair and a thick dark mustache. Like a villain. Even from this distance, he seemed shorter and stockier than Dad. Not nearly as handsome. His long stride and bouncy step reminded me of a cartoon character.

Margot stood on her tiptoes and looked out the window. "What are you doing?"

"Watching."

Behind her, Uncle Chuck downed the rest of his drink.

Marianne jogged out to meet Tony halfway between the little house and the Victorian cottage.

I glowered at them.

"Mary! What's hanging, old lady?" Tony set down the box and scooped Marianne off her feet.

"Is she really that horny?" Uncle Chuck asked.

Auntie Beth crossed her arms in the kitchen doorway. "Chuck. The kids."

I knew the term. *Gross.*

Marianne gave Tony a smooch on the cheek. "How was the drive?"

He set her back down. "I hit rush hour traffic in Kokomo, if you can believe it, but otherwise, not bad."

Their volume dropped and I struggled to hear over the sound of a motorboat passing by.

Margot's gaze was locked on Tony too. "He's not what I expected. Have you met him before?"

"It's all new to me."

His black hair blew away from his face and he seemed to look right into the window at me. "Wow, look at this crib. Right on the lake and everything. This is your pad?"

"My mother's. I can't afford it, I'm a starving artist, remember?" Marianne said. "I can't wait to hear what happened with your boss at Indy Graphics. Did you show him my work?"

"Later, babe. I want to see more of this Victorian crib."

I already hated him. Margot looked up at me with a mixture of pity and empathy.

Uncle Chuck's eyes locked on Tony when they entered. Tony greeted him with a dopey smile. "What's hanging, my man? I'm Tony Gennaro." He vigorously shook my uncle's hand.

"Charles Thallman." He loosened his wide tie. "You must be Marianne's friend."

Friend? He destroyed our family, I thought. I stood in the doorway with Margot at my side. I couldn't take my eyes off him.

"That's right. My lucky day, meeting her." Tony swung an arm around Marianne.

Marianne clung to his arm. "Beth, this is Tony. Tony, my sister Beth."

"My lady…"

I tried to remain hidden and peered past the doorframe as my aunt awkwardly shook his hand.

"No jiving. I can dig it. You are a pretty lady too, just like your sister. Are you a swinger?"

"Swinger?" Auntie Beth asked.

"What's a swinger?" Margot whispered. "Like at the circus? Those trapeze artists? Why would he think my mom–"

"Shh." I put a finger to my lips.

"Beth's very, um, married," Uncle Chuck said. He put his arm around her and pulled her close.

"So you're her old man. Maybe the four of us—"

"No, Tony." Marianne shook her head. "How about that drink?"

"I can dig it. Where can a man get a glass?"

I didn't want to eat with the adults. I didn't want to sit with Tony. I headed out through the living room, and Auntie Beth stopped me. "Where are you going? Come sit with the rest of us, Daphne."

At the table, no one spoke much. The sounds of chewing made me nauseous. I let my food go cold.

Brandon dropped his sloppy joe on his plate and wiped his fingers on a greasy paper napkin. He was the one who broke the awkward silence. "Is he the reason Dad kicked you out?"

"Brandon!" Marianne said.

I choked and laughed into my hand. Leave it to Brandon to put Marianne on the spot.

Duke nosed Brandon's elbow.

"What? It's true, isn't it?" Brandon asked.

"Don't be like that . . . " Marianne said.

"Dad's not here. I'm not doing what you say."

"Your mom and dad had their differences, can you dig it?" Tony said. "I'm just a friend. I can be your friend if you want, Brandon."

Brandon pushed his chair out. "Can I be excused?"

I hid my smile. My brother and I were on the same side in this battle.

"Me too," Sammy said.

"Go ahead," Marianne said.

"Sit back down, boys." Uncle Chuck had taken his place at the head of the table. His final say overruled Marianne's.

Brandon slumped back into his chair. "Aww, come on."

"No backtalk. You'll stay until everyone's finished," Uncle Chuck said. "Samuel, I haven't seen you all week."

Under my breath, I said, "God." I set my mouth in a thin line and pushed my plate away.

"We're building a giant card house," Sammy said.

"Chuck, they can go," Marianne said. "We're not following strict supper etiquette this summer."

Uncle Chuck took a swallow of his drink. "You're not following any etiquette, Marianne. You do exactly what you want. So do your kids."

Marianne and Tony shifted uncomfortably in their seats.

"I haven't seen you since Easter," Uncle Chuck added. "How's divorced life?"

"It's good." Marianne smiled, but I knew it was a fake one. "I have everything I could possibly want."

"Is he such a good lay?" Uncle Chuck asked.

Auntie Beth said, "Not at the dinner table, Chuck."

"Quiet, Beth."

Uncle Chuck gave Tony another once-over. Swirling his drink, he began his interrogation. "So what do you do for a living, Tony?"

"Tony works for Indy Graphics," Marianne said. "He offered me a chance to make money drawing commercial art. I'd be doing what I love."

Tony chuckled and began a long description of his work.

Brandon and Sammy quietly played with their silverware and looked into their laps while the adults talked. And like everyone else, I shrank. This family dinner—if it could be called that—was so unlike anything we had with Dad.

CHAPTER 8

"SISTER GOLDEN HAIR"

Lara

All the days blurred into one. Had it only been a week in Lake Carlson? It felt like a month. Lara stared out the window of her bedroom in the summer home. The gray lake churned with the wind. Father had rented the house from a friend who was spending the summer someplace much better than Northern Indiana. Someplace like Cancun or Puerto Vallarta. Someplace exotic and hot in all the right ways. Along the shore of this Lake Carlson house, foamy lakeweed floated on the surface under their dock. She longed for it to be as crystal clear as the blue Caribbean Sea. She stepped away from the window.

Sticking another eight-track tape in the player, the twangy guitar of America played *Sister Golden Hair,* but Lara was bored. She left her player on and dragged her feet down the hall to Lewis's room.

She knocked on the door, but he didn't answer, so she went down the stairs slowly, tipping the frames of fake reprints on the wall until they were all off kilter. In the living room, Lewis sat on the couch holding his video game controller. He'd brought along his new game with the stupid name—Pong—and hooked it up to the TV.

"Where's Mother?" Lara asked, watching the white ball bounce between sides of the television screen.

"Out. She went to a tennis lesson, I think." Lewis kept his gaze on the screen.

"Did you ever wonder? When did she start playing tennis?"

"This summer, I guess."

Lara plopped down on the couch and stared at the TV for a few numbing minutes. Lewis had become good at the video game. She envied his innate abilities to learn things quickly. Father loved that about him. That was why Lewis was the favorite.

Not Lara. Father told her she was pretty. He said it was the only thing she had going for her. He said she wasn't smart like Lewis, or athletic like Phillip. And she believed it. If she let it, it saddened her to be thought of by everyone as such a perfect Barbie doll. Instead of letting her feelings bring her down, it was easier to pretend it didn't hurt. And to hurt others along the way.

Sitting there in his navy shorts with the little anchors on them and his white Polo shirt—such a Goody-Two-shoes—Lewis jiggled the controller.

Lara couldn't stand it anymore. She sat back and casually raised her arm behind him, out of his sight line. Gently, so gently, she tickled the back of his neck.

He swatted the irritation but kept his eye on the game. He didn't miss the shot.

Stronger tactics were needed. She smacked the back of his head.

"Leave me alone!" Pent-up rage exploded out of him. He shoved Lara off the couch so fast she cracked her elbow on the coffee table.

"What the hell?" Lara rubbed her elbow.

"Leave me alone. Find someone else to bother." Lewis picked up the game controller without giving her a second glance.

She stood and brushed herself off. "What difference does it make? If you win Pong again today, you'll have nothing to do the rest of the summer."

"Go listen to your music and stare at yourself in the mirror. There's gotta be makeup that can cover that ugly thing on your face."

"What ugly thing?" Lara's hand floated to her cheek. When she put foundation on today, she didn't notice any pimples.

Lewis threw the controller down and moved to her side. "It's right there." He leaned in as if scrutinizing something and raised a hand to point to her face.

"Do I have a zit?" She felt her brow crease.

"It's bigger than that. Right here." Lewis flattened his hand and shoved his palm into her nose.

"Goddam it!" Lara backed away and rubbed her sore nose.

Lewis laughed and returned to the couch.

"Fuck you," she said.

"Fuck you." He settled back into his game.

What a butthead. She wandered to the kitchen. Only ten o'clock. It was going to be a long day. The phone hung on the wall near the fridge. She'd memorized Phillip's number at Carlson Academy. It rang three times before he picked up.

"What are you doing today? I'm so bored."

"I'm heading to my first class. I don't have time to talk right now."

"Are you teaching again?" She knew he was the hockey camp instructor for ten- and eleven-year-old kids, but she wanted to talk to him. She had nothing better to do.

"I really have to go."

"Come over tonight. Bring some pot. I need to get stoned."

"Sure. Geez, Lara. Go swimming or take the boat out. Find something to do."

"Please, Phillip? Tonight?"

"Sure." He hung up.

It was only five after ten. *Crap. Now what?*

Her gaze scanned the kitchen and landed on a cabinet between the kitchen and dining room. Yesterday, Mother had stocked the shelves with boxes from the liquor store because she didn't go a single day without her vodka tonics. Lara found herself perusing the shelves. Cuban rum, Jack Daniels—too strong for this time of day—vodka and . . . *here we go.* Peach schnapps.

She opened the bottle and took a swallow.

CHAPTER 9

THE ESCAPE

Daphne

With Uncle Chuck visiting, no one could relax. In a few days, he'd imposed his rules. Strict bedtimes, and meals together. He made us all sit up straight and keep napkins in our laps. No one was allowed near his boat, and no one could go swimming within two hours of eating. The boys weren't allowed to play in the living room, only in their bedroom. And at the end of the day, when he sent all the kids to bed early, it was fine with me. I was happy with any excuse to get away from him and Tony Baloney.

Margot put her nightgown on and clipped on her headgear. "What's wrong?"

"Nothing." I closed the closet door tightly before lying on the bed. Even on a school night, I didn't go to bed this early. I didn't feel like reading, sleeping, or talking. I itched to go outside and take a walk. I wanted to run. Look at the moon. Feel the night air and hear the cricket's song.

"I don't believe you," Margot said. Sometimes she was more intuitive than she let on.

"I'm not tired, are you?"

"Not really." Margot closed her book.

The adults had turned on the radio, which had only one static-free music station, broadcasting from Plymouth, Indiana. Laughter and Barry Manilow's "Mandy" rattled pictures on the walls while they drank and played card games downstairs.

I rolled one of my itchy earring studs between my thumb and index finger. "Let's go for a walk."

"What? Now?"

"Yes, now." I swung my feet to the floor and slid my jeans and T-shirt back on.

Margot's thick eyeglass lenses magnified her eyes. "We'll get in so much trouble."

"We'll sneak out the back door."

I was surprised and delighted that she agreed. When she was ready, I turned off the bedroom light and gripped the crystal doorknob. The smell of cigarette smoke wafted upstairs. On the floor near the top of the stairway, Duke lifted his head and wagged his tail.

"This is exciting," Margot said. "Like we're Nancy Drew on a case."

"Shh."

Duke got to his feet, eager to join us.

"Stay, Duke." I patted him on the head and hoped he would stay. Though Marianne had trained the big dog, he wasn't good at following commands.

"Come on." Pressed against the wall, we avoided the creaky third step. In the living room, Auntie Beth and Marianne sang "Last Dance" louder than Donna Sommer. As the refrain repeated, I stopped at the bottom of the steps and took a deep breath. I furtively peeked around the corner and saw them dancing between the couches by the fireplace. Tony sat at the card table with his back to the stairs.

Where's Uncle Chuck? *If I can't see him, he can't see me.*

Duke stood at the top of the stairs wagging his tail.

I gave the signal and dashed around the newel-post into the darkened back hall. Margot followed quickly and quietly, but Duke gamboled down the stairs loudly with the tags on his collar clanging.

We tiptoed past the bathroom near the kitchen. Light streamed from under the door and the toilet flushed. Duke was now at our heels, crowding into the tight hallway with us.

"No, Duke," I whispered and gave him the signal to stay, and the big lug sat down in the doorway, blocking Margot's exit.

I pushed open the screen door and ducked under the kitchen windows. Hoping Duke would stay put, I held the door and my breath as Margot appeared in the doorway, making eye contact with me.

The bathroom door opened. "Margot? What are you doing out of bed?" Uncle Chuck stood right behind her.

Margot turned away. "I needed a glass of water."

"Do you know where the glasses are?" he asked.

"Yes." Margot sounded nervous.

"Does Duke want out?"

"No, I . . . I think he heard something."

"With all that racket from your Aunt Marianne's singing? I'm sure it's nothing. Come on." He directed Margot into the kitchen and, at the last minute, looked out the door.

By then the screen door had closed, and I was huddled in the shadows.

EVERYTHING IS BEAUTIFUL

Daphne

Once it was safe, I crept beneath the light thrown from the kitchen windows and stole along shadowy Aubenaubee Creek. Tree frogs and bullfrogs croaked complicated rhythms in five-part harmony. Crickets and cicadas buzzed a keyless soundscape. Free from the structure of a metronome, free of form, measure bars, or tempo markings, the sounds gave shape to the darkness and meaning to my escape.

I avoided the well-lit street and crossed the small wooden bridge that led into the neighbor's hillside yard. Not the Vaughans' yard. I wouldn't be caught dead going that way.

I ran from tree trunk to tree trunk through shadowy mowed grass and followed the creek bed through the golf course. I crouched low until I was far from the houses. Until I was sure no one would spot me. Last summer, Auntie Beth told us the police caught a gang of local teenagers stealing flagpoles and carving up the greens. Someone had seen them from their lake house and called the police.

I stayed low. The smooth rolling hills of the course provided little shelter, but those same hills hid me from watchful eyes where the ground dipped. At times, I lay down on the cool grass and looked up at the Milky Way. The stars were so bright they decorated the sky all the way to Kokomo. Or Chicago. Or Timbuktu. Trees were fewer here, and the night song diminished to a mezzo piano. My footsteps and heartbeat gave a steady beat to the frogs' songs.

I walked along the trees on the far side of the fairway and recalled the Vaughans. Lewis's mussed up blond hair like a halo. His life was probably perfect. His parents weren't divorced. A bad feeling combined with prickles ran from the base of my neck to the backs of my knees. I ignored them and thought of his sister. She looked so pretty with straight hair down to her waist. I ran a hand through my regrettable short haircut.

The crescent moon hung like a stage prop in the sky. The mowed fairway stretched out before me. On East Shore Drive, the headlights of a single car shone brightly. It turned into one of the driveways and the lights flicked off. I listened as the car doors opened. Their voices carried. But as those people went inside, I heard something else. Whispered laughter and footsteps. In the shadows, three figures moved along the trees at the edge of the fairway.

I crept to a group of shrubs near the creek bed. Crouching down, I watched the figures strolling toward the huge white gazebo on the top of the hill. I ran light-footed beside the creek, following, stopping when they stopped. Listening to their high laughter bouncing off the hills.

At the tree line, I tried to blend into the landscape, hoping my long legs echoed the shapes of tree trunks and my arms looked like branches.

Painted white pillars and scrollwork on the gazebo glowed in the moonlight. The threesome entered it and sat down, their chatter sprinkling the night air with a sense of fun and adventure. In the moonlight, I made out a girl with long hair and two young men.

The Vaughans?

Drawn to them like a bee to the sweet scent of the deadly pitcher plant, I crept closer. Goosebumps tingled on the back of my neck, but I dismissed them. I longed to be one of the cool kids. I'd do just about anything to win their friendship.

"It's so boring without my friends." The girl lazily twirled a strand of hair in one hand.

"You think you're bored. I'm stuck babysitting a pack of eight-year-old boys." I was sure that voice was Lewis and Lara's older brother Phillip, whom I hadn't met yet. His mop of dark curly hair was nothing like his siblings' straight blond hair.

"Coaching," Lewis corrected. "You're coaching the hockey players, not babysitting. It's a real job. At least you can get away from Mother."

"Father hates it. He'd rather I had a job assisting the elections this term."

"Volunteering at the polls isn't the same thing as making real money," Lara said. "That's what he says to Mother all the time."

"I've worked hard for his approval my whole life. Trust me, he's not proud of my hockey scholarship. He wants me to go to business school and get a real degree." Phillip lit a cigarette. The coal brightened with his inhalation and illuminated his features. After he blew the smoke out, he passed the cigarette to Lara, and it looked like a hand-rolled joint.

"Sometimes I just want to . . ." Phillip stared into the trees—straight toward me—and tensed.

I squatted in the bushes balancing on my toes, my fingertips touching the ground.

"What?" Lewis stood to see what Phillip stared at.

"Nothing," Phillip said.

Nana said nothing is always something. I wished I could see his face. I kept squatting in the shadows as he gazed in my direction.

"Dad's not that hard to please," Lewis said.

"Says the son who can do no wrong." Lara slurred the words.

I lost my balance and fell on my butt, causing a twig to snap.

"Hey!" Phillip said. "Did you hear that?"

Lewis peered into the darkness. "Who's there?"

I considered running but doubted I'd get far before they caught up to me. Instead, I stepped out of the shadow into the moonlight. "It's me, Daphne. I'm your neighbor."

Phillip strode toward me, his elbows cocked back and head forward as if ready to fight. "Are you following us? What are you doing out here?"

The odor of pungent, skunky smoke hung in the air, confirming my suspicion they were smoking pot. Torn between the temptation to run and the desire to join them, I backed away. I just wanted them to like me. "I just . . . I was out here too."

"Are you going to narc on us?" Phillip stood within a foot of me now. His shadowed features looked dark and long. His sweeping arm movements reminded me of a conductor coaxing music from the orchestra. His eyes lit with a fire and when he looked right at me, I thought he understood me. I decided at once that I'd follow him anywhere. Do anything he asked. To gain his approval.

"Oh, my god, you're that kid who was playing with dolls next door."

He remembered? "I wasn't playing with dolls," I said. "I'm fifteen. My cousin is . . . she's twelve. I was just . . . I was hanging out with her." My words stung like betrayal.

"You see, Phillip?" Lewis came out of the gazebo. "She's not a kid. She's the same age as me."

"Says the baby," Lara said, staring at the moon.

Phillip put a hand through his curls. "Go back home, little girl," he told me.

"I won't tell on you," I said.

The Vaughan siblings all stared as if expecting me to perform Debussy's "Arabesque" on the piano.

"Let her hang out with us, Phillip," Lewis said.

"As long as you're not a narc."

"I'm cool." I wanted so badly to earn that title.

Phillip shrugged. "Maybe."

I followed them back to the gazebo, where Lewis took a seat across from Lara. I sat between them while Phillip lit another joint, then passed it to Lara. She put it to her lips.

"Do you smoke?" Lewis asked.

"Oh, yeah. I've been smoking like, forever." I pinched my new earring stud and tilted my head. I didn't want to look like a dork. I'd never hung out with anyone who smoked pot. My middle-school friends were a lot like me. They were spelling bee champions and history club nerds. They sang in the choir and helped backstage with school plays. None of them drank alcohol, not even Amy—who found a bottle of Jack Daniels under her brother's bed.

Lara closed her eyes and held the smoke for six beats before slowly exhaling into the wind.

"Don't Bogart the joint, Lara. Pass it along," Phillip said.

I took the joint and hoped I looked as cool as Lara when she drew in the smoke. It tasted earthy, not bad at all, but it burned the back of my throat. I inhaled deeply and tried to hold it but my body betrayed me immediately. I coughed hard, expelling all of it.

Lewis patted me on the back. "You okay?"

At his touch, I sensed something wrong. I wanted to be afraid for Lewis, but that feeling didn't stick. My head was suddenly swimming in clouds that blocked the view. I felt light and heavy at the same time and the tiny tingles scattered down my spine, then went away.

"She said she's been smoking forever." Phillip laughed and took the joint from me.

"Shut up, Phillip," Lewis said. "Can't you be nice to anyone? You're such an asshole sometimes." He took the joint and I noticed his missing finger again.

"Baby." Phillip looked away.

"I'm not a baby," Lewis said. He lounged back on the gazebo after taking his turn, his arms limp at his sides.

It occurred to me that Phillip was calling Lewis a baby when he saw me playing with Margot. The thought came and went as quickly as a lightning bug's flash.

I was here. In the gazebo.

Actually, I was in awe of all three of them. Lewis's odd finger strangely made me more curious about him. He looked like a Greek god, sculpted and athletic. I imagined him with angel wings and smiled, wondering if he could fly. Phillip pranced around like a dancer. Graceful and muscular, he was acrobatic and agile. I could hear songs from a musical rustling the trees and in the crickets chirping. I wanted to dance with him. And Lara smiled at me like we were best friends. I wanted to hold her hand.

I was hanging out with the handsome and wealthy, perfect Vaughans. Everything was beautiful.

CHAPTER 11

PHILLIP THE PIED PIPER

Lara

Lara couldn't keep her eyes off Daphne. She had the body of an Olympic ice skater or a superbad tennis pro—legs as long as the day—and her cute haircut brushed against her long neck. She was like a daisy among the thorny thistles. A butterfly in a wasp's nest.

Lara hated her.

While Phillip and Lewis smoked the rest of the joint, Daphne asked, "Are you from Indianapolis?"

What a stupid question. Didn't she know who they were? "Duh," Lara said. "I heard you go to Orchard Park private school."

"Lara will be a senior," Lewis said. "I'll be a freshman."

Daphne's gaze shifted to him. "I'll be a freshman too."

Lara wanted the new girl's attention back. "I haven't seen you at the country club, so how does Mother know your aunt?"

"They went to school together at Orchard Park," Daphne said. "That's why my grandmother is sending us there in the fall. Family tradition or something like that."

"Our mother graduated from Orchard Park in '55," Lara said. "She was going to Wellesley College when she met Father. Our father's a famous lawyer."

"He's the Marion County Prosecutor," Lewis said.

"What difference does it make?" Lara said. What mattered was she owned the bragging rights. She had no idea what her father did in the courtroom. She tried to pay attention when Father talked about his work, but it was boring. And though he didn't pay any attention to her, she longed to have his love and affection. She wanted it more than anything. She asked Daphne, "Isn't your dad a cook or something?"

"He's a trained chef," Daphne said. "He opened a natural food deli called The Asparagus Sandwich in Broad Ripple. Maybe you've heard of it?"

"I've never heard of it. It must be very small."

"He bakes all the bread and makes vegetarian sandwiches, egg dishes, and pastries," Daphne said. "It's really good."

Lara looked at her fingernails as if she could care less, but Daphne's forthright admiration for her dad made her jealous. Still, there was something cool about their new neighbor. And Lara could use a friend.

"Do you cook?" Lewis asked Daphne.

"He's teaching me." Daphne's smile lit up her face. "What about you?"

"The only thing Lewis knows how to make is a bowl of cereal," Phillip said.

"I can make a mean TV dinner." Lewis was flirting with Daphne. "Salisbury steak is my favorite."

"Cooking is for housewives," Lara said. "I'm going to college in New York. I'm going to model for magazines."

"No, you aren't. You're too old." Phillip was climbing the sides of the gazebo like it was a jungle gym.

"I can model for *Glamour* or *Vogue*. The photographer wants me. He said I have the look."

"Mother will never take you back to New York," Lewis said.

"It doesn't matter what she wants. I graduate in a year." Lara dug the flask out of her back pocket and downed the last of it.

"I wasn't as lucky as my spoiled brother and sister," Phillip said. "Dad sent me off to boarding school. Said I needed discipline." He stepped up on the bench and swung around the post, hanging on the gazebo like a big ape—his leg kicking out as he howled at the moon. He leapt onto the grass outside the gazebo and started jogging toward the road. "Let's go, people. We gotta keep moving so we don't get caught."

"Wait. I don't want to get caught," Daphne said. "I heard the groundskeeper has a gun."

"He does." Phillip's eyes were as big as soccer balls.

"He's exaggerating," Lara said. She used to love that about him. She loved his stories and the way he took her mind off their bickering parents. Now Phillip was just another person getting in the way of what she wanted. Lara stood and a wave of dizziness forced her to grab the bench.

"Come on." Phillip started walking toward the shelter of the tree line.

Lara followed because she wanted to talk to Daphne. The more they talked, the harder it was to hate her. She was a nice kid, Lara realized. Uncorrupted.

"Where are we going?" Daphne asked.

"That's the question, isn't it?" Phillip marched along the tree line. "'You have to go on and be crazy. Craziness is like heaven.'"

"What does that mean?"

Lara caught up with them. "It's a famous quote by Jimi Hendrix. Phillip quotes a lot of famous people like he thinks he's one of them."

"I can hear you, Lara." Phillip turned right on the unlit country road, walking away from the lake, toward darkness.

Phillip the Pied Piper. By now, Lara was so stoned, she couldn't tell if she'd said it out loud or not.

Phillip strode ahead. "'In order to change the world, you have to get your head together first.'"

"Who says that?" Daphne said, looking at him like he was a god or something. Lara wanted her to get a clue. Phillip was a controlling, egotistical jerk. He would get them all into trouble.

"Jimi Hendrix," Phillip said. "Don't you know anything?"

"Where are we going?" Lewis asked.

"Almost there."

A single streetlamp illuminated a darkened building on the corner of the street.

"Behold. The corner store." Phillip took off, jogging toward it. He darted from window to window, looking for a way in as Lewis tried to stop him. Baby brother. Everyone's hero.

Daphne remained near Lara by the side of the road. "What are they looking for?"

"He's going to break into the store," Lara said.

The smell of something sour and rotten rose in the breeze and turned Lara's stomach. Maybe it was the vodka and grapefruit juice she drank at dinner. Bile rose in her throat.

Lara gripped Daphne's elbow unsteadily.

"Are you okay?" Daphne asked.

"I'm great." Lara focused on the pavement at her feet.

Phillip darted from window to window, pressing his face against the panes. A half mile away, headlights from an approaching car crested a hill.

Breaking glass shattered the hushed quiet.

Fucking Phillip. He's going to get us into trouble.

"A car's coming!" Daphne pushed Lara behind a tree trunk. "What's Phillip doing?"

"Breaking into the store, I told you." *Wasn't it obvious?* But Lara didn't want the kind of attention Phillip brought. Each one of them had tested Father's anger. His bristling rage. Father. Prosecutor Vaughan. Even his name evoked a kind of supreme justice and punishment. Phillip and Lewis had their own ways of avoiding it. Lara tried hard to be the perfect daughter. It wasn't enough. It was never enough.

She dropped to her knees. "I don't feel good." Her stomach lurched.

The car crawled closer. It sat at the stop sign for a long time with its headlights illuminating the corridor of trees along the road. The crickets and frogs became eerily silent.

Lara crawled into the bushes and hid behind a tree. Her head was spinning. *Maybe I drank too much peach schnapps?* Wooziness overcame her, and she retched on the ground.

Daphne smoothed Lara's hair away from her face as she threw up in the bushes.

WHAT THE CAT DRAGGED IN

Early hours of June 12ᵗʰ: Mark

Mark had been lucky. He'd been out for a week and Pops knew someone who could get him a job.

Pops had known Red, the owner of The Bar, since they were kids. Years ago Pops had done Red a favor—though Mark had no idea what that was—and now asked for one in return. Pops made the phone call within an hour of Mark walking in the door. Because Pops sure as hell couldn't support Mark on his welfare check and food stamps.

"My boy needs a job."

"The one in prison?"

"He got out on good behavior. He's a good boy. I promise you'll be satisfied."

Mark had to seek permission from the judge. As a parolee, he wasn't allowed to drink or go to any establishment where alcohol was served. But since Pops was on welfare, the judge allowed it with a stipulation that Mark didn't drink.

Cool. I don't want a drink, Mark thought. Since he was only seventeen when he was convicted, he didn't really know how booze affected him. But he was pretty sure alcohol would loosen his temper and he'd end up back in prison. He couldn't let that happen.

Behind a stained and cracked wood bar, Mark hand-washed glasses and put them away. An old RCA box television set sat precariously on the edge of a narrow shelf in the corner of The Bar where Walter Cronkite talked about Jimmy Carter's election campaign. The country was getting pumped up for the bicentennial.

The boom of thunder outside shook the building. Mixed with some early fireworks, it was hard to tell the difference between celebration and storm.

The crack of billiard balls drew moans and a "Right on!" from regulars Randy and his brother Watson shooting a game of pool. Others had gone home.

At the end of the bar, Red leaned on his elbows with a cigarette hanging from yellowed fingers. He and his longtime friend Guy were huddled together like an old married couple. They talked quietly below the hum of Cronkite's deep, thoughtful voice.

One elbow propped up Red as he waved his glass at Mark. "Pour me another beer, boy."

Mark was no boy. He'd just spent seven years in prison. Seven years seemed more like ten because he was tried as an adult.

"What time you closing tonight?" Mark asked.

"Same as usual. 'Round midnight. Got somewhere to go?"

"'Course not."

Red took another cigarette from the pack in his pocket, tapped the inch-long ash from the one burning between his fingers and chain-lit the new one. Inhaling deeply, he covered his thin lips with his fist and coughed.

Mark grew up out here between farms and country roads that trailed off to nowhere. Cornstalks as far as the eye could see in July. The only thing this area had going on was Carlson Academy. Those folks brought money to town. Without the school and the summer vacationers, this town wouldn't really be on the map.

In the fifties, Red and Guy parked a double-wide on the six-acre lot outside of Carlson and built the bar. No windows and nothing fancy about it. It became a hangout for locals who drove twenty miles to get away from their trailers and farmhouses. Didn't even have a name. The Bar sign in the window and a neon Budweiser light over the door said it all. Red and Guy had made this bar their life. They lived here from noon till midnight every single day.

Guy pushed his glass forward. Mark nodded, refilled it with ice, Jack Daniels, and Coke, and passed it back. Both turned toward the TV, Cronkite, and Carter, the soft-spoken Democrat. The hope.

Nineteen seventy-six was a big election year. Especially in the wake of the Watergate scandal and Nixon's resignation. "I am not a crook." Mark could relate. Doing time just made him regret everything. He'd take it all back if he could.

God, what he'd do if given half a chance.

Randy and his brother Watson circled the pool table, eyeing the lay of the balls. Watson was nicknamed after Sherlock Holmes' assistant, the doctor. Though this Watson was no doctor, he was fiercely loyal to his brother—his only family. They had no future as far as Mark could see. But they'd grown up here like Mark, in a trailer home. They were janitors at the academy and farmhands during fall harvest and otherwise had no prospects.

Like Randy and Watson, Mark was anchored here by birth and something he couldn't quite grasp. Not that he was tied down. He just couldn't leave. Like a dog on a leash. Like a man with a record.

The evening was just about over when the door to The Bar sprung open and slammed into the wall. Night air blew in, making the rank beer and cigarette smells seem stronger somehow.

The young man who opened the door staggered inside and tripped on a bar stool. He was a stocky, athletic looking guy, wearing a Carlson Academy polo shirt and jeans. His dark hair was messy, and his brow seemed to be raised just to keep his eyelids open.

"Can I get you something?"

"Gimme a shot of Crown and a beer," Sporto said and white-knuckled the edge of the bar as he swayed in place.

Mark glanced at Red, who shook his head.

"I don't think so," Mark said. "Some other time, pal."

The guy smirked. "What? Do you need ID?"

"No. We're closed. Go home."

"Fuck that!" The guy looked around the bar. Randy and Watson didn't take notice. With his cue chalked and ready, Watson leaned over to take another shot.

"Hey! Hey you! The bartender here won't pour me a drink." Sporto let go of the bar and staggered forward.

Randy laughed. "Give him one, Mark. Maybe he'll pass out."

Sporto crossed the floor like on ice skates. He had Randy by the throat and backed up to the pool table faster than an Indy car on time trial day. Watson grabbed Sporto by the shirt and Randy punched him in the face.

Shit.

Mark flew around the end of the bar. The last thing he needed was to get in another bar fight. He pulled the guy off Randy and threw him to the floor.

Watson wasn't ready to give in. He dropped to one knee and raised his fist. "Don't hit my brother! Don't hit my brother!" His fists crunched Sporto's nose and blood splattered. He drew back to hit him again and Mark caught his arm.

"Watson! Get off him!" It took both Mark and Randy to pull Watson off the guy.

An hour and a half later, a lone cricket chirped near the wet parking lot. As the thunderstorm moved away, moths, mosquitos, and other winged nightlife swarmed to the light of a single streetlamp. Mark and Randy had carried Sporto outside and dropped him on the ground. Passed out and drunk, he still lay there with the toe of one shoe in a puddle.

Mark watched Randy and Watson looking down at the guy as they walked to their car. Watson clutched his bruised knuckles close to his chest. "I'm so sorry. I didn't mean to."

"I know, Watson," Randy said. "It wasn't your fault. You just didn't think it through."

Randy and Watson walked off, Watson muttering with his chin dropped to his chest.

Mark sat on the concrete step in front of The Bar. His car, a used Mustang he bought in Plymouth, and a kelly-green Toyota Corolla, were the only ones left in the lot.

"See you tomorrow?" Red asked Mark when he came outside.

"Yep."

Red locked up and he and Guy walked back to their double-wide.

A cricket hopped across the crushed gravel drive, stopping at Sporto's leg. Blood had dried on his face around his mouth and nose. His white academy polo shirt meant he either went to the school or he worked there. Either way, the dude probably had more money than Mark had seen in his whole lifetime.

"You're gonna wake up with a nasty hangover," Mark said. He didn't know exactly why he stayed. It was important to him that Sporto got home safely.

While the guy lay passed out on the pavement, Mark pulled Sporto's wallet from the back pocket of his jeans. He had a Wisconsin driver's license with the name Harold Zienkiewicz, age thirty-five. This guy wasn't that old. Mark dug around and found a student ID for the University of Wisconsin, Madison. The name on that ID said Phillip Vaughan. An Indiana driver's license matched. Age twenty.

Vaughan. "No shit."

Mark would never forget that name. He tossed the wallet on the ground beside Phillip.

Prosecutor John Wesley Vaughan III had sent Mark to prison. Not juvie like the other kids his age, prison. And the crime wasn't even Mark's fault. Could this guy be related to Prosecutor Vaughan? Maybe his son?

That was too big a coincidence. Mark stubbed out his cigarette and flicked it away. "Hey? You awake?"

Phillip moaned.

Mark rolled him onto his back. Dust from the gravel driveway coated his cheek and jeans. Blood specked his white shirt. He wasn't so clean anymore. "Hey! Wake up."

Phillip started and covered his eyes against the glare of the streetlight. "What the fuck?" He rolled back over and pushed himself up on his elbows and knees.

"If you're gonna vomit, please do it off the road."

Phillip crawled to the grass and collapsed again.

Mark looked away and dug a new pack of smokes out of his shirt pocket. Tapping them down to pack the tobacco, he asked, "Do you live in Carlson? I can give you a ride. You sure as shit shouldn't drive." He pulled off the cellophane and tapped them again.

Phillip picked up his wallet and stood, running his mouth across his sleeve. "Been worse. Thanks for the offer, though." He made his way toward the Corolla. When he got there, he dug through his pockets for the keys.

"Looking for these?" Mark held them up. In the back of his mind, he thought about ways to get revenge. He needed to find out if this kid was related to Prosecutor John Wesley Vaughan III. The man who stole his youth and prospects for a decent life.

CHAPTER 13

TONY BALONEY

Daphne

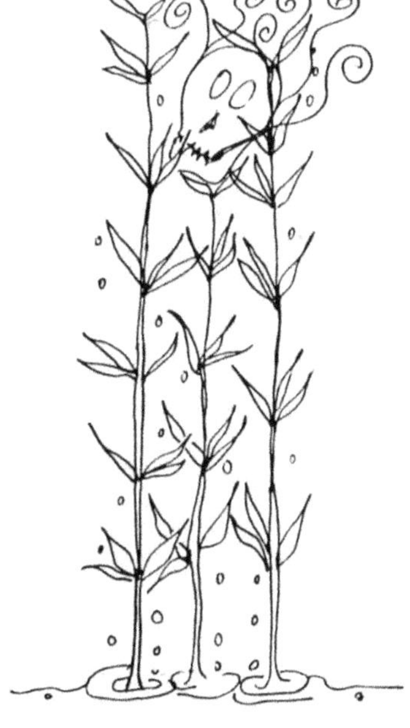

The house smelled like bacon and coffee. After breakfast, I went up-stairs to be alone. Out the window, waves from the lake splashed against the retaining wall, thrumming with thick noxious whispers. I ignored them. Because for the first time in over a year, I felt alive.

When I'd snuck back inside last night, Margot was sleeping. The adults were still listening to music. I hadn't told anyone—last night I was hanging out with the Vaughans. *The Vaughans!* The memory sounded like my favorite piano concerto, Rachmaninoff's third. With sweeping arpeggios and uplifting phrases that made me think of angels singing in heaven.

Before Lara was sick, and even after, she'd carried herself with an air of royalty. I didn't just want to be her friend, I wanted to be Lara. Not sick Lara. The Lara I met in the gazebo. She was so pretty. Her long hair fell over a fashionable halter top that showed off her boobs.

I reached for my new bathing suit with little triangles on the top and wondered when mine would ever grow.

Lewis had moved with athletic poise like one of those jungle lions from the movie *Born Free*. Every time I'd looked at him, he stared right at me with a warm smile. He wasn't like the kids at school who bought into Ruth's story. *Who was I kidding? It was my story too.* At least Lewis didn't know.

And Phillip was unlike anyone I'd ever met. He seemed so carefree. Like I wanted to be. Free of parental rules. Free from the stigma of divorce. And . . . I giggled at the next thought.

I smoked pot with them! I was actually hanging out with the cool kids.

As I changed into my bathing suit and a pair of shorts, unfamiliar voices rose from downstairs. I threw a T-shirt over my bikini and crept barefoot down the stairs. I peered around the corner into the living room.

Two police officers, a man and a woman, were talking to Uncle Chuck and Tony.

"The kids went to bed early," Uncle Chuck said. "We were here all night, though. We didn't hear anything."

Auntie Beth and Marianne sat at the card table sipping from coffee cups. Margot looked at the officers over the edge of a book she was reading. Brandon and Sammy pretended to build a card house on the floor while listening to every word.

"It was a minor break-in, but the owner wants the thief caught. You understand. There was damage to the property," the male officer said. He wore a tan uniform with the sleeves rolled up and his hands folded at his belt. His brown hair was combed and neat with long sideburns that framed his face.

Was Phillip caught? Am I in trouble? Heat rose suddenly to my cheeks and neck. I couldn't tear my gaze from the guns on the officers' hips.

"Are you sure the kids were in bed?" the officer asked.

I froze when he looked my way. Though his pale blue eyes held a stern gaze, there was softness around his mouth and something kind about his face. His name tag read Deputy Marshal Brant Simmons.

In a flash, like a Rolodex flipping through a series of photos in my mind, I saw him helping me out someday.

"There you are, Daphne," Uncle Chuck said.

Marianne looked up from her magazine but didn't say anything. Uncle Chuck introduced me. "The kids went to bed early," he said. "I made sure of it."

"There are lots of kids her age around here. Do you have any friends? Maybe someone at the academy?" The officer had directed the question at me.

I opened my mouth but couldn't speak. *Are you going to narc on us?* Phillip had asked. My face heated up. I didn't want to get Phillip in any trouble. I'd only just met the Vaughans. I wanted them to like me.

"She's only fifteen," Tony said. "She went to bed with the rest of the kids."

At least he defended me. It didn't make me like him any better.

The officer smiled kindly as the female deputy behind him touched his elbow, with a nod. "Well, if you hear anything about the break in, I'd appreciate a call." His gaze locked on mine, and I turned away.

"Have a nice morning." The female officer backed out of the room.

I was so relieved they didn't ask me any more questions.

"That was interesting," Uncle Chuck said after they left.

"Good to know the pigs are Johnny-on-the-spot."

"Tony. There are kids," Auntie Beth said.

"We'll have to start keeping the doors locked at night," Uncle Chuck said.

Marianne wore dark glasses and moved slower than usual. Next to her, Tony put his hairy arm around her. "Who wants to go skiing?" she said.

I slipped out the door past the adults. Lewis had invited me to go skiing today, but now how would I explain getting to know them?

Where were you last night? Were you with the Vaughans? Did you see the break-in?

I imagined the whole conversation and it didn't turn out well for me.

Why didn't you tell that nice police man you saw the boy who broke into the store?

Would it make me an accomplice? Probably. I watched *Kojak* and *Barnaby Jones.* I knew how these things ended for the criminal.

Meeting the Vaughans had to be kept secret. And I was fine with that. I smiled and cherished it. The secret was mine, and mine alone.

Swarms of mosquitoes and no-see-ums hovered near the ultra-calm shore. The sound of the boat lift ticking echoed off the lake like a count-down clock as Marianne lowered the Hydrodyne into the water. Tony carried a Styrofoam cooler. Sammy and Brandon ran out on the dock with their towels in hand.

"No running on the dock!" I told Brandon for the hundredth time.

Thrilled to go for a ride, we all piled into the boat. The cooler filled with pop and beer sat between Auntie Beth's feet. Margot held onto her baseball cap at the stern and the boys lay on their bellies on towels, their faces to the wind. Life vests remained under the seat benches because Tony told the boys that big kids didn't need life vests. Auntie Beth and Uncle Chuck let it ride. Everyone just wanted to have fun.

So far, Tony was winning points from everyone except me. I didn't like him, or the way he'd schmoozed his way into the family's good graces. I watched him slide an arm around Marianne and narrowed my gaze at him, willing him to remove his arm.

He caught me staring and a single brow rose. *What are you looking at?*

I looked away and hugged a sun-warmed towel to my chest. I couldn't figure out what Marianne saw in this loser. He was trying too hard to fit in. And he was nothing like Dad.

Dad should be here. Tony Baloney was not family.

At the helm, Uncle Chuck sped across the lake in search of the smoothest water for skiing.

The sun was warm, but there were clouds on the horizon. Another storm? When they reached the far south side of the lake, Uncle Chuck shouted over the wind and engine roar, "This looks like a good spot." He slowed the boat near the shore, and the Hydrodyne sank into smooth-as-glass water. "Who's up first?"

Brandon and Sammy both answered the call. Brandon clamored loudest.

"Okay, okay, little man." Uncle Chuck shut off the engine.

The family leapt into action. "Here's your ski vest, Brandon. Make sure it's tight." Marianne adjusted the straps and opened the vest for Brandon. "I'll get your skis."

Auntie Beth untangled the ski rope and Margot moved out of the way. Sammy put his vest on and peered over the aluminum side rail. Brandon unlocked the flimsy gate and cannonballed into the water, splashing everyone.

My aunt groaned but Tony laughed. "Good one!"

Marianne tossed the skis to Brandon one at a time, and he slipped them on his feet.

"Tips up!" Marianne shouted.

"I know." Brandon gripped the handle of the ski rope. He'd learned to water-ski when he was six.

Sammy took the seat next to me as Uncle Chuck put the engine in idle.

When the end of the rope was taut, Brandon shouted, "Hit it!"

Uncle Chuck eased the throttle and Brandon bobbed out of the water like a cork. He skied halfway around the lake before wiping out on a big boat wake, then laughed about it when he climbed back on board. Sammy didn't have as much stamina, and he let go of the rope after zipping back and forth across the wake a few times. Margot didn't want to slalom, though she'd learned last year. She skied on two all the way to the academy and back again.

"Good run, Margot," Auntie Beth said. "You kids have become such experts. I'm proud of you."

I shivered as I put on the cold, wet vest Margot had worn. My tiny boobs were tender, and I loosened the upper straps.

"One or two skis?" Auntie Beth asked.

"Just one."

"Show off," Brandon said.

"She's a pro," Tony said.

"I taught her everything she knows," Marianne said.

Since it was impossible to dive gracefully with a ski vest on, I jumped in feet first. Though the vest prevented me from going too far under, the cool water momentarily took my breath. I wiped my eyes and caught the slalom ski gliding across the surface. I slid my foot into the boot and looked for the rope. It landed with a small splash beside my shoulder.

I took the handle with an alternating grip. Uncle Chuck put the boat in gear and idled. The rope reached its length and grew taut. At first, I struggled to keep the ski straight and the tip dipped below the surface. I quickly got my bearings, muscle memory kicked in, and I found my balance. "Hit it!"

The boat roared ahead, dragging me through the water as it accelerated. I squatted and stabilized the ski. In no time, I was standing on water. No feeling in the world was as exhilarating or as powerful. Ahead of me, the Hydrodyne flattened the water into a V-shaped wake. Outside the wake, the glassy surface of Lake Carlson invited me to play.

This year my legs were longer and stronger. I had more confidence on the water ski than ever before. Bearing into the ski, I zigzagged across the wake. After several sweeps, I settled into the centerline again. Auntie Beth clapped above her head, and the boys pumped their fists in the air. Uncle Chuck's gaze was on me when another boat with a skier headed toward us.

I pointed. The other driver didn't swerve. Uncle Chuck cut right to avoid a collision and dragged me through rough water. I hung on, but then he turned the boat sharply. It forced me outside the wake and into a patch of rough water. Waves swallowed the tip of my ski, and I tumbled across the surface.

When I came up for air, my shoulder ached. I looked around for the ski. In this section of the lake, the water looked darker because a thick patch of lakeweed grew close to the surface.

Slimy dark-green weeds twisted around my ankles. I tried to kick them away, which only got my feet tangled even more. As I fought the weeds, I heard a whisper. My breath shallowed as I peered under the surface. Between the creepy strands, a white body rolled slowly upward with the water's surge. A face turned toward me.

Save me!

The water muffled my scream. I kicked the leafy tendrils away and swam as fast as I could.

A person? Or had it been a dead fish?

I paddled hard to the ski. The Hydrodyne was still turning around and seemed miles away. I retrieved the ski, winded, my heart pounding the tremolo bass line from Beethoven's *Pathétique* Sonata.

The Hydrodyne finally returned to pick me up and the entire family hung off the starboard side.

"Are you okay?"

"That was some wipeout!" Brandon said.

"Are you hurt?"

"That was cool!" Sammy said.

I swam toward the boat, keeping my gaze and my feet above the surface of the water. Tony held out a hand, and I only took it because I needed to get out of the water quickly. I needed to shake the feeling of dread.

As soon as my hand locked on Tony's, images filled my mind. *Smoke, pot, pills, and a wad of cash.*

I fell into the boat and looked up at him. I knew who he was. He was someone who broke the law. He was someone I couldn't trust, and Marianne shouldn't be dating him. Tony was a criminal.

"What's the buzz, my friend?" Tony caught me staring.

"Are you hurt?" Marianne asked.

"I got the wind knocked out of me," was all I said.

Weirdo! Freak!!

CHAPTER 14

DORITOS AND A DEAD BODY

Daphne

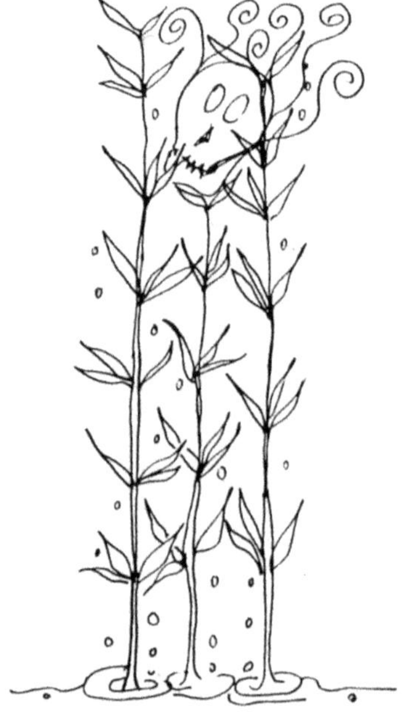

It was a white face with milky eyeballs and an open mouth. It could have been a dead fish, but I wasn't sure. It also could have been a dead body. I couldn't get the image out of my mind.

Out on the dock, I lay on my stomach on a blown-up floatie. The sun heated my back. Nearby, Uncle Chuck and Tony leaned over the prize-winning vintage Chris-Craft and discussed the fine points of the boat. To me it was just a boat. I could count on one hand the number of times I'd seen my uncle take it out for a drive. Even though Auntie Beth had to scrape ice and snow off her windshield every morning to drive Margot and Sammy to school, he kept the boat in his garage during the winter.

Marianne sat up from her towel and checked the wet ski vests drying over the aluminum rail on the Hydrodyne. "How's your shoulder? That was quite a spill you had."

"I'm fine." But the thing I saw, the bloated dead head, made me wary of getting back in the water.

"I have Tiger Balm in my bedroom. If you rub some into the sore areas, it should take the sting out of it." Marianne started collecting towels destined for the clothesline.

"Why can't you leave me alone?" I said to her. I wasn't a baby. And my shoulder didn't hurt that bad.

"The inboard engine is the original, ninety-five horsepower engine," Uncle Chuck said. "It's 239 cubic inches of pure power."

He lowered the Chris-Craft partway into the water. "The propeller is tucked under the hull. See that Mastercraft next door? It's got an inboard engine too. A cheap imitation."

"Whoa," Tony murmured.

I sat up. I'd been watching him ever since he'd pulled me out of the water. Tony Baloney. *What a loser.* I rubbed Hawaiian Tropic dark tanning oil on my arms. When he'd helped me out of the water, I saw things. He gripped my hand, and it was like he told me everything about himself—without ever saying a word—things he probably didn't want me to know.

"Whoa is right, my man. Let me show you." Uncle Chuck climbed along the lift and untied the heavy tarp cover from the bow. With Tony's help, he carefully rolled it back to the windshield, exposing the multigrain woodwork, shiny, polished, and gleaming in the sun.

Both men whistled.

Marianne gathered her towel and plastic glass and prepared to go back to the house. "How about lunch, Daphne?"

"I'm not hungry." I wanted to learn more about Tony.

"She's a beauty, Chuck," Tony said. "Can we take her out? I'd love to see how she feels out on the water."

Uncle Chuck lowered the boat the rest of the way, then hopped in the water. "I don't use it for water-skiing. But I toyed with purchasing raw maple planks to construct a swim platform for the back of this baby, like that Mastercraft next door. Just to make it easier to climb back into the boat. It would be a lot of work sanding and staining planks to match the finish. Though practical, it would ruin the integrity of this classic antique."

He waded around to the far side of the boat. Waist-deep in the lake, he untied the tarp that protected his cherished and valuable craft. "Help me with this, will you? Pull it toward you, but don't let it drag on the finish. It'll scratch."

"Got it, my man." Tony rolled more of the cover back, exposing the windshield and oiled, red leather seats.

Marianne had her towel folded over her arms and an inner tube the boys played on. "Are you coming?" she asked me.

"I said I don't want lunch." I wanted Marianne to leave me alone.

In the water, Uncle Chuck moved around the boat. "What the . . . How'd this get untied?"

Tony lifted the tarp off the back and under his breath said, "Uh-oh."

I looked up. I'd seen Brandon sneaking around the boat but didn't want to get him in trouble.

"What do you mean, uh-oh? Did you scratch it?" Uncle Chuck strode over as fast as he could in the chest-deep water.

I stood behind Tony as he pulled the cover back even farther, revealing a pillow stuffed into the corner of the back seat where someone had lain down. There was a flashlight and an empty bag of Doritos on the bench.

"No scratches. But . . ." To his credit, Tony didn't complete the sentence.

Inside the boat were discarded Snack Pack pudding containers and empty chip bags. Crumbs were scattered all over the back seat and ground into the leather.

Brandon had been sneaking junk food from the kitchen. I'd seen him carry stuff out on the dock. The trash always mysteriously vanished.

Marianne seemed nervous. "Now, Chuck, don't be mad."

"What do you mean?" Uncle Chuck hustled up the ladder. Dumbfounded, he looked into his boat. "What the . . ." He turned to me. "Did you know about this?"

I shook my head, but I was more afraid for Brandon, so kept my mouth shut.

Marianne held out a hand. "Now, Chuck—"

"Who did this?" The redness of anger flowered on his neck and chest. His sharp blue eyes bored into me. "Daphne?"

"It wasn't me."

"Chuck, listen. They're kids," Marianne said.

His eyes narrowed, wrinkling his forehead. "I suspect you do know, Daphne. You're just not saying."

I flinched.

"Don't blame her," Marianne said.

"Not that big a deal," Tony said, "I'll clean it up." He started to climb into the boat.

"No, wait," Uncle Chuck said. "Leave the evidence. I'm going to get the boys." He stormed back to the house.

"Chuck, stop." Marianne tried to keep up with him as he stomped off the dock. "Chuck . . ." She tossed the towels in the grass and kept going.

I watched them go and Tony came to my side. "I hope Brandon doesn't get in too much trouble."

I shot a look at him before taking off at a run. Hoping Brandon didn't get a spanking, I skidded to a stop outside the screen door.

"Stop defending him. Your boy has been acting out since you and Jeremy divorced, and he needs to face some consequences. He's known for years that my boat is off limits." Chuck's face was beet red.

Even Marianne looked frightened of him. "Are you angry with me? Or are you upset that he broke the rules? Those are two separate things. He makes forts at home all the time. It's harmless fun."

"You never should have divorced Jeremy. He was the only thing keeping that boy in line."

"That's not true."

"It is, and you know it." Uncle Chuck moved to the bottom of the stairs. "Brandon?"

I cringed as Brandon appeared at the bottom of the steps, within arm's reach of my uncle.

He grabbed Brandon. "What were you thinking? You know the rules. Never ever take food into my boat. Understand?"

"Stop, Chuck." Marianne touched Uncle Chuck's shoulder. He slapped her away, knocking her onto the floor.

I fought the urge to go inside and help my mom. Auntie Beth appeared out of nowhere. "What's going on?" She helped Marianne up.

Marianne scrambled to her feet and brushed her away. "Don't you lay a hand on him, Chuck."

"Someone needs to take the blame."

"He's just a boy," Auntie Beth raised her voice. "Whatever he did, it can't be that bad."

"What the hell, Beth! You too?"

Brandon took off out the screen door. I grabbed his arm to reassure him and the look of fear in his eyes went straight to my heart. He pulled away and ran down the shore.

"When are you going to do something about that boy?" Uncle Chuck said. "Your family is out of control, Marianne."

"My family?"

"Your entire life! You and your sexual freedom! Do you even know Tony? What the hell is he doing here?"

Marianne blushed. "How did this turn into a fight about me and my choices?"

I stared through the screen door with the same question.

"Because this is your fault," he said.

Pushing Auntie Beth out of the way, Uncle Chuck stormed off through the kitchen. The other screen door in the front of the house banged open, slammed shut.

Tony came in from the dock and, passing me, he asked, "Did Chuck kill anyone yet?"

Uncle Chuck did seem like the murderous type. He was self-centered, possessive, and volatile. I wondered if Tony had killed anyone. "What do you care?"

His face grew long. "Dude."

I took off after Brandon, knowing I'd find him walking along the shore. I wanted Marianne to do something. She needed to stand up for herself and for us. Tony didn't belong here, but Marianne wasn't strong enough to send him away. Dad would have told Uncle Chuck to back off.

He would have protected Mom and Brandon. He cared about his family. If Tony cared, he would have stood up for Marianne. Pills? Cash? Pot? I'd seen those things when he lifted me out of the water. What did it all mean?

CHAPTER 15

The Prosecutor's Son

Mark

After driving Phillip home that night, Mark made sure to get a phone number. He made sure to make himself available in case Phillip or his friends needed anything.

Phillip stopped by The Bar each afternoon after his last coaching sessions at the academy because he could use his fake ID there. He became conversational and blabbered on about his job, his prospects as a hockey player, the kids he coached. And more importantly, he talked about his father.

And guess what. Phillip Vaughan was the son of the asshole prosecutor. The man who incarcerated Mark when he was seventeen.

Mark had scored the biggest goal of his life.

"He hates me," Phillip told him from his spot on the bar. "I didn't turn out the way he wanted, you know." He picked at the bandage on the bridge of his broken nose. His dark eyes looked more menacing because of the bruising and swelling beneath them.

With his back to Phillip, Mark wiped down the sink. At the end of the bar, Red and Guy drank draft beer and watched the news. The whole country was in an uproar about the 200th birthday of the country. Mark wasn't feeling it. He had hell to pay.

Phillip was a first-class jerk—just like his father. Entitled. Rich. And he sat here crying about how *Daddy doesn't love me. Idiot.* Phillip didn't know what really mattered.

"Count your lucky stars," Mark said. "You've got a lot more than most folks."

"Not me. I'm working my ass off. Father won't support my career. He's not paying my tuition. What else could he possibly want from me? I mean, the Minnesota North Stars scout is watching me."

"They're the best hockey team in the US."

"You follow hockey?"

Mark followed sports. He'd been a basketball player in high school. Fuck. He'd been the best basketball player the state had ever seen. It won him a scholarship to IU, where basketball players were treated like gods. Then he was wrongfully convicted of assault with the intent to kill.

He tossed the towel aside and leaned against the sink. "Sure. I follow hockey." In prison, few hockey games were televised. He used to sit in the TV room and listen to one of the inmates yell about it.

"Did you play?" Phillip lit a cigarette.

"Once." It was half the truth. When he was a kid, he and his friends would go out on the frozen lake in winter and bat around rocks or chunks of ice. "My folks didn't have enough dough to send me to the academy."

Mark was envious of those kids. They were also the ones who had landed him in prison. All his chances were ruined the day he went to the north side of Indianapolis after working on the highway. At the age of seventeen, he was working road crew to help Pops pay for groceries. The kid provoked him. Egged him on. It wasn't Mark's fault that he hit the kid. He was just in the wrong place at the wrong time.

Meanwhile, this Phillip had prospects. He had a chance to become something. And instead, he sat here drinking and smoking. If Mark had so much as a hope of playing hockey with an NHL team, he'd spend all his time on the ice. He would not sit around The Bar like this dope. He would make it happen.

Now it all seemed so ironic.

Phillip's head had hung. Eventually he said, "It's all a game, isn't it?"

"Got that right."

"'Like a true Nature's child, we were born to be wild,'" Phillip said.

"What's that mean?"

"Steppenwolf. You haven't heard their music?" Phillip took a drag of his smoke.

"No." Mark stifled a grunt. In prison? They didn't play Casey Kasem's Top 40.

"If it were up to me, 'There wouldn't be no such thing as establishment,'" Phillip said. "Jimi Hendrix."

"Right on, man." Now more than ever, Mark wanted Prosecutor Vaughan to pay for ruining his life. He leaned closer to Phillip and wiped the counter. From this distance, he could grab his throat and choke him to death. How would Prosecutor Vaughan feel about that? His son, murdered by the kid he put away. The one who was innocent.

"Hey, man, do you know where I can get a dime bag?" Phillip said.

Mark got a grip on his emotions. He wanted to prove he could come through for Phillip. He'd heard some of the locals talking about weed yesterday. "Sure, man. I hear a guy is coming up from Indy. He has good shit."

Phillip took out his wallet and thumbed through a wad of bills. He laid some money on the bar and said, "Can you get it for me?"

Mark pushed it back toward Phillip. "Wish I could. I'm on parole. If I get caught, I go back to the slammer."

"No shit?" Phillip locked his gaze on Mark while he pocketed the cash. "What did you do?"

It was too soon to tell Phillip that his old man had prosecuted him. He looked Phillip in the eye. This little brat didn't know what was coming.

"Never mind, man." Phillip looked away, seeming nervous. "You're cool in my book. Hook me up with the guy?"

Two steps closer to ruining the prosecutor, Mark thought. But could he go through with it? His head involuntarily shook his answer, no. He didn't really want to hurt anyone. Phillip was only a kid. But so was he, once.

Gooseflesh rose on Mark's arms. His breath clouded the air in the Carlson Academy ice dome. He was meeting Phillip at the rink after his coaching session. Phillip needed pot and, since Mark couldn't make the transaction, he had agreed to connect Phillip with a guy drumming up business at The Bar. A guy spending the summer on Lake Carlson.

On the other side of the boards surrounding the rink, tykes in thick hockey shoulder pads and helmets chased a puck straight toward Mark. Their exuberance about the game brought a smile to his lips. As the kid with the puck shooshed around the ice, a string of players followed, awkwardly speeding along on their skates. One fell down.

In the center of the ice, Phillip wore long black pants and a zippered jacket with the Carlson Academy logo on it. He shouted names and encouraged them. He kept glancing at a tall blond girl in the stands. Hunched over, she wore shorts and an orange poncho and rubbed the backs of her arms. She looked bored and out of place here.

A shorter kid with number 17 on his jersey sped ahead of the pack and circled in front of the net. He raised his stick and slapped the puck. It went flying toward the goal and the goalie shuffled to the side and lunged. The puck slipped between his elbow and knee, right into the net.

Number 17 raised his arms and cheered with his teammates. Phillip blew the whistle. "Good job, guys! Take a water break." He shooed them toward the benches on the side of the rink. To Mark, who'd never worn a pair of skates in his life, Phillip skated like an Olympic champion.

As the kids zigzagged toward their bench, Mark waved and Phillip met him at the gate. The bruises under his eyes had turned sick shades of green and yellow. "Did you bring him?"

"He'll meet us outside."

"Cool. Class is over in like twenty." Phillip looked over Mark's shoulder at the blonde in the poncho. She had come down from the stands and stood beside him.

"Why did you make me come here?" she said. "It's freezing cold in this place." She rubbed the backs of her arms and Mark wondered if she were his girlfriend.

"You didn't have to come," Phillip said to her.

"I did so. You won't bring me any weed."

"Can you keep your voice down?" Phillip looked around. "This is the guy you want to talk to. Mark, this is Lara."

She looked him over, head to toe, with an expression that Mark couldn't read. "You can get weed?"

"No, but I'll hook you up with the guy who can."

"Let's get out of here then." Lara took him by the arm. "It's fucking freezing in here."

"I'll meet you outside." Phillip skated back to the kids.

When Mark stepped outside the dome, the summertime heat hit him like a blast from a hot oven. He pulled a key chain out of his jeans pocket as he walked to his car. When they got to his Mustang, Lara leaned back on the hood like she was a model posing for the money shot. "What do you do? Do you work at the academy too?"

If only. "No, I'm a bartender. How do you know Phillip?"

Lara smiled and stared at him a few beats. Her shoulder twitched and she looked away. "Where's this guy we're meeting?"

"He'll be here in a few minutes." Mark eyed Lara. He wasn't sure how old she was. She looked young, like maybe college age, but it was hard to tell. It had been a long time since he'd actually hung out with a woman. He liked her long smooth legs.

She tipped her chin downward and looked up at him through dark eyelashes. "Do you live around here?"

"Grew up near here."

"In Carlson? What's there to do around here besides get high?"

"Not much," he said. "Are you here for the summer?"

"Yeah. Rented a house on the lake." She slipped her fingers beneath the buttons on Mark's white and blue plaid shirt. She was suddenly so close to him that he could smell her shampoo.

He kept his hands in his pockets. "Are you flirting with me?"

"What's it look like?" She ran her hand down the leg of his jeans.

"But what about Phillip?"

"Screw Phillip. I'll pay for the weed myself." Her breath smelled sweet and minty and her eyes . . . She was so close he could see the little flecks of gold in her irises.

Mark wasn't sure what came over him, but he didn't notice the car parking next to his or the guy strolling up to them.

"Mark Walters?"

"Yep?" He unlocked his gaze from Lara's and stepped back. His contact had arrived. "Hey, man. This is Lara. She'd like to buy some weed."

"That's what I'm here for." The guy stuck out a thick-fingered hand, and she shook it. "Name's Tony. What do you need?"

CHAPTER 16

A CRINGY, PRICKLY FEELING

Daphne

I was relieved when Uncle Chuck returned to Indy, but he left a wake of bitter feelings and sadness. I saw it in Margot especially, who retreated to books and playing with horses. Brandon came back out of his shell, but Sammy pouted in his room. Auntie Beth sat alone on the dock, dangling her toes in the water.

And Tony stayed, lingering like a bad taste in your mouth. He tried but failed to make jokes and act cool. He was a dweeb in every sense of the word, but beneath that, I sensed something more dangerous. I wished he would leave too. *Tony Baloney.*

He wasn't the only thing bothering me. The image of that head floating in the water haunted me. Since there was no television at Aubenaubee Lodge—Nana wanted to keep it that way—I went looking for a distraction. And like some creeper in a van offering to show me his puppies, that eerily defective old piano sucked me in.

I sat down and played a somber tune. It was easy. I hit any combination of keys and rueful sounds filled the room. Like Erik Satie, or John Cage. I wondered if this was how they began composing—on an out-of-tune piano. I tentatively opened the Chopin *Études* music and tried to practice, and my lips curled into a sardonic smile. The melody was so discordant, laughter started deep in my chest. A tickle bubbled up. Then it rose and grew. Suddenly, tears streamed from my eyes, and I doubled over.

"What's so funny?" Brandon said. He and Sammy had stopped on their way outside. Beside them, Duke wagged his tail.

"Nothing. Inside joke."

"Whatever. Weirdo." Brandon led the troops outside.

At the window, I watched the boys go.

Weirdo.

Tony stumbled downstairs with his hair in disarray. "Mary? Where's that bottle of Excedrin?" He smelled like an old ashtray. Not at all like Dad, who smelled of baked bread with sometimes a hint of garlic and onion mixed in with sweet Royall Spyce cologne.

"Behind the coffee cups," Marianne called from the patio. "Daphne, show him where it is, please."

The silliness fled from my chest. I went to the kitchen and opened the cabinet with clean coffee cups. I handed the Excedrin bottle to him, and he chugged what was left in the coffee pot to wash down three pills.

"I'm going out for donuts," he said.

He was up to something. I chased after him. "Can I come with you?"

Tony reeled. "Uh . . . There's no room in my car."

For some reason, I suspected he'd say something like that. He left me standing in the yard, wondering where he was really going.

When he returned with donuts, he smelled like cigarettes and funk.

The mid-June temperatures climbed into the nineties and, since the old cottage didn't have air conditioning, everyone cooled off in the water. Around lunchtime, Marianne and Auntie Beth sunned themselves on the dock. Tony sat in a folding chair in nothing but swim trunks. I averted my eyes from his hairy body. Sammy and Brandon floated on rafts.

I'd just come in from a swim when Tony looked at his watch and said, "I could go for a tuna sandwich. Anyone with me?"

"We're all out of tuna," Marianne said.

"Then I'll run out and get some." A set of keys magically appeared in his hand.

"Are you sure? We have turkey and bacon—"

"No, thanks. I have a major craving for tuna. I'll be back." And he took off again.

Marianne and Auntie Beth didn't seem curious why he kept leaving the house.

I dried off and threw my shorts and Dr. Scholl's back on.

I waited near the road along the tree-lined golf cart path across the street, where red and white daisies grew four feet tall.

Behind me the low hum of a golf cart came to a stop. Lewis wore a lime-green polo shirt with the white Polo symbol. "Hey."

"Hey." I dropped the flowers behind my back.

"We're going water-skiing later, wanna come over and play Pong with me?"

It was really two questions. I smiled because I wasn't sure how to answer.

"What I mean is, Lara and I can't ski by ourselves. We need a third. If it doesn't work out, I have Pong. We could play a tournament."

"That sounds good." I was thrilled for any invitation to get out of the house, but if it involved water-skiing, I was skeptical. That disembodied head . . .

"Come over after lunch?"

I couldn't wipe the stupid grin off my face. "Okay."

Lewis took off and shortly, I heard Tony's car. He drove in from the south, which surprised me. Carlson and the grocery were north. *Had he driven all the way around the lake? Where had he really gone?*

I ducked behind the thick trunk of an oak tree, watching as Tony parked in the carport and opened the trunk. There he stooped over and reached for something. He seemed to be rearranging boxes, or whatever he had in the back of his car. Then he shook out a blanket and draped it over everything before closing and locking it. He looked over his shoulder as he walked back to the house without a grocery bag, or any tuna as far as I could tell.

At lunchtime, I made a turkey sandwich in the kitchen. "I was looking forward to tuna fish." I fished for an explanation from Tony.

"The store was all out of Chicken of the Sea. Can you dig it?" The color of Tony's cheeks deepened.

He was lying. I was sure of it.

After lunch, I told Marianne I was going for a walk.

Margot hopped up from the card table. "Can I come with you?"

Ugh. I planned to go to the Vaughans' house and play Pong with Lewis. But I didn't want to tell anyone. "I need to be by myself," I lied.

The dejected look on Margot's face made me feel so bad.

"Stay, Duke," I added. He sat at the screen door looking just as crestfallen as Margot.

Ducking behind the parked cars and the carport, I furtively made my way to the Vaughans' house and knocked on the kitchen door.

"Hey. Come on in." Lewis seemed to have been waiting for me. I glanced at his hand—at his missing finger—and a macabre *Moonlight Sonata* echoed in my mind with a swirl of watery sounds.

I looked around the kitchen. It smelled like pine-scented air freshener, not like roasted turkey or bacon or coffee. Not like ours. "How's it going?"

"Good. Lara's not here right now, so we can't go skiing." For safety reasons, everyone knew you needed a driver, a skier, and a spotter.

"That's okay." I was actually relieved we weren't going skiing for a number of reasons. One: my family would see me on the Vaughans' pier, and I hadn't told them where I was going. Not that Marianne would care. But Auntie Beth would push for punishment. Two: I was not ready to get back in the water with that dead head floating around. I didn't know if it had been my overactive imagination, or real. I still hesitated to tell anyone.

He led me to the living room.

I looked around. The Vaughans' summer home had modern furniture and a television set in the living room. It was nothing like the cottage where—except for the old RCA radio bought in the fifties—Nana kept Aubenaubee Lodge free from modern electronics.

"Have you ever played Pong?"

"Once. But it's been a while." Ruth's big brother had hooked the game up to their TV. I pushed her memory away. And like a curtain opening on a stage, I saw the baby grand piano appear behind Lewis and remembered Adelaide had invited me to play for her.

"You have a piano." This piece truly set the Vaughans' summer home apart from ours. Suddenly I was drawn to the shiny black Baldwin baby grand like a kitten to a saucer of milk.

"Who plays the piano?" I asked.

"No one. It came with the house."

I couldn't imagine having enough money for a baby grand that no one wanted to play.

Lewis dropped into an overstuffed leather La-Z-Boy chair. He picked up a square device attached to the TV by a wire, and I noticed his missing finger again. "There's an Atari, but the only game we have is Pong. I beat that game when I was twelve."

My gaze remained on the piano. The Baldwin sang songs without being touched. I glided toward the beautiful instrument and before I even realized it, I was sitting on the bench. My fingertips gently brushed the keys, and my right hand began a light staccato melody. My left followed in a perfect round, echoing the tones in a game of copycat—the notes that made up the Bach *Two-Part Inventions* No. 8—until the harmonies intertwined in beautiful counterpoint.

When I finished, I caught Lewis's wide-eyed gaze and his smile of pure enjoyment. "That was amazing. What was it?"

I told him. "I learned it last January for a recital at the Second Presbyterian Church on Meridian Street."

"You performed there? That church is enormous."

"I wasn't alone. Twenty-five other music students, violinists, and cellists played too. We had to perform pieces from two different eras. I chose this and Debussy's Rêverie."

My fingers found the starting phrase of the Romantic Era piece and the rest flowed from me as I tried to channel the composer. The peaceful music calmed me and quieted my mind. When I looked up, Lewis was staring with his mouth open.

"You're good."

"Well, I practice a lot. The humidity ruined the piano at our house. I just hope Nana's new piano arrives soon."

"You can practice here any time. I don't think anyone will mind."

A creepy feeling came over me. I felt like I was in some scary movie. The part where the killer is outside watching, but the main characters don't know it. I peered out the windows to see if anyone next door was watching the house. I'd never seen Aubenaubee Lodge from this vantage point and checked all the windows before I was satisfied. The cringy feeling persisted, a prickle on my arm and ear.

CHAPTER 17

MARK WALTERS

Lara

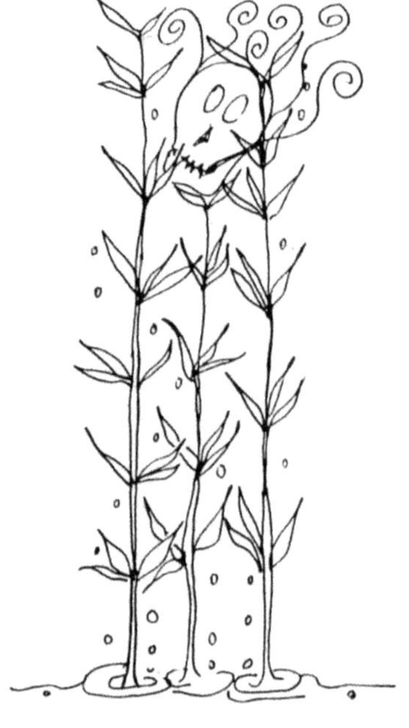

Mark Walters, Mark Walters, Mark Walters. Lara couldn't keep her mind off him. She recalled him running his fingers through his chin-length curly hair. His tight T-shirt stretched over muscular shoulders. He seemed a little bit shy around her. His awkward behavior and slightly off-kilter social skills were endearing. Like when she snuck up on him and he startled. "Don't do that. You scared the shit outta me." It made her laugh.

Mark was dreamy with a little bit of a bad-boy vibe like John Travolta in *Welcome Back, Kotter.* He was mature, kinda cute, and easy to be with. He didn't have much money, so he wasn't pretentious like the boys at Orchard Park. He didn't go to college, so he didn't have goals to be the next senator. The way he checked her out, his eyes lingering on her tits, she knew she'd hooked him. And he grew up in the sticks.

Perfect. Father and Mother would hate him.

After calling his house a few times and getting no answer, she took her towel and a pillow out on the dock.

Lake Carlson was a drag. Mark was the only thing interesting in this stupid little town. Television reception and programming from the surrounding small towns were terrible. *Days of Our Lives* droned on, and the only other choice was a money-raising telethon. It sucked even worse than watching old black-and-white movies. Lara had already listened to her entire 8-track tape collection—America, the Beach Boys, Shaun Cassidy, and Elton John—a half dozen times.

She was frustrated and needed someone besides Lewis to entertain her.

Greasy with tanning oil, she lay on her beach towel at the end of the dock. She watched Lewis swim laps out to the buoy and back while she browned in the sun. He'd been swimming for an hour when he climbed the ladder and shook his hair out, spraying her with cold lake water.

"Hey!" She shaded her eyes from the sun and sat up. "Dry off somewhere else."

"Don't be so much like Mother. She hates getting wet."

"Don't compare me to Mother. I'm nothing like her."

"You are." Lewis clawed his fingers and snarled at her. "Meow."

Lara rolled to her stomach and propped her head so she could watch the activity next door. That girl, Daphne, was sunning on the dock too. Her brothers, or whatever, were swimming and yelling. They were loud and obnoxious. Lara glanced toward their ugly old cottage. The girl with braces was reading on the patio.

How boring. Lara couldn't wait for the weekend when Phillip would be off work. He'd bring pot to light up this dismal vacation. He had a direct line to Tony, the Weed Man.

Lewis sat on the end of the dock. His head turned toward the kids next door too. He watched Daphne stand up and throw a raft to one of the boys.

"What are you looking at?" Lara asked.

"Daphne. She was nice, don't you think?"

Lara shrugged. Daphne was nice. She'd held Lara's hair when she got sick on the side of the road. Still, she was boring. Lewis's dreamy gaze was locked on Daphne as she took off her sunglasses, went to the edge of the pier, and performed a long shallow dive. When she came up for air, Lewis's mouth slackened, and his lips curled into a slight smile.

"Why don't you go over there and talk to her?" Lara asked.

"What? No." He blushed. Lewis clearly had a crush on the girl next door.

"Oh, no." Lara smiled. It would give her no end of pleasure to watch him squirm. Now she knew just what to do to ease the boredom. "We're going over there. Let's invite her to go skiing."

CHAPTER 18

YOU BE CAREFUL, NOW, YOU HEAR?

Daphne

A second week passed without a piano and it was nearing the end of June. Or so I thought. I had no idea what day it was. Nana said a new one was on its way, but waiting was torture. Though Lewis invited me to come by any time, I still didn't want anyone to know about that night. Besides, it was a little awkward to just stop by *anytime.*

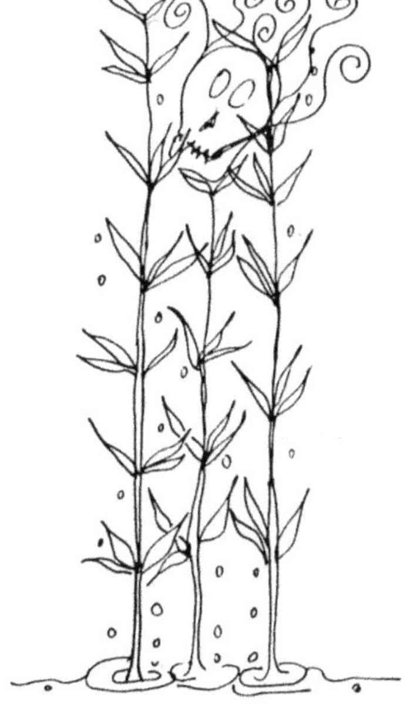

So, late one afternoon, I plunked out a tune. The *Moonlight Sonata* came out sounding darker—if that was possible—like a dissonant and macabre piece. Toward the end, I heavy-handed the chords, *forte,* not *pianissimo,* until sound filled the house like everyone's dark emotions.

And before the final chords, Marianne shouted from the kitchen. "Can you stop that awful racket, Daphne? Someone's here for you."

I sank my fingers into the final chord—*fortissimo!*—and stood when the Vaughans entered. After a day on the pier, I still wore my bikini top with a pair of shorts. I smelled like tanning oil and my air-dried hair curled left to right.

Lewis's soft gaze fell on me. Horizontal stripes on his tight-fitting polyester T-shirt accentuated his buff shoulders.

"Hi." I stepped away from the piano.

Lara lurked behind Lewis with her shiny hair brushed to perfection. She lifted her fingers in a tiny wave. "Can Daphne come with us to the A&W? We're going to grab dinner."

I tried not to act too excited. "I like A&W."

Margot looked up from her book. The boys became quiet.

"Isn't that nice," Marianne said. "Is your mother driving?"

"I'm driving. I'm seventeen." Lara jangled a key ring with a half dozen keys and a miniature tennis racket.

"How nice of you to offer. Daphne, you, and Margot can both go."

I wondered, if Margot came along, would she find out about the pot? And if she did, would she tell Auntie Beth? The blood rushed from my face.

"Okay. But I don't think Margot wants to come."

Margot lengthened her neck and sat up tall. "Yes, I do."

"There's room in the car for everyone," Lara said.

When I'd first met the Vaughans, I was shy and jittery. I wanted so badly to fit in and if they were smoking, I wanted to do it too. I liked it. But babysitting Margot put a damper on my plans.

"There's money in my purse, Daphne." Marianne held the door open for Lewis and Lara, who hustled out the door.

I followed with money in my hand. Margot came up behind me and whispered in my ear, "I thought you didn't like them."

But I couldn't meet her gaze.

The car radio blared a new hit single by Blue Oyster Cult, "Don't Fear the Reaper." Lara sped past bikers and dog-walkers on the narrow and curvy East Shore Drive. Sitting between Lara and Lewis in the front seat—more like a leather sofa—I had nothing to hold onto, and my feet straddled the center hump on the floor of the car. I couldn't help leaning into Lara's, then Lewis's shoulders.

I was dying to ask Lewis if Phillip got in trouble for breaking into the store. If they arrested him. But I'd never talk about it in front of Margot. I didn't want her to know I was with them that night. And now, I hoped neither Lara nor Lewis mentioned it either. Nervous, I pushed the uneasy cactus prickles away.

"Mother went shopping in Plymouth today." Lara was driving with one hand on the wheel and her left elbow resting out the open window.

Lewis looked like a young jock—like someone who would eventually be the star football player on the varsity team. I found my gaze wandering to his thighs and developing chest. His sculpted jaw and bright eyes. Despite the attraction, I tried to keep my foot from touching his tennis shoes. Every time it did, an army of invisible ants crawled up my leg.

Freak.

The wide beast of a car swerved. Margot snapped on her seatbelt.

"She always goes shopping when Dad puts another criminal behind bars. Like my new top?" Lara waved her arm in front of me. The orange poncho had three-inch kelly-green fringe sewn around the edges. It looked too warm for the summer, even though she wore it over shorts.

I smoothed out my T-shirt, realizing it wasn't stylish or cute. It was pale blue and had the words from a hamburger commercial on it. "Two all-beef patties special sauce . . ." More than anything, I wanted my new friends to like me.

The car veered into the other lane. "Lara!" Lewis gripped the dashboard.

"Don't tell me how to drive until you have a license."

Both hands on the wheel hardly improved Lara's driving. She chattered about all the new garments her mother bought, the elephant ear pants and her new stylish, lace-up sandals. "Do you have any lace-ups?"

"Shoes with laces?" Though I always wore my favorite Dr. Scholl's sandals I suddenly didn't like them anymore.

"No, silly, like these." Lara lifted her left leg to show off a pair of white sandals with laces crisscrossing up her calf.

Envy wrapped like morning glory around my chest. "Those are cool. Where did you buy them?"

"There's a new JC Penney in Plymouth. Mother took me there last week." Nearing town, Lara sailed right through a stop sign.

Margot gasped.

Lewis snagged his seat belt and pulled it on. "Are you watching the road?"

"Phillip's coming home from hockey camp tonight," Lara said. "He might bring Mark and we're going boating. Mark is older than Phillip, old enough to get my parents' attention. I decided to date him this summer."

Lewis peered around me at his sister. "You can't date Mark. He's a towny."

"So? What do you care?"

"I don't care, but Mother will have a fit."

"That's the point, isn't it?"

The high chirp of a police siren got everyone's attention. My heart-beat skipped.

Lara glanced in the rearview mirror. "Small-town fuzz. Don't they have anything better to do?"

"Oh no!" Margot gazed through the rear windshield with her mouth agape. "He's signaling you to pull over."

"You're in so much trouble if you get a ticket," Lewis said. "If Father finds out, you'll be grounded until Christmas."

The wheels squealed as Lara turned sharply onto a side street lined with single-story homes. She slammed on the brakes. "He won't find out. Will he, Lewis." She leaned forward to look around me at Lewis.

His leg pressed against mine and it stung like I'd brushed against a hot thistle bush. I pulled away, rubbing my leg. *Was it because of the policeman?*

Lewis glared at his sister. "If you'd been paying attention and not jabbering about your new clothes, you might have seen the stop sign."

"I saw it, I just ignored it," Lara said.

"You're going to get a ticket," Margot said.

The squad car pulled up behind them and a swaggering deputy with a bushy mustache and his hand on his gun belt approached the window.

"Oh, look. Here comes Hutch. Where's Starsky?" Lara rolled it down with the turn crank. "Hello, officer, can I help you?"

Neither of my parents had ever been pulled over before—at least not while I was in the car. Swallowing my pounding heart, I made eye contact with Margot. We would be in trouble too, if Auntie Beth found out.

The deputy peered into the car, taking stock of each passenger. His eyes finally rested on Lara. "Did you know you drove through the four-way stop sign back there?"

I recognized the cop—the same one who'd asked about the break-in at the corner store—and my heart rate sped up again. Deputy Simmons. Did he know we were there during the break-in? I hid my face in case he recognized me.

"I did?" Lara's hand fluttered to her chest. "I must've missed it. I'm so sorry. We just came up for the week." I envied her ability to lie so easily.

I built up the courage to speak. "We're new to the area."

The deputy put a hand on top of the Lincoln Continental and tapped three times. "Do you have your driver's license?"

"Yes, sir. It's in my purse."

Lewis groaned and sank deeper into the wide passenger seat, tossing Lara's white crocheted purse across my lap. Fringe splayed across Lara's bare legs as she dug around inside. Pulling out a small leather wallet, she removed her Indiana driver's license and handed it to the deputy.

He tapped the roof of the car again. "You wait right here, now, you hear?"

"Yes, sir." Lara batted her eyelashes.

When he took the license back to his car, Lara leaned over me and poked Lewis's thigh. "Father is *not* going to find out, Lewis. You better swear."

With an exasperated groan, he said, "Fine."

"Swear it!"

"I swear, okay? What more do you want from me?"

I looked back at Margot, trying to get out from the middle of the sibling quarrel. Margot slunk down into the seat as if trying to make herself small. Her thick eyeglasses magnified her wide eyes.

When Deputy Simmons returned with Lara's license, he said, "I know your father. He's a respectable man."

"Yes, sir."

"I also know that he rents a summer home every year here on Lake Carlson. This isn't your first time here, is it, Miss Vaughan?"

"No, sir."

"I'm not giving you a ticket today." He handed her license through the open window. "Consider this a warning, and you be careful now. You hear?" He tapped the roof of the Lincoln three more times, then went back to his car.

We were laughing when we pulled into the A&W Root Beer stand. It seemed like I hadn't laughed in years.

Lara deepened her voice, mocking the deputy. "You be careful now, Miss Vaughan." She parked in the diagonal slot between a VW bug and a convertible town car. "Did you see that? Daddy's so famous, the fuzz in Carlson can't even touch me."

"You know that's not true," Lewis argued. "He said it was a warning."

"I can get out of anything. And even if I can't, Father will bail me out just like he does with Phillip."

A girl wearing cut-off jeans roller-skated up to the car window. Her T-shirt had the word Groovy in slanted bubble-letters. She took a pad and pencil out of her back pocket. "What'll you have?"

The menu board on the side of the small shack listed Papa Burgers, Mama Burgers, and Teen Burgers with French fries and cold fountain drinks. As the name suggested, the drive-in featured A&W root beer exclusively.

Though Margot seemed traumatized by the close encounter with the fuzz, I was thrilled. I liked hanging out with the Vaughans. It seemed they could do nothing wrong.

Lewis tried to include Margot in the conversation as we ate our meals and sipped root beer milkshakes and ice cream floats. Margot nibbled and picked food out of her braces without saying much. She clearly didn't fit in. It would make it easier for me to ditch her the next time.

SPEEDBOATS AND SCHNAPPS

Daphne

I instantly regretted diving into the lake. Something slimy wrapped around my ankle and a scream burst from my chest. I swam back to the dock as fast as I could. On my way past Brandon, he grabbed my leg and stopped me.

"Let go!" I didn't mean to be so rough, but I kicked him away.

He laughed and said, "Weirdo!"

When I climbed out, Lara and Lewis were there.

Lara had a tie-dyed wrap covering her bathing suit. "Hey," she said. "Lewis wants to water-ski."

"It was your idea," he said.

"No, it wasn't." Lara flashed him a devious smile and I wondered what was up between them.

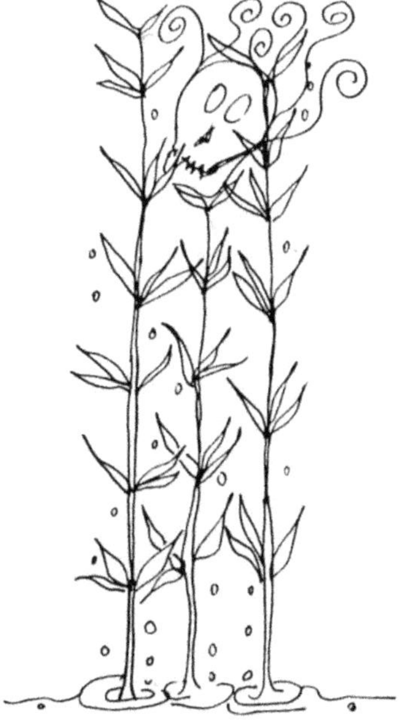

"We need a third," Lara said. "Come with us?"

As much as I loved skiing, and wanted to hang out with them, the last place I wanted to be was out in the middle of the lake. The image of that white disembodied head floated into my mind again. It was pale and the lips had turned the most awful shade of blue. Its eyes, open in the dark cloudy water, had a distant, vacant look.

Lewis and Lara waited for an answer while Brandon and Sammy played under the dock and Margot watched from the patio on shore. Lewis's sweet eyes pulled me in, and I heard myself say, "okay," against my better judgment.

I grabbed my towel, and we darted back to their place.

I braced myself, standing in the center of the Vaughans' Mastercraft speedboat, gripping the windshield.

"You're going too fast!" Lewis yelled into the wind. In the rear-facing passenger seat, he gripped the dashboard.

I squinted at the sun's sparkling glare as spray from the bow hit my face. My hair whipped around my head, and I hooted and threw both hands in the air. My aunt would have had a heart attack if she knew I wasn't holding on to anything. But it was exhilarating.

"I can go faster if you want!" Lara stood with one hand on the throttle and the other on the steering wheel. Her mirrored aviator sunglasses reflected the sky, and her hair flew behind her.

As we raced across the choppy middle of Lake Carlson, the boat leapt across the rough water, slamming into the waves. I clenched my teeth so I didn't bite my tongue. Behind us, the white foam of our wake made S-curves on the surface of the lake.

"Watch out, Lara!" Lewis shouted, "There's a boat—"

Lara swerved, zigzagging across the water. I tumbled into her.

"Sit down!" She pushed me into Lewis's lap.

I scrambled to grab hold of something.

Over the wind and engine noise, Lewis hollered, "Goddammit Lara! Stop!" He held me by the waist, bracing for the next swerve.

Ahead of us, a triplet of boat wakes rolled toward us. Lara turned into it and accelerated again. The boat caught the first wave and rocketed into the air.

I shrieked and bit my tongue.

The boat came down on the second wave with a jarring lurch, then hit the third and skipped across the surface.

Lewis yelled, "Stop!"

When Lara cut the throttle, it threw us forward. Lewis hit his head on the corner of the dashboard.

"Shit, Lara!" He rubbed his head and narrowed his gaze at his reckless sister. "Stop being such a spaz. Someone could've gotten hurt."

"Are you okay?" I asked him. When Lewis's head impacted the dash, it triggered something like déjà vu. Like I'd seen this happen before.

"You'll be fine, little brother." Lara patted his head and rubbed his hair. "It's nothing a little schnapps can't cure." She popped open the compartment under the windshield and pulled out her flask.

"You're going to get in trouble," Lewis said. He popped the tab on a Coke and dropped the aluminum tab ring into the can before taking a sip.

"Okay, smart aleck, why don't you drive." Lara leaned back, letting the sun hit her face.

"Can I?" I asked. Dad and Marianne never taught me how to drive the boat. I didn't question it until now. But I couldn't wipe the smile off my face. I hadn't had so much fun in my whole life.

"Go ahead."

I sat in the driver's seat and looked at all the dials. "I don't know how."

"No way." Lewis pushed Lara out of the way and pointed. "Here's your speedometer, and this is the tachometer. It shows RPMs. This is the throttle and—"

Lara reached across and fired up the engine. "It's not hard. Push the throttle forward and go."

I smiled at the power I held in my hands. The boat moved forward. "Can you get a speeding ticket in a boat?"

"Nah. You'd have to drive like a maniac."

"Like Lara?" I said.

I drew a laugh out of my friends.

"What time do you have to be home?" Lewis asked.

"They don't care." I figured Marianne was drawing at her easel, and Tony was tanning his hairy chest. Margot probably sulked with her baby toys in the side yard. When I left, Duke had followed me to the gate like he was the only one who gave a damn.

I drove the Mastercraft past the academy and along the east shore past Aubenaubee Lodge. There, I cut the engine, and Lara passed me the flask.

My shoulders blazed pink. "I think I'm getting sunburned."

Lewis stripped off his white polo shirt and tossed it to me. "Put this on."

"Thanks." I inhaled deeply as I pulled it over my head. The shirt smelled like Polo cologne and Lewis.

He put his watch in the glove compartment, climbed up on the big square engine cover in the middle of the boat.

"What are you doing?" For some reason, I didn't want Lewis to jump in the water.

"Swimming, of course."

"Wait—" I reached out, but he vaulted into the water, cannonballing as he hit.

Despite my mounting fear, I looked over the side of the boat. Foam and strands of lakeweed floated on the surface, hiding the forests below.

"Come on in. It feels great!" It didn't bother Lewis, but I wasn't about to get in with him.

"Don't drown!" Lara passed me the flask again. "Father couldn't handle it if something happened to Little Lewis. He's Father's pride and joy. Screw the rest of us."

"I'm sure your dad loves you just as much."

"You'd never know it."

Following Lara's lead, I stripped down to my string bikini and stumbled to the stern. She sat on the back of the boat and posed like—I imagined—a model or sunbathing beauty in a fashion magazine. Though they'd invited me to go skiing, the water was far too rough. I was glad. I didn't want to swim out here.

The images of the head in the weeds filled my mind again. Since I was drunk, I giggled at it. I made fun of the dark whispers. I took the flask and another swallow helped ease my worry.

Lewis treaded water off the port side. "Come on in! The lake is waiting."

"That sounds creepy," I said.

"Like we're in some horror film." Lara lay back on the padded engine cover.

Lewis made his voice deeper like a TV-show announcer. "While most of Lake Carlson vacationers slept, they didn't know the lake was alive. Swallowing swimmers for breakfast."

I laughed nervously. "You're the one swimming in it."

"No, wait." Lara deepened her voice and played along. "Little did they know that beneath the ultra-calm surface, a great white monster lurked. Duhn-duhn, duhn-duhn, duhn-duhn . . . Rawr!" Lara opened her arms wide with her fingers rounded like the jaws of a big shark.

"Have you seen *Jaws*, Daphne?" Lewis said, still swimming around the boat.

"My parents wouldn't take me."

Lara sipped from her flask. "Lewis was afraid to use the toilet for a week."

"You know what?" Lewis said. "It's showing in Carlson this weekend. We should see it."

I wanted to see *Jaws*, but then again, I didn't.

CHAPTER 20

DUHN-DUHN, DUHN-DUHN, DUHN-DUHN

Daphne

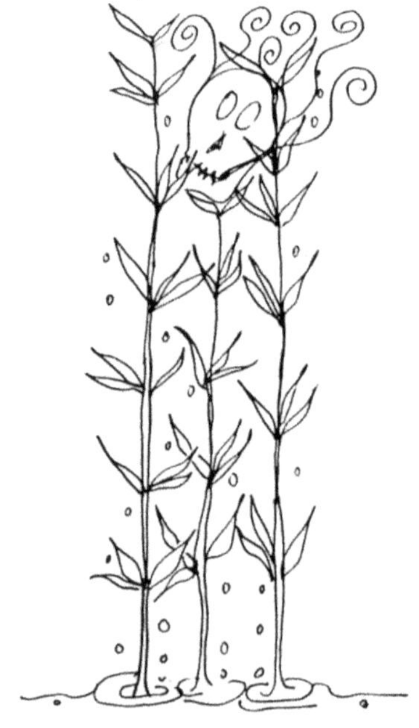

That weekend, Lewis and Lara took me to see *Jaws* at the Carlson movie theater. I sat between them in the second row. Campers from the academy and summer vacationers filled the faded velvet seats. The small theater had an old-timey-quality to it and smelled like popcorn and cake because of a bakery next door. Lewis bought a large bucket of buttered popcorn, enough to share, but I didn't want any. My stomach was nervous and queasy, and the movie hadn't even started.

Lara sank into her chair, stretching out her long legs over the seat in front of her. She rested her head on the seat back, and sang the theme music, "Duhn-duhn, duhn-duhn, duhn-duhn. Are you scared yet?"

"I'm not scared. The shark's just a dumb model. Everyone knows sharks don't get that big in real life."

I used to love scary movies. I loved the edgy, nervy feeling. The fear creeping up my chest. I enjoyed them because in the end, monsters weren't real. Like the disembodied head floating in the water. *It wasn't real,* I kept telling myself. The thing was, I had trouble believing it.

"It's not the special effects that are scary," Lewis said. "It's the anticipation."

My shoulder rubbed against his as the lights went down, and a chill skittered up my neck. *It's nothing. It's just the movie,* I thought.

Lara held out a box of Good & Plenty and shook a few out in her palm. "Want one?"

"No thanks." Licorice wasn't my favorite.

"I brought rum too." Lara opened her purse. "When the movie starts, I'll pour some into your Coke if you want."

When the lights went down, I opened the lid of my cup.

We doubled over laughing as we exited the theater. I'd jumped so far out of my skin watching *Jaws* that I almost ended up in Lewis's lap.

"You screamed so loud." Lewis put a finger in his ear and laughed.

Lara strode to the car. "Who's up for a swim when we get home?"

"I'll pass." Lewis laughed again. "Could you believe that girl at the beginning of the movie? Swimming at night all alone? She might as well have worn a big sign around her neck that said Free Dinner."

"I'm not afraid." Lara dropped into the driver's seat.

Lara had been drinking, but she was the only one with a driver's license. "Are you sure you're okay to drive?" I asked.

"Have you been drinking?" Lewis asked. He didn't see her pour rum from a flask into our cups.

If Lewis didn't know about the flask, I wasn't going to tell him.

"Of course not. I'm not a lush like Mother." Lara started up the car. "When we get home, I'm going for a swim."

Lewis looked at me for a response. With wide eyes, I shook my head. The movie spooked me. The idea of swimming at night with my feet dangling in the dark water—in those weeds—terrified me. Apprehension gripped me like during the ice storm two years ago. Only this time, I refused to tell anyone I was afraid that someone would die.

The mosquitos were thick outside when we returned to the Vaughans' summer home and the sound of wailing guitar floated out the windows. The Beatles' "Got to Get You Into My Life" reminded me of my Dad.

Lara ran ahead and disappeared into the house. Lewis held the door open for me. "Phillip's taking us out on the boat. Are you coming too?"

I mean, I was elated he invited me, but the idea of going out on the boat at night . . . Stinging nettles crept up my arm. I stopped on the threshold and pushed the feeling away in favor of hanging out with the cool kids.

In the Vaughans' doorway, Lara bumped into me on her way back out the door. She had her fringy purse draped over her shoulder and the car keys still in her hand.

"Where are you going?" I asked.

"My boyfriend invited me out. I'm meeting him at the bar where he works."

"You're going to a bar?" *Lara's so cool.*

"He thinks I'm 21." She smiled. "But I gotta run. Have fun with little Lewis and Phillip." Lara darted to the car and peeled out of the driveway.

I watched her go. The tingles and worry subsided as she drove away. Inside, rock music played so loud the dishes on the counter seemed to vibrate while Phillip loaded a cooler with beer and ice.

Lewis asked, "Where's Lara going?"

"She went to meet someone," Phillip said. "There was a phone message from Mark."

"What?" Lewis leaned against the counter with his arms crossed. Father will be furious when he finds out she's dating a townie."

"Shit." Phillip dug through a brown paper sack "She took the bottle of Jack Daniels." Resigned, he opened a beer and slid the pull tab into the opening. After chugging the whole thing, he wiped his chin on his arm. "This party is dead, man." He picked up the cooler and backed out the door. "I'm not sticking around. Have a good life."

Lewis didn't seem too broken up that his siblings had left. "Want to go someplace quiet?"

After a year of Ruth turning everyone against me, I wanted more than anything to make new friends. "Yes."

A cloud covered the crescent moon behind us. Though Lewis's mom was out for the night, lights were on at Aubenaubee Lodge. I still worried Auntie Beth or Marianne would see us smoking. We sat in the dark at the end of the dock, hidden behind the boat lift.

Lewis passed me a joint. I took a small hit this time, careful not to embarrass myself like I did in the gazebo.

The pot made me super aware of Lewis sitting close by. I'd never sat this close to any boy, not like this. It made me both hopeful and afraid at the same time. *Does he like me?* Nervous that I'd do something stupid, I passed the joint back to Lewis.

We smoked in silence, listening to the crickets and cicadas. I brushed mosquitos off my arms and gazed up at the stars. As Lewis dangled his feet in the pitch-black water, I squinted into the depths. Waves of sensation, like silverfish crawling under my skin, spread all the way to my toes. I didn't dare dip my feet in the black water. The urge to pull Lewis back on the dock—back to safety—was overpowering.

PRAYING TO THE PORCELAIN GOD

Lara

Lara peered out the window, watching for Mark's gold Ford Mustang. Though it was hard to keep track of the days of the week—it all blended together up here at the lake—Lara knew it was Sunday. Mark had the day off. Last night at The Bar he'd let her sit in his lap. She'd wrapped her thin arms around his neck and rested her head on his shoulder. His arms were strong, and he smelled like cigarettes. Like a man. And now he was on his way to pick her up.

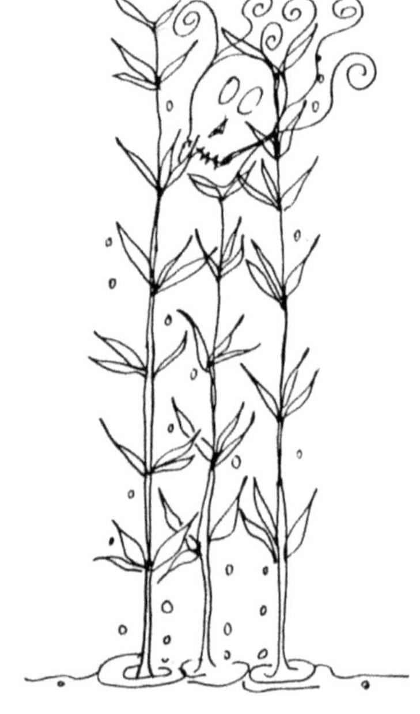

While waiting, she perused the liquor cabinet. Mother kept the cabinet stocked with exotic liqueurs. To impress her friends, she mixed up fancy drinks like Grasshoppers, Pink Squirrels, Stingers, and Harvey Wallbangers from a fat book of cocktail recipes.

Lara had just topped off her flask with Mother's peach schnapps and dropped it in her purse when Adelaide walked in and lit a cigarette. She wore her pure white tennis skirt and tight Polo shirt with a thin pink stripe around the collar. Her neat little socks had pink puffballs on the heel and her tennis shoes glowed white, without a scuff on them. Adelaide didn't play tennis.

"Where are you going?" she asked.

"Out. It's boring here, anyway."

"You're not going out with that Mortensen girl, are you? Lewis told me Daphne came over last night."

"No. What do you have against her, anyway?"

"Her mother is the laughingstock of the country club."

"So? Daphne's nice."

"I don't want you hanging out with her, and I certainly don't want her coming over."

"What's your problem? It's not like her mom comes with her."

Adelaide took a drag, letting the ash of her cigarette get even longer. "She'll tarnish your reputation."

Lara kept one eye out the window, looking for Mark's car. "Like you fooling around with the tennis instructor hasn't done enough damage."

"Lara!"

"Everyone knows you screw the tennis pro, Mother. Even Father."

The ash from her cigarette fell on the floor. "You can't speak to me that way."

"What are you going to do? Ground me?"

A car horn beeped in the driveway.

"Who is that?"

"Mark. He's a friend of Phillip's. And he's twenty-five."

"I forbid it. He's too old for you."

Lara turned on her heel and opened the back door. "Really? Wouldn't that mean you're too old for your tennis pro?"

Adelaide's mouth gaped.

Lara let the door slam.

The breeze from the lake blew Mark's hair back like he was the star of a film. His chin dropped as he lifted his shades for a better look at Lara. "You're one hot chick, Lara."

"Where are we going?"

"I'll take you wherever you want." He held the car door open for her.

She sank into the low bucket seat of his Mustang and Mark took off, spewing gravel behind his tires as he accelerated away from the house.

She laid back her head and laughed. "Let's go to Chicago and dance the night away."

His brow twitched as he sped around the curves of East Lake Shore Drive. "Did you bring any money?"

"I only have a twenty."

"I thought your dad's loaded."

"He is. But I'm not."

"I guess Chicago's out, then. How about Plymouth instead?"

Lara pulled her flask out of her purse and took a swig. "Want some?"

He upended the flask and wiped his lips. "Sweet like you." He handed it back and leaned in for a kiss.

She pressed her lips against his for a long—and she hoped sensuous—kiss. Lara had given head in the boy's bathroom at school. She'd almost done it with Andrew Walsh. At an aftergame party this spring, they went to the master bedroom and made out. She let him get all the way to third base. Her top was on the floor and his hand down her pants when the parents arrived unexpectedly and sent them all home. She would have gone all the way. She wanted to.

She laid her hand on Mark's thigh and squeezed. "Do you have a spare joint to smoke on the way?"

He winked and smoothed his hair. "Yes, I do."

The smell of rancid whiskey and cold pizza woke Lara. She lay on still-damp sheets and the burning between her legs helped her recall the night before. Sleepy, she rubbed the raw skin on her lips and cheeks. As the sun split the greasy curtains like a knife, it stabbed open her eyes. Her head felt like she'd been hit by a hammer.

She pulled the sweaty sheet over her face and the smell of her peach whiskey and pizza-breath gagged her. She leapt out of bed, entirely naked, and rushed across pumpkin-orange shag carpet that had seen better days.

Lara kneeled in front of the toilet. She pulled her hair away from her face and thought of Daphne. Of that time she held her hair for her. Perfect Daphne. *I bet she's not praying to the porcelain god this morning.*

When Lara set out to make her mother and father angry, she thought ruining their virginal image of her would show them. Last night, Mark popped her cherry. The first time, she straddled him in the Lincoln. Then they did it in a shadow, against a tree by the Carlson public pier. The sex had been fine. Even enjoyable.

After barfing, all that was left was the hollow sensation she had done something wrong. Everything hurt. The back of her head where Mark's fist had gripped her hair. The skin near her swollen vulva. Her thighs. Even her jaw from remaining open for so long. She thought she was going to die.

She showered with a tiny bar of orange soap and rinsed her hair. She didn't have a hairbrush or toothbrush, so she swiped a finger around in her mouth and spit in the sink. After drying her face on a washcloth, she stood in the bathroom door to survey the damage in the room.

Wearing only his white Fruit of the Looms, Mark was crashed, face-down, on the sweaty, wrinkled sheets. The array of crushed beer cans and cigarette butts in the full ashtray made her head hurt. The empty fifth of Wild Turkey lying on its side and the smell of the greasy pizza box with two cold stale slices and chewed-up crusts made her stomach flip again.

"Holy . . ." He rolled onto his back.

She took her underwear and top to the bathroom and put her clothes on.

"Morning," he said.

In the bathroom mirror, she watched Mark pull on his jeans and light a cigarette. One hand combed back his hair as he sat back down. "You okay?"

"I'm fine." She sat heavily on the side of the bed. She wouldn't admit to Mark how lousy she felt. Her purse lay on the chair nearby. She grabbed it and dug around inside for an aspirin, an Excedrin . . . anything. She needed something to help get rid of the strobe-light headache pounding in her head. She dumped the contents of her purse on the bed.

"What are you looking for?"

"I have a headache." She scanned the items from her purse.

Mark opened the last beer. "Hair of the dog?"

"Couldn't hurt." She took a hit. Alcohol—even warm beer—made everything easier to swallow. Mother's demands. Father's neglect. Phillip's rage and Lewis, who was so fucking perfect. She could forget how crappy this summer was going to be when she drank.

"When will you see Tony again? I need drugs."

"No, you don't. That shit's bad for you."

"You're not my father." *What an absurd thought.* She added, "Don't get all preachy on me. You can't tell me what to do."

Mark tilted his head and gazed at her. His eyes narrowed, like a bright lightbulb had come on in the room. "How old are you again?"

Lara couldn't remember what she'd told him. "Twenty . . . one?" She tried to smile, but knew it fell flat.

"Are you kidding me?" Mark shot out of his chair and yanked his shirt over his head.

Guilt burned at her cheeks and lips. But she had used Mark for what she wanted. Father would be plenty angry when he found out. And that was the point, wasn't it?

"What are you worried about?" she said. "In Indiana, the age of consent is sixteen. I'm older than that."

"Are you?"

"I'm a senior in high school, for god's sake."

Mark picked up his keys and walked to the door. "Don't come looking for me, Lara."

He's leaving? No one had ever walked out on Lara Vaughan before. "Wait. It's not what you think."

"What is it then?"

Lara looked at her knees. Her head throbbed from the booze, but she didn't regret it. A smile grew on her lips. "You liked it, didn't you."

Mark slammed the door.

Back at the lake house, she showered again. All the Crabtree & Evelyn shower gel and Herbal Essence shampoo in the world couldn't wash away the feeling that something was terribly wrong.

CHAPTER 22

MIND YOUR OWN BUSINESS

June 18th: Mark

The dogs were barking again when Mark drove up to the trailer. They probably hadn't been fed. Pops' four hunting dogs, two gangly hounds, a shaggy mutt that looked like Benji in that movie, and an old golden retriever named Jenny, stayed in a chain link pen outside the trailer. There wasn't room for them inside the trailer home, though sometimes Pops let Jenny sleep with him at night.

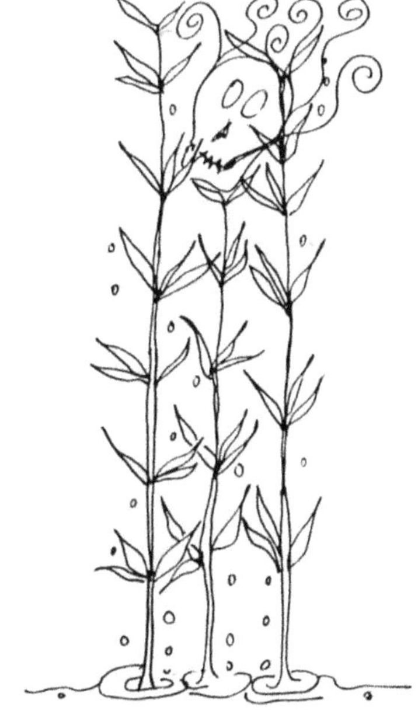

"Pops? Are you home?" Mark hollered loud enough that Pops would surely hear him.

The noonday sun heated the door handle to the trailer. Inside, Pops lay on the couch with his arms crossed and his mouth open. He still had his clothes on. An empty fifth of Jim Beam lay on the floor beside him.

Pops barely stirred as Mark picked up the bottle and tossed it in the trash can. He went to the sink and splashed chilly water on his face. Last night with Lara was the first time he'd ever tied one on, as his old man liked to say. If his parole officer found out, he'd be in deep trouble.

When he was younger—*Lara's age? Shit*—he drank with the guys at work. That's what got him into trouble, wasn't it? Alcohol hit him hard back then. Like last night at the motel.

Damnit. Lara was just a kid. He wanted so badly to believe she was older. *Why did I fall for her?* She had a magical pull on him, that was for sure.

He changed his shirt and left his room. Empty bottles and dirty dishes cluttered the narrow kitchen galley. The reek of last night's fried chicken, leftovers from the KFC near Plymouth, coated his nostrils. He scraped the chicken bones and the greasy cardboard bucket into a paper grocery bag and set it by the door.

Outside, the chirp of a car horn caused another round of barking from the dogs. The sound of gravel crunching beneath tires warned that a car had pulled into the driveway and the dogs went wild.

Mark threw a wadded towel at his dad, then peered through a dirty window to make out a black Pontiac. "Shit."

Pops grunted and rolled toward the back of the couch.

Someone pounded on the door. "Mark Walters? You in there?"

Mark pushed open the door. "Can I help you?"

Underneath a bulletproof vest with a state seal on it, the guy wore a navy-blue polo shirt and khakis. He had a gun belt and a military haircut. Dark glasses hid his eyes. He cocked his head and peered into the home. "Name's Jim Strickland. Are you Mark Walters?"

He knew who this guy was. He'd seen the name on paper. He just didn't expect him to show up today of all days.

"I'm your parole officer. Let's talk."

Jenny's hackles were up, and the other dogs continued to bark. Mark closed the door and stepped outside. "Shut up! Jenny! Brandy! Calm down."

"Ferocious." Jim kept his distance from the cage. "You didn't come home last night."

"You keeping tabs on me?" Mark walked over to his Mustang.

Jim followed. "It's my job to check in on you. Make sure you're playing nice. How's the adjustment going?"

"Good. Can't complain."

"I saw you got a court order, an okay to work at a bar around here."

Mark shoved his hands in his pockets. "Pops can't afford me on his salary. There's not that many jobs in Carlson." Not many employers would hire an ex-con.

Jim looked at the hazy white sky. "I heard they're looking for janitors at the academy."

Mark coughed. "No, thanks."

"Probably pays better than bartending."

Mark shook his head. No way in hell would he work around all those snotty rich kids.

"Your dad sleeping one off? I smelled booze. You're not drinking, are you?"

"Pops went on a bender. Give the old guy a break." Mark could still taste Wild Turkey from last night, but he had no intention of letting Jim know. "I don't mean to be rude, but is that all?"

Behind him the dogs started barking again. A black-and-white patrol car slowed at the driveway and pulled in. The local cop stepped out of his car and Mark recognized him—his cousin Brandt Simmons, one of his mother's sister's kids. He didn't know Brandt had become the Carlson deputy. Though Pops burned most of those bridges after Mom died, Mark occasionally ran into the cousins around town. Mom's family were good people. It gave him hope that maybe someday . . .

Brandt walked up to Mark with his arms out. Mark shook hands with his cousin.

"Been a while," Brandt said. "How are you?"

Been better? Never better? Mark didn't know how to answer. He just nodded.

Jim introduced himself and the dogs began to bark again.

"Jenny! Brandy! Shut up!"

Jim tucked his thumbs into his belt. He asked Brandt, "Mark causing any trouble, officer?"

"Not at all." Brandt swatted a fly away from his face. "Assault with the intent to kill. That was harsh. I bet you thought so too."

Mark cringed at the reference to his charges and subsequent

conviction. Since Brandt didn't tell Jim they were family, Mark kept it under wraps. "Look, I don't have time for social hour, I gotta get ready for work."

"I'll get to the point." Brandt's gaze drifted past Mark to the dogs. "Know that little corner store off East Lake Shore Drive? They reported a couple break-ins over the last two weeks."

Mark just nodded again. Was it a coincidence? He had only been back in Carlson for a few weeks.

"Whoever's doing it didn't steal much, just a couple cases of beer," Brandt said. "But they broke the window. Last night they tore the boards off to go inside again. Insurance won't cover it, so Peggy Bursaw, the owner, wants justice. And it'll be two weeks before the glass shop in Plymouth can send someone to fix the window. Got any idea who's breaking into shops to steal beer?"

Mark had an idea, but he didn't want to share that information. Not yet anyway. "No, sir."

Jim scratched his nose with the back of his hand. "Mark wasn't in prison for stealing."

"I know," Brandt said. "Mark, you're working at Red's bar out near Knox. I know you hear things. I'd like to become your new best friend. Find out what you know."

A burst of air escaped Mark's lungs. Almost a laugh. "I don't need any friends."

"Sure you do."

"I also know you did your time without a single incident. What a good guy, that Mark Walters. That's what my friend in the Marion County prison says to me. But just so you know, that doesn't mean a thing to me. Just 'cause you did your time and got past all them folks without raising any red flags doesn't mean you can get past me. I know better than that."

The family reunion was over. Mark narrowed his gaze. "Look, I'm minding my own business and I'd like to keep it that way."

"My point is, I don't think you intended to hurt that boy as bad as they say. You didn't do anything to him that wasn't warranted. You just happened to punch the wrong asshole at the worst possible moment.

Then, no fault of your own, Prosecutor John Vaughan used you as a means to an end. To get something he desired. Know what that was?"

Mark did know. He'd followed the news articles and learned all he could about John Vaughan the Third. He knew his kid Phillip was working at Carlson Academy this summer. He knew Phillip drank a lot, did drugs, got into fights, and was a petty thief. Mark didn't have to work too hard to get revenge. Phillip could do that all on his own.

"John Vaughan wanted to be appointed Marion County Prosecutor."

At least someone else saw through the prosecutor's bullshit. "So what's your point, officer?"

"I don't believe anyone's above the law. Not even the prosecutor's kids. Phillip Vaughan is working at the summer camp. Mrs. Vaughan and the two younger ones—both in high school, I believe—rented a house on the East Shore. Did you know that?"

Mark shook his head. Phillip didn't say anything about the rest of his family. Then the realization hit him between the eyes. Pretending she was older, Lara was staying on East Shore Drive for the summer. Phillip introduced him to Lara. They never said they were siblings, but what were the chances they weren't?

Blood drained from Mark's face. He cleared his throat. "What are you saying?"

"I don't want anything to happen to them. Do we understand each other?"

"I think so, sir."

Jim Strickland tilted his head and stared at Mark. "The prosecutor's family is here for the summer. That's good to know, Deputy Simmons."

"No need for formalities. Call me Brandt."

"Jim."

"Jim and Brandt, it's been real," Mark said. "I need to get ready for work." Blood returned to his face, but the cold feeling of dread hadn't left his extremities.

"I'll see you around, Mark. It's been a long time," Brandt said.

Mark watched the patrol car pull away.

Jim remained. "Stay clean, Mark. I'll be back to check on you."

Mark watched him go too. Of course Mark knew who was stealing from the corner store. Prosecutor Vaughan's son, Phillip, was a drunk and an idiot. His dear old daddy had enough money to buy the frickin' store. But what about Lara?

She had to be Vaughan's daughter. Thoughts of revenge returned.

I KNOW WHO YOU ARE

Daphne

It was a cloudy and windy day, uninviting for boating or marine sports. I wanted to play cards, but Margot avoided me. Brandon disassembled his latest Erector Set project. Sammy dumped a bucket of Hot Wheels cars out, making a loud, metallic racket. Even Duke was uninterested in fetching his ball.

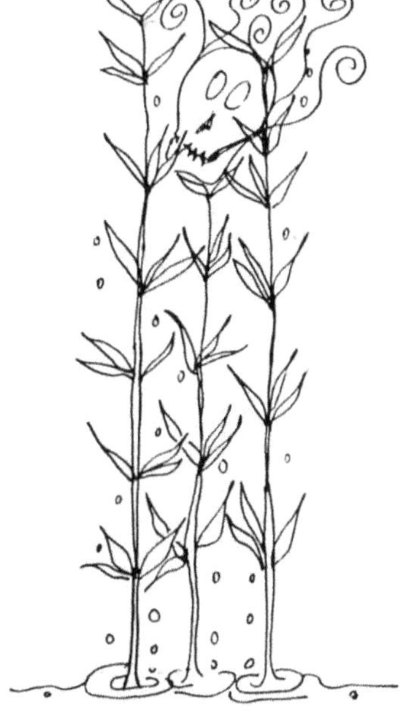

Before lunch, Tony snuck out the back door and jogged to his car through the drizzling rain. I watched him go and wondered why he had so many errands. When he went out, he returned with beer for a boating excursion, or A&W root beer floats for the boys. Sometimes he brought home donuts. The lingering sense that he was up to no good remained lodged in the back of my mind.

"Everything okay in here?" Marianne walked through the living room on her way to the patio.

"It's fine." Brandon pouted.

"What time did you come in last night?" she asked me.

Guilt heated my cheeks, but I only shrugged. No way would I tell Marianne what time I snuck in. "When does Nana's piano arrive?"

"It should have been here by now. I'll call Mother today and ask."

When Marianne took her iced tea and drawing tablet out on the patio, I snuck upstairs to Marianne and Tony's room. I wanted to see if Tony had left any evidence, though I didn't know what I'd do if I found something. Duke followed me, his collar jingling all the way up the stairs. I patted his head and told him to lie down on the floor.

Duke didn't lie down. He followed at my heels, sniffing around piles of clothes on the floor and under the unmade bed. Tony had pushed the two twins together and made it into one. The thought of Marianne sleeping with him made my lips curl. Empty beer bottles littered the bedside table on one side. A small pipe lay on the table with a few stems—the pieces of the marijuana plant you don't smoke.

Where's the weed?

When Tony helped me out of the lake that day, I saw baggies of weed, stacks of dollar bills, and bottles of pills. Sometimes I smelled pot at night, when the adults stayed up late. *He must keep it somewhere,* I thought.

I peered out the door and down the hallway to make sure no one else was upstairs. Except for Duke sniffing and snorting at the piles of clothes on the floor, I was alone. Marianne's folded flowery shirt lay on top of a clean pile of laundry. I loved that shirt. I quickly changed into it, and I went to the dresser. I looked in the mirror, then combed my fingers through my hair. It was growing out, but I still looked like a dork. I found Marianne's mascara and dabbed my lashes with the wand.

Looking for Tony's pot, I opened drawers and found a baggie containing seven rolled joints underneath Marianne's nightgown. This wasn't the huge stash I imagined when Tony helped me into the boat that day.

I looked over my shoulder again and opened the bag. *Tony won't miss two joints.*

Footsteps padded up the creaky stairs and I stopped to listen. Brandon's voice carried, complaining about not being able to go swimming in the rain. "There's nothing to do."

Tony's heavier footsteps followed. "Your old lady's right, dude. You brought toys. There are games and puzzles. Go find something to do."

I quickly put the joints in the pocket of my cutoff jean shorts and shoved the drawer closed.

"What are you doing in here?" Tony stood in the doorway. Duke sniffed his shoes.

I spun. "Nothing." My cheeks blazed.

"Right. Stealing your mom's shirt?"

I looked down at the wide sleeves. "Borrowing."

"Sure." His gaze landed on the pipe on the bedside table as he stepped into the room, blocking me from the exit. "This room is off-limits, you know. What are you looking for?"

At that moment, I'm not sure what came over me. But I said what was on my mind. "I know who you are."

"What do you mean?"

"Does Marianne know you're dealing pot?"

Tony smirked and tossed a leather satchel on the bed. "You have no idea what you're saying, kid."

"I do know." I wanted to tell him I would go to the police, but the words got stuck in my throat. Would I get in trouble too? Would Marianne?

Tony took me by the arm and pulled me toward the door. His hand was hot through the sleeve of Marianne's shirt, and I didn't like the sudden meanness in his eyes. "Stay out of our room, kid. Don't you be snooping around in my business. This is a warning. Got it?"

He pushed me so hard out the door that I landed on my hands and knees. The door slammed behind me.

I jumped up and brushed off my knees where the carpet burned my skin. Holding back tears, I darted down the stairs and out the door.

Lewis was on the couch playing Atari when I arrived. I went straight to the piano and sat on the bench. "Our new piano still hasn't come."

"Go ahead and play if you want." Lewis wiggled the joystick and remained focused on his game.

With my right hand, I played the opening phrases of the Chopin, *Trois Etude* No. 1. The quarter-note triplets, set up a feeling of sorrow and abandonment. After four measures, my left hand began eighth note arpeggios in a counter rhythm. When the two joined, the counterpoint and eerie melody expressed everything I felt about this summer.

Phillip entered with a six-pack in one hand and his boom box in the other. "What's that droll stuff you're playing?"

I stopped playing. The burns on my knees stung.

"How about a little rock beat, like "Piano Man" by Billy Joel?" Phillip plopped down on a chair and set the beer on the table.

"My dad can play it by ear, but I'd need to see the music," I said.

"Can't you improvise?" Phillip asked. "Like Hendrix or Steely Dan?"

"Steely Dan isn't the name of the guitarist, it's the name of the band," Lewis said.

Phillip took a long draw on a beer. "What about that crazy Brit, what's his name?"

"Elton John. My dad can play "Candle in the Wind.""

"Forget that. I've got Pink Floyd." Phillip popped a tape into the slot. A song from the spacey *Dark Side of the Moon* filled the room. He said to me, "Tired of playing dolls with the children?"

My cheeks heated. "It's not like that. My mom's dating a total loser. She should be with my dad."

"Huh. Rich kid problems, don't you think? I wish my mom and dad would separate. Then I might not have to see my fucking father ever again." He didn't have medical tape on his nose anymore but the yellow bruises under his eyes made him look angry.

"If you behaved like an adult, he'd treat you like one," Lewis said.

"Shut up, baby." Phillip swigged his beer.

The rug burns on my knees still stung as I stood up from the piano and sat beside Lewis.

"You look nice today," he said. "What happened to your—"

I covered the red spots. "I had an accident." I wanted to show him the joints I stole from Tony, but it didn't seem like the right time.

"We have some Bactine antiseptic spray." Lewis led me to the bathroom, where he opened the medicine cabinet. "Here's some Band-Aids."

"Thanks. Actually, it wasn't an accident. Tony pushed me down."

"Tony?"

"My mom's boyfriend. I was searching their bedroom for pot. I think he's dealing."

"And he pushed you? That's so uncool." The sad look on Lewis's face told me I'd made the right choice telling him. "I'm sorry he did that to you."

"Thanks. I'm not sure my mom knows who he really is."

"Maybe she does."

He was right. Maybe Marianne did know Tony dealt pot. Maybe that was even why she was with him.

Out in the living room, Lara looked different. There was something about her that seemed off. I couldn't tell for sure what it was. "Mark's on his way," she said.

"You invited him here?" Phillip asked.

"Why not?" Lara said. "Mother's playing bridge with the ladies down the lane. She'll be gone all afternoon."

"He's a towny. He was in prison."

Lara's face turned white, but she seemed to recover quickly. "So. You hang out with him."

"That's different." Phillip lit a cigarette.

Those stinging nettles crawled up my arms. "Mark was in prison? What did he do?" My curiosity got the better of me. I'd never met someone who'd gone to prison.

"He killed someone." Phillip took a drag of his cigarette and acted so cool—like killing someone was nothing. Like killing someone was so cliché.

"You're just saying that." Lara glared at Phillip until he shrugged.

"Maybe. Maybe not. Ask him." Phillip took a drag of his cigarette and flicked the ash into a nearly full ashtray.

Lara took a long sip from a glass of iced orange juice. "Want a screwdriver, Daphne?"

Whatever Lara was drinking, I wanted one. "What's in it?"

Someone knocked on the door and Lara almost spilled her drink on the way through the kitchen.

"Everybody, this is Mark. Mark, this is everybody." Lara swept her arm in a grand gesture toward the room.

Mark looked around the room with his mouth set in a thin line. I noticed right away that he was older. He seemed nervous and I got the sense things had been hard for him. Did that make him a bad person? He didn't look like a killer, but there was something tense about him. He didn't look mean, or angry. Or evil. But then again, neither did Tony until he shoved me out of the room. What did it take for someone to want to kill another person? How angry did they have to be?

He's been to prison.

Lewis shook Mark's hand. He introduced me and I waved from my spot in a chair.

"What's up?" he asked. "What are you guys doing today?"

Lara tried to put her arm around Mark, but he backed away. There was something unspoken between them. Something like an argument or misunderstanding.

I smoothed out the Band-Aids on my knees. After introductions, it became awkward when no one spoke. Mark looked around the house like he thought someone would jump out from the shadows. Tension in the room—between Lewis and his sister, between Phillip and Mark, between Mark and everyone—fell on us like the descending chromatic scale in the first movement of Beethoven's *Piano Sonata in C Minor*, the *Pathétique*. I looked forward to getting high.

"Well, come on. Let's get the party started," Lara said. She brought out a pitcher of orange juice and a bottle of vodka and set it on the coffee table.

Mark sat on the couch with his shoulders hunched. His mouth and brow pinched. "How old are you guys?"

"Old enough," Lewis said. He'd come out of the kitchen with two Cokes. He handed one to me. I remained quiet.

Mark looked right at me. "I don't want to get you in trouble or anything."

"I won't get in trouble. My mom's not paying attention. Anyway, I stole these from her." I carefully dug the two joints out of my pocket.

Lara laughed. "Wait. You stole those from your mom? Cool!"

"She must be the coolest mom in the world," Phillip said.

Cool wasn't the word I'd use to describe Marianne.

We smoked one of my joints, then Phillip passed the bong around. Mark only smoked cigarettes, I noticed. So why was he here?

When the rain stopped, Phillip loaded the cooler with beer and ice and a bottle of Crown Royal—whiskey I guess—while Lara stacked towels and plastic cups. We paraded out on the pier with armfuls of gear. Mark carried the boom box, and I followed him with a box of cassette tapes. Looking over my shoulder at Aubenaubee Lodge, I half expected Marianne or Auntie Beth to come running out and stop me.

Mark set the boom box down and we waited while Phillip and Lewis lowered the boat into the water. A crackle of fireworks sounded down the shore. The Fourth of July was next week.

"Known the Vaughan family long?" Mark asked me.

"Not really. Just met them this summer. They seem cool."

Mark laughed.

I stared up at him. "What's funny?"

"You're pretty naïve, that's all. How old are you?"

"Fifteen. Why? You're older, aren't you?"

"Yeah." Mark's cheeks had turned red. He must have realized he was too old to hang out with high school kids.

I wondered how old Tony was. He didn't seem much older than Mark. "Phillip's twenty-one. You can't be that much older."

"I'm not here to cause trouble," Mark said. He had an aura of kindness.

"I know." Even though I was high, *I knew.* He didn't want to hurt anyone, but I still questioned his motives.

As the sun parted the clouds, we all climbed into the boat and crossed the lake to an undeveloped part of the shore. Phillip cut the engine where lakeweeds had grown out of control. I cringed looking over the side of the boat. Their slimy, leafy tendrils waved below the surface.

"Why'd you stop here?" Lara asked. She pointed to the water. "We can't swim in the seaweed."

"It's everywhere," Mark said. "They say it's the worst it's ever been."

"It's the heat." Phillip drank from the bottle of Crown.

"I'm not swimming in that." Lewis leaned over the side of the boat and Phillip gave him a playful shove from behind.

"Hey!" Lewis caught himself, but I almost lost it.

My nerves caught fire as a wave of strong tingles ran from my fingertips to my toes. "Don't do that!" I shouted.

"Wow." Lara said. "We never should've taken you to see *Jaws.*"

"What do you mean?" I said.

"You just seem more scared of the water today."

"No kidding." Phillip laughed.

Mark and the Vaughans all stared at me. "That bad, huh?" Mark said.

"It's just that . . ." I grew defensive. Maybe I was high, or maybe I needed them to understand. "Can I tell you something?" I said.

They nodded. Mellow guitar moaned from the double speakers of the boom box. Mark took a Coke from the cooler.

"When I went skiing a few weeks ago, I saw something in the water."

"Duhn duhn, duhn duhn," Lara said. She leaned on the square engine cover like a model on the cover of a magazine. Mark seemed to be trying not to look at her.

"It wasn't a shark," I said.

I told them the story about the day Uncle Chuck took us all skiing. I described what happened, about falling in the weediest part of the lake, and stopped.

Everyone stared, waiting for more. Lara sank into the cushioned seat and pulled a small flask out from under her poncho. She tipped the flask to her lips and then handed it to me. "Cinnamon schnapps. Mother doesn't buy it often, but when she does, she can never figure out how it disappears so quickly."

The spicy liquor heated a path all the way to my belly.

"So?" Lewis asked.

"So," I said, "under my feet, caught in the weeds, there was a human head."

"What?" Lara grimaced.

"Gross." Lewis looked at me with something like disgust.

Phillip threw back his head and laughed. "Was the body attached, or did the lake piranhas eat it?"

But Mark quietly asked, "Did you report it to the police?" He believed me.

"No. I wasn't sure it was real."

Lara said, "There aren't any lake piranhas."

"I might be able to find out if someone in the area went missing," Mark said.

"Could you?" I asked.

He nodded. And suddenly I trusted him with my life.

CHAPTER 24

THE BICENTENNIAL BANG

July Fourth, 1976: Daphne

Fourth of July weekend finally arrived. The entire country celebrated the biggest birthday party anyone had ever had, the Bicentennial. Two hundred years. Red, white, and blue banners hung from awnings and porches all around the lake. People dressed in stars and stripes and fireworks boomed all day long. Cars drove past with their horns blaring and kids held thick, two-foot-long sparklers over the lake. The American flag was pasted in windows and flew from every pole and staff.

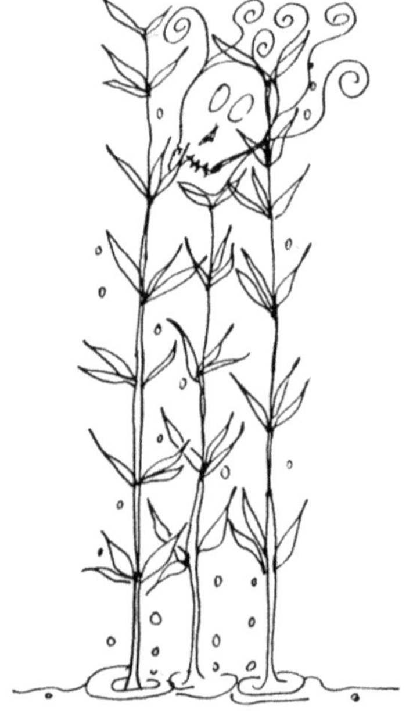

In Carlson, the Carlson Academy marching band led a parade down Main Street. The Black Horse Troop followed them and then came a half dozen old cars, and farmers driving tractors.

Tony gave Brandon and Sammy a string of five hundred firecrackers and a box of wooden matches. The random pops made Auntie Beth jump every time.

On that day, I found an old, tattered music sheet in the piano bench: "The Star-Spangled Banner." Duke laid down at my feet as I rested the soft, worn pages against a hardcover book. When I dug my fingers into the keys, Duke got up and left. The disharmonious cacophony unsettled rather than uplifted my mood. I ended the song abruptly with a terrible chord.

"That sounds awful," Auntie Beth said as she examined puzzle pieces spread out over the round table in the living room.

I closed the key cover. "When will the new piano arrive?"

"I'm not sure. Mother said the new piano arrived at her house yesterday."

"How did that happen?"

"They confused her address with the delivery address. Someone wrote it down wrong, I guess. They had to leave the new piano in front of the window in her living room and you know how small her house is. She was livid. I think they're scheduled to pick it up next week and bring it here."

I let out a sigh. I wasn't comfortable asking to practice next door, but playing this ruined out-of-tune piano was worse.

"Hello? Anyone home?" Dad's voice carried through the house. He entered with Duke at his side. The big dog wagged his tail so hard it thumped the wall.

I leapt up from the bench and ran to him. "Dad!" His warm embrace was exactly what I needed.

He wrapped me in a fatherly bear hug. "I missed you!"

Brandon thundered down the stairs, followed by Sammy. They welcomed Dad with hugs and pats on the back. When Marianne entered from the back patio, she said, "Hello, Jeremy," and her eyes twinkled with happiness.

I was glad to see her look so happy even though Tony was still lurking around. Maybe Dad would convince that loser to leave.

Lightning bugs, with their own light show, blinked random patterns as dusk settled. Dad grilled salmon and served it with his home-baked bread. I cooked with him, tossed a salad with avocados from California and made homemade dressing. Auntie Beth bought a festive cake decorated like the flag.

All day, Tony competed with Dad for Mom's attention. He kept trying to one-up Dad in skiing, driving the boat faster, telling funnier jokes. Dad was better at everything in my eyes. And Marianne put up with it without saying a word.

When Uncle Chuck arrived, the added tension had everyone on edge. The whole family dynamic made me cringe. Every cell in my body fought to leave the table during the evening meal—Dad at one end of the table and Tony by my mom's side—but none of the adults seemed phased by the strangeness of us all dining together.

By the time we carried dirty dinner plates into the kitchen, the sinking red sun reflected off the lake. While Auntie Beth and Marianne did dishes, Dad, Tony, and Uncle Chuck carried an arsenal of fireworks onto the dock. Despite my fear of the water, I let my feet dangle off the dock. Dad was here. Everything was good.

"Dad, Dad, Dad!" Brandon peered into a box with wide eyes.

"Brandon, Brandon, Brandon!" Dad replied.

"Did you bring parachutes?"

"What would the Fourth of July be without parachutes?" He pried open a cardboard box, pulled wooden matches from his pocket, and struck a flame. "Stand back!"

The bottle rockets soared into the air and when they exploded, soft parachutes floated to the ground. Brandon and Sammy ran to retrieve them.

Dad smiled like a kid at a baseball game. "I've got the big sparklers you like too."

I hadn't seen Brandon so happy in months. Dad lit the sparklers and told the boys, "Hold them over the water."

Brandon and Sammy oohed and aahed over the bright display. Margot, with her feet in the water, pretended to ignore me. When we were up in our room, I'd told her I was going next door as soon as I could get away. Margot had asked, "What do you see in them?" and turned her back when I didn't answer.

"You're not too old for a sparkler, are you, Daphne?" Dad asked. "How about you, Margot?"

"Sure." Margot stood next to me twirling the sparkler in a slow circle. Sparks arced like little knives into the water, lighting up the murky depths.

As the sky darkened, the smells of bug repellant and sulfurous explosives clouded the air. Dad and Tony found common ground—lighting explosives—and opened a bottle of scotch. Uncle Chuck joined them.

"Why can't I light fireworks this year?" Brandon complained.

"Next year, little man." Dad shooed him away.

I kept my eye on the house next door as I herded the boys, Duke, and Margot off the dock. "Brandon, you've got the best seat in the house," I said. "The Vaughans' fireworks are going to be so far out."

"When did you start using that expression?" Auntie Beth asked as she approached the boys with a green bottle of bug spray.

I shrugged. "Lara says it all the time."

"Lara, Shmara." Margot huffed and walked inside.

"Put this on." Auntie Beth handed the spray bottle to me as Tony lit the first series of bottle rockets. Pop-poppity-pop.

The Vaughan family emerged from their house with friends. Ladies in sundresses and men in slacks went out to the dock. Phillip, carrying more explosives, joined Mr. Vaughan on their dock. Lewis stood apart from the group with his hands in his pockets. Mrs. Vaughan chatted with her friends. They were the perfect family, I observed. A mom and dad and siblings all playing together. Not broken and bandaged, like mine.

Lara wore a red-white-and-blue halter top with white hot pants. I rushed toward her, meeting her between our two yards so that we didn't have to shout. "Get me outta here!"

Lara squinted toward the end of the dock. "Wait. Which one's your dad?"

I pointed. "The tall one in the blue shirt."

"Who's that with him? He looks familiar."

"Uncle Chuck?"

"No, the other guy. I know him."

"How could you know him?"

"He sold me some pot in the parking lot of the academy ice rink."

I think my eyes grew as big as a buoy. "I knew it."

"What's he doing at your house?"

"That's Tony, my mom's boyfriend."

Lara's white straight teeth practically glowed. "Your mom's so cool."

"She's not." I grimaced. "Come on! Let's get out of here."

Lara slipped her hand into mine, and we took off toward her house. As soon as she touched me, I knew what was wrong. I was as sure as the day Ruth fell on the ice. I knew. Lara was pregnant.

CHAPTER 25

BURNED

Daphne

We ran in the Vaughans' back door, into their kitchen, where Lara filled two glasses with ice and rum. "It's called a Cuba Libre if you add lime, but Mother doesn't have any lime or Coke. Only Tab."

She didn't notice me staring at her. I sensed that she didn't know about the baby yet.

After what happened with Ruth, I kept my lips zipped. I didn't want to be the one to tell Lara about the baby. A string of firecrackers went off outside the window.

I took the plastic glass and followed her out past the ladies sitting in folding chairs on the lawn. My dad stood in the grass between the fiery blasts and the boys. On the dock we saw colorful blasts and sprays of pyrotechnics up and down the shore. Across the water, a bigger display had begun at the academy. Thunderous booms echoed off the lake.

Lewis emerged from the shadows and came to my side. "Hey."

"Hey. This is some Fourth of July, isn't it?" I sipped the strong rum drink and tried to get the image of Lara and her baby out of my head.

Lewis shrugged. "Not really."

"What's wrong?"

"Lewis, get over here and light one of these big ones," Mr. Vaughan said.

"Come on, Lewis," Phillip said.

"Light some, Lewis. Have fun for a change. Stop being such a downer." Lara climbed into the Master Craft and posed on the padded engine block.

Lewis seemed resistant. He didn't want to do it. He shrank away from the explosives, and I sensed that he was afraid. It gave me something besides Lara to focus on.

With a cigarette hanging out of his mouth, Mr. Vaughan lit three small rockets. They fizzed for a few seconds before zipping into the sky and exploding like meteor showers.

I joined Lara in the boat and chose a vantage point where I could see Dad's display as well. Lewis hung back in the shadows, rubbing his right hand with the missing finger.

"What's wrong with him?" I whispered.

After a big boomer, Lara said, "Lewis hates the Fourth."

"Come on, Lewis," Phillip said. "It's your turn. Light a few firecrackers."

"I don't want to."

Phillip lit a firecracker with his cigarette coal, held his arm out, and looked away as it exploded in his fingers. "See? Nothing to be afraid of."

"Light a few, Lewis," Mr. Vaughan said.

Phillip took Lewis by the shoulders and looked him in the eyes. "Time to grow up, little brother. Come on. Play with fire. Show us what you're made of."

Lewis pushed Phillip away and he stumbled backward into their father. "Leave me alone."

"Lewis." Mr. Vaughan held out the lighter. "Come on."

Lewis crossed his arms. "No, thank you."

Mr. Vaughan bent down and lit the fuse on another eight-inch rocket. At that moment, Phillip jumped on Lewis and dragged him over to the burning explosive. "Scared of a little fire?"

Lewis fought Phillip's grip but he didn't have any leverage.

I held my breath.

Phillip kicked Lewis's feet out from under him. Lewis dropped to his knees. Pinned over the quickly diminishing fuse, Lewis struggled to get free while his dad looked on and laughed.

I leapt to my feet. "Stop it!"

A moment before the firework exploded, Lewis swept his hand along the dock and knocked the rocket into the lake. It exploded under water, and the hot sparks fizzled out.

Mr. Vaughan laughed. "You'll always be Little Lewis."

Phillip let go and Lewis fell onto the dock. Even in the dark, Lewis's face was red with mortification and anger. He jumped to his feet and stormed past.

I flew after him.

PIPE DREAM

Lara

Alone in the docked Mastercraft with fireworks going off all around the lake, Lara watched Daphne run after Lewis. *Let them go.* She didn't care. Earlier, she'd happened to be looking out the kitchen window when Daphne's dad arrived. When she saw how he hugged everyone—the joy, the pure love—Lara burned inside, like someone lit a string of firecrackers in her heart.

Things weren't like that when John Wesley Vaughan III came home. He expected his family to stand at attention.

She thought back to when Father had finally joined them at the summer home yesterday. She'd been holding onto the stair rail, wearing her bikini top and a pair of hot pants when he drove up. Mother had said, "For God's sake, make yourself presentable, Lara. Go put a shirt on."

"God, what difference does it make?"

"Go!" Adelaide said.

Lara groaned and went back upstairs to put on a frilly red-and-orange blouse. It seemed like she was never thin enough, never pretty enough, and never good enough for Father. For Prosecutor Vaughan.

This spring he'd hit the campaign trail, and appearances were *everything* to him. He wanted to become the next Indiana State Attorney General and elections were coming up in the fall. It was the only thing he talked about anymore.

Lara didn't care about that. She just wanted him to hug her. A bear hug. Like the ones Daphne's dad gave so freely to his family.

She spritzed Opium perfume on her neck and chest to cover the smell of alcohol that lingered on her breath and went back downstairs to meet her father.

Adelaide bustled around picking up used glasses and full ashtrays. "Who's been smoking so much?"

"You have, Mother." Lewis straightened the pile of magazines and tucked in his shirt.

"I don't smoke that much. And I don't smoke Winstons."

"You smoke a lot, Addy." Father had walked into the living room with his tie hanging loose around his neck and a suit jacket slung over his arm.

"You're early, John. How was your week?" Adelaide took his jacket and brushed out the wrinkles.

"It was hell. My Democratic adversary, Ralph Seidel, is claiming I'll refuse to follow the Supreme Court decision on Roe versus Wade. He's making it into a big campaign promise to uphold the ruling in the state of Indiana."

"But you're not opposed to it, are you, John?" Adelaide lit a cigarette.

Lara knew about Roe versus Wade because it was all her father talked about the year it was in court. She didn't agree with his stance at all. Women should have the right to choose. Besides, what if they got pregnant because of something bad? What if it wasn't planned? What if they were too young, or didn't have any means to support a family? Lara was definitely in favor of the Supreme Court ruling. She was in favor of abortion.

"Of course I'm against it," Father said. "Those women are killing babies."

Mother took a drag and crossed her arms over her chest. "Women have every right to make the choice. Especially in certain circumsta—"

"I disagree, Addy. Shelve it! Look. I'm not discussing this here at home. It's been a long week." Father always spoke the last word.

Lara took the opportunity and opened her arms. "Daddy!"

John held his daughter at arm's length. "Since when did you start calling me that? Daddy? Really, Lara. And wash that perfume off. You smell like your mother."

"I missed you, Father."

Her father only nodded before moving on.

Behind their backs, Lara made her way to the liquor cabinet. She poured a strong shot of whiskey and downed it.

Now Lara sank into the back seat of the Mastercraft. She sipped her drink and watched as her father lit another rocket and watched it fly. He'd been home for a full twenty-four hours and he still hadn't talked to her. He'd pulled Lewis aside many times. Five times if Lara were counting. Lewis gained his approval and his support like they were old cronies, and now that Phillip was here, all John's attention was on him despite the fireworks.

"How is teaching ten-year-old boys the rules of hockey going to help you when you're forty, Phillip?" Father asked. "You can't play the game forever, eventually the sport will wear you out. Then what're you going to do? Work at a drugstore?"

Phillip crossed his arms over his Carlson Academy polo shirt. "The North Stars' scout likes me. I'm favored to play center for one of the best NHL teams in the world. I'm good at it. This is what I want to do."

"And what if you don't get the position? You're throwing your life away."

Adelaide came out onto the dock with her group of hens. "John, can't we have a peaceful holiday?"

"Shut up, Addy. Phillip and I are having a conversation."

"Kind of one-sided, don't you think?" Phillip dug another firework out of the box.

"Well then? Defend yourself, goddammit! Tell me why this is the best life path for you?"

"How the hell can I? Nothing I do is good enough." He tossed the rocket back into the box. "I could win a fucking Olympic gold medal and you'd still be harping on me because I didn't do things your way!"

"Watch your language."

"What's it going to take to win your approval?"

"What's there to approve of?" John's voice grew louder. "You chose to play sports instead of getting a real job! You're teaching summer camp to little boys instead of making real money in a career that will keep you employed for a lifetime."

One of Mother's friends put her cardigan on and nervously approached them. "Oh Addy, it's probably time we get going."

Lara sank even deeper into the bench on the boat and glowered at them.

"I don't want the life you want for me," Phillip said. "Don't you see? If the North Stars draft me? The best hockey team in the country? It still won't be good enough."

"Phillip, of course it will," Adelaide chimed in.

"That's a pipe dream, and you know it," John said.

Phillip stormed off the dock. All of Father's berating and chiding hadn't molded Phillip into a miniature version of himself. Instead, the lecturing and castigating was only turning Phillip against him.

The women dragged Adelaide away, leaving Father with his arms crossed. Though she wanted Father's attention, Lara didn't want him to target her next. She stayed quiet inside the boat, hoping he didn't notice her. And to her disappointment, he didn't.

IMAGINING THINGS

Daphne

Fireworks all around the lake lit up the sky. When I caught up to Lewis, he strode fast across the street toward the golf course as if running away.

I jogged to catch up with him. "Lewis, wait. What was that all about?"

"Nothing. They're messed up." He ducked under trees and charged toward the creek.

"Wait! Can I come with you?"

He looked back, his expression sad and confused.

"My family sucks too," I said. After witnessing Phillip torture Lewis with a burning rocket and their father—cheering Phillip on!—my small admission felt like a lie.

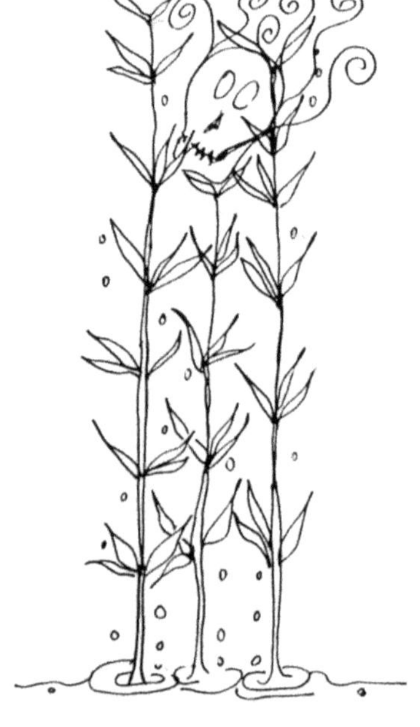

"Come on." He darted behind trees and rushed through the shadows. I followed close behind.

And we ran.

The moon brightened the golf course, turning the grass and trees gray. Shadows came alive, creeping up on us like ghouls.

Over the fairways and past the seventh green, we leapt across the creek and hurried along its grassy bed. Our shoes barely touched the ground. Frogs and crickets went silent as we passed. When we reached the line of trees on the far side of the course, Lewis finally slowed.

I fell into the grass, slightly out of breath, and rolled onto my back. "We did it. We escaped!"

Lewis dropped to his knees beside me. "It's so great to get away from them." He flopped on his back and gazed upward. The sadness I'd seen in him earlier seemed to have lifted.

I pointed to the sky. The nearly full moon hid behind a few clouds. "Isn't it beautiful? I could stay here forever."

"Me too," he said. "Do you golf?"

"No. But my grandmother does. I heard she hit a hole in one twice."

"Once is lucky. But twice? That's insane. Mother bought a membership to this golf course for me this summer. Want to come with me? I have a tee time, tomorrow."

Lewis likes me. He really likes me! I didn't know what to say, but a smile grew on my lips. He wasn't like other kids. He never pressured me or made fun of me. What I liked best was his easygoing nature. I could probably tell him anything. Almost anything.

I wouldn't tell him I thought Lara was pregnant. It was just a feeling, anyway.

Plus, when I had told Ruth about my premonition, when I'd warned her not to go out on the ice that day, Ruth did it anyhow. *I have a bad feeling about it,* I'd told her.

Weirdo.

I knew I was strange. I'd been lucky to meet Lewis and Lara this summer. As lucky as Nana hitting two hole in ones. At school I was a nerd. An outcast. I touched people and saw wild images. I wasn't one of the cool kids. Not like the Vaughans.

I sat up. I couldn't tell Lewis about any of that. "I'd like to golf with you, but I'm probably really bad at it."

"I'll teach you."

The smile on my face grew and I reached into my pocket. "Before this summer, I didn't know my mom smoked pot. Now, it's like everyone does it. When my mom and Tony Baloney went to the store today, I stole two more joints from their room."

"Lara's a bad influence."

"Well, maybe I learned a few things from Lara. I took a pack of matches too." I opened the matchbook from The Huddle restaurant in Indianapolis. I struck the match and cupped it in my hand, igniting the tip of the joint. I coughed with the exhale and handed it to Lewis.

He took it with his thumb and index finger. His stubby ring finger—the fourth finger for pianists—wriggled between the other two. With his exhale, he said, "When I was little, Phillip and I used to put cherry bombs in the neighbor's mailboxes then run. They were like tiny little bombs. When they went off, they blew the doors off the mailboxes and shredded envelopes flew like confetti. One time, a cherry bomb went off in my hand. The explosion took my finger off." He turned his hand. "Phillip still kids me about it."

"Phillip is a jerk." *A handsome, confident jerk.*

Lewis dropped the joint in the grass. He took my hand. "I like you, Daphne."

My mouth hung open.

He pulled me close and the next thing I knew his lips were on mine. He put a hand behind my head and held me in place. Gritty, grainy images like on an old TV screen flicked in my mind. I saw Lewis heckling kids. I saw him hitting Lara. I saw how much he hated everything. The images were dark.

I pushed him away.

"Sorry." He scooted closer. "I just really like you."

I was speechless. Smoke streamed up from the joint suspended between blades of grass, but I didn't pick it up.

Freak.

He dug the joint out of the grass and took another hit, blowing the smoke away from us.

The silence was too much. I tried to explain. "I'm not dating anyone. It's not like that."

"I thought you liked me."

"I do!" I took another hit of the joint, willing the prickles to go away. "I . . . I'm a . . ." *Don't tell him you've never done it with anyone.* "I just need time."

Lewis looked into my eyes, and I tried to hold his gaze. Something was wrong. He was dangerous, but I didn't know why.

He quickly and smoothly changed the subject as if nothing happened. "I wanted to volunteer for Father's election campaign this summer. He's running for the State Attorney General. He promised that I could go back to Indianapolis with him. Today he said I have to stay here."

The feel of his lips lingered on mine. I tried to get the images out of my head, to focus on what he was saying. He kept talking about politics as I took another hit from the joint. I looked at the grass or at his expensive track shoes. I liked Lewis a lot, but I didn't really know him. *He'd kissed me. He wants more from me. But I don't want to get pregnant like Lara.*

"I want to intern at his friend's law firm in the fall because I'm going to study law when I graduate," he said. "I want to be a lawyer. What do you want to do when you graduate?"

I rubbed my fingers along the tips of the short, mowed grass. Marijuana numbed my skin and turned off the strobe-like visions. Waiting for the high to kick in, I sat at attention, and avoided contact with Lewis.

"I love playing the piano," I said. "I want to take violin in the fall and try out for orchestra. I think I want to be a music teacher."

"Cool," he said. He passed the joint back to me, and I took a hit, willing the cactus needles in my arms to go away.

I'm imagining things, that's all.

We took our time walking back to the house. Lewis didn't kiss me again, but he was nice and seemed interested in what I had to say. Outside the Vaughans' kitchen door, I asked, "What time are we golfing tomorrow?"

"I'll call you. Father's leaving early and I want to ask him one more time about helping with the campaign," Lewis said. "What's your phone number?"

I gave him the Aubenaubee Lodge number.

Lara was standing inside the kitchen door. "What's your phone number?" she said, mocking Lewis with her arms crossed. "You two are too cute."

"Shut up, Lara."

When he passed his sister in the doorway, she gave him a look. I couldn't decide if she was serious or teasing. My head buzzed from the pot. It was late, and all decision-making faculties were gone.

"I'll see you soon." I turned to go home. It was past curfew.

"Wait, Daphne, I want to show you something." Lara held the door open. "It will only take a minute." Lara smiled like the crew of the Love Boat welcoming committee, and I followed her inside. We hurried upstairs to her room and shut the door. Lara snagged her flask off the bedside table and climbed up on the bed. "I want to tell you a secret."

I sat on the bed with Lara but looked around the room for a clock. I needed to go home.

Lara took a sip, then passed me the flask. "I'm seeing Mark!"

It wasn't a secret. I'd met Mark. Now I wondered, *Is he the father?* I took the flask from Lara's pushy hands and bit my tongue. I couldn't tell Lara she was pregnant. She'd find out soon enough, wouldn't she? "Isn't he a little old for you?" I said.

"That's the point. I like older men. Don't you?"

"Did he really go to prison?" I was more worried that Mark would go back to prison. That would make family life difficult. It would certainly upset Lara's mother.

Lara shrugged. "So what if he did? At least he's not a little boy." She tilted her head. "Don't tell me. You have a crush on Lewis? That's so middle school."

I liked Lewis, but I'd never admit that to Lara. "He's nice, that's all. We'll be in the same grade."

"He's *nice*? Lewis is a puppet. He does what anyone tells him to do. Take a drink. It's peppermint schnapps. You'll like it."

"So why do you like Mark?" I asked.

"Mark's a man. He's hot."

"Have you had . . ." I raised my eyebrows and nodded. ". . . you know."

"Sex? Of course! Lots of times."

Was that proof? I chugged a big gulp of sweet schnapps, and the thick liquid coated my throat like cough syrup.

"I keep forgetting you're only a freshman," Lara said. "Are you, like, a virgin? I don't know why you don't go for someone older too. You're so much more mature than Lewis."

Coming from Lara, this was a big compliment. "I am?"

"You're as mature as my senior friends." Lara hopped off the bed. "When you get to Orchard Park, all the seniors will want to date you. You're really cute. Hey, want to have some fun?" She went to her dresser and grabbed a small case and a mirror.

"What's that?"

"Makeup from my photo shoot in New York." She opened the case, like a fishing tackle box, and displayed a dozen boxes and brushes, bottles, and creams. "I want to show you how pretty you are."

My smile grew. I had wanted Lara to include me, to be my friend. Maybe this was proof that Lara liked me. It made me feel so special, like Lara was my best friend.

I scooted closer and let her go to work.

A UNIFIED FRONT

Daphne

Lara transformed my face from that of a little girl to a *Vogue* magazine cover model. She brushed my cheeks with blush, painted sea-green eyeshadow on my lids, and put mascara on my eyelashes. A dab of bright pink lipstick on my lips made me feel so Stevie Nicks.

Right up until I tiptoed back into our cottage at two in the morning.

A light was still on in the living room. Dad was sitting in one of the floral wingback chairs, with a magazine folded open. "Where've you been?"

"Next door." I wiped lipstick off with my fingers.

"You know your curfew is eleven. You were supposed to be home . . ." Dad

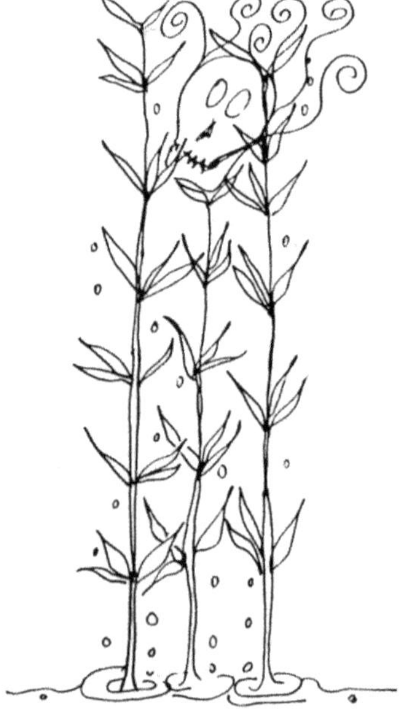

looked at his watch. "Three hours ago." He set the magazine on the side table and pushed himself up to his feet. "Go to bed. We'll talk in the morning."

An early morning breeze blowing in through the sliding door cleared out the musty air in the little house attached to the carport where Dad was staying. Though Auntie Beth had invited him to stay in the big

Victorian, Marianne had the final say. Maybe she drew the line at both her husband and boyfriend sleeping under the same roof.

With a clean face and the taste of bubble gum Lip Smackers on my lips, I slumped in the middle of a modern green, half-circle couch with wooden peg legs. In front of me, a white egg-shaped coffee table had rings from sweaty drink glasses. My parents had grounded me for the day. I had no hope of golfing with Lewis, which was just as well. I knew he wanted more than just kissing and I wasn't ready for that.

On the radio, Casey Kasem counted down the top forty. "Number four on the countdown this week is Daryl Hall and John Oates with 'Sara Smile.'"

On either side of me, my parents' heads bowed as they contemplated my punishment.

Marianne wore a scarf over her hair and gold hoop earrings. "You're drinking and smoking pot, Daphne. And that's what concerns us."

Smoking hadn't come into the conversation until now. My face heated. "You would know." I hoped the words cut like a knife.

"Tony said he's missing a couple joints."

"You're such a hypocrite," I said. "You and Tony smoke all the time." I recalled what Lara said the night before—that Tony was dealing—but kept it to myself. It only confirmed that my vision of him with stacks of money, pills, and weed was true. Dad would flip out if he knew.

Marianne blushed and shot a furtive glance at Dad. His mouth fell open. "This isn't about me," Marianne said. "I'm an adult."

The skin between Dad's eyebrows folded. "You're supposed to be one, Marianne," he said. "Lately I'm beginning to think of you as one of the kids."

Marianne walked to the sliding door as if avoiding Dad's scrutiny. Outside, the boys ran around and threw balls into the center of a giant inner tube.

I was in trouble, but Marianne had a part in it. I wanted Dad to see who Marianne had become now that they were divorced. I hoped he had something to say about Tony.

"Anyway. I'm glad you've made some new friends," Marianne said.

I shrugged.

"What are their names?" she asked. "Larry and—"

"God, Marianne. Lewis. And Lara."

Dad leaned forward, resting his elbows on his knees spread wide. "Is Lewis into sports? He looks like an athlete."

"Can we not talk about them?" I said.

"I'm just curious about your new friends. I'm curious about you, Daph," he said.

I kept my gaze out the window.

"What do you guys do when you're hanging out?" Dad asked.

"Nothing."

"Phillip's old enough to buy beer, isn't he?" Marianne asked.

I didn't answer. Technically, he wasn't. But Marianne dated a drug dealer. That was so much worse. "Can I go now?"

"No," both my parents said.

I hung my head and wished I could disappear. This wasn't how I imagined their reunion. I didn't want to be a point of argument between them. I got no satisfaction in bringing them together like this. Why couldn't they be more normal?

Dad looked down at Duke, sleeping on the orange-and-yellow carpet. "Sweetie," he said to me. "I can't speak for your mom, but I'm worried about you. Are these kids pressuring you into drinking and smoking pot?"

Pressure? The Vaughans had seemed like the coolest kids I'd ever met. "No."

Marianne sat back down. "We set a curfew for a reason. And we expect you to follow it."

"I just, I lost track of time."

"Daphne, your dad and I talked about it, and we know you're at an age where you're going to experiment with alcohol and weed. When I was your age, my uncle Barty would give us glasses of wine with dinner, and sometimes I would sneak a second or third."

I shook my head. "What are you saying?"

"I'm saying I know what you're going through."

"Sara . . . smile . . ."

Marianne placed a hand on my shoulder. "Look, I'm not angry that you're experimenting. I just want you to be safe."

"I agree." Dad looked me in the eye. "Don't ever get into a car with friends who've been drinking."

"Exactly. I'm happy to pick you up if you ever need a ride." Marianne lowered her head to make eye contact, but I kept my gaze on Duke licking his paw.

"Call me. Or call your mother if you need help. If your friends are drinking. If you feel pressured or if you just want to come home." Dad put a hand on my knee. "We love you."

Marianne added, "We love you, Daphne."

Once again, they were a unified front. I was relieved they weren't fighting anymore, but I couldn't look them in the eyes. There were too many things I didn't feel comfortable talking about. So I turned my head and looked out the sliding glass door.

I CAN SEE THE FUTURE

July 10th: Mark

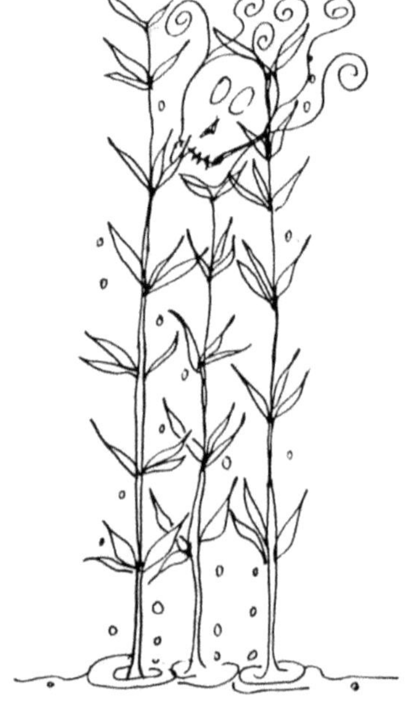

The week after the Fourth of July, Mark found himself at the Vaughans' again. Lara wanted him there. Phillip wanted to party. It was awkward, a young man like him—just out of prison—hanging out with a bunch of teenagers. But his reasons for being with them outweighed all the strangeness. For one, this was like reliving those lost teenaged years. Living it like he should have. Partying and having fun.

Because instead of living the idyllic life he'd been promised—scholarships, college basketball, a future in sports—he'd been in prison with a bunch of grown men. Rapists, murderers, gang members, and men who would just as likely sleep with your little sister as cheat at a game of rummy.

Mark scowled. He was just like them now. And he couldn't stay away from the Vaughans.

They had a strong magnetic pull, and for some reason he was drawn to them like lemmings to a cliff. Revenge was no longer his primary motive. He showed up because his curiosity got the better of him. Those kids were doing a great job of fucking up their lives. The prosecutor would be horrified if he only knew.

Mark smiled at the irony.

Lara called constantly. She found the number of The Bar in the Yellow Pages, and somehow, she'd found his home number. He thought he knew what she wanted, but sex wasn't the whole of it. He sensed she was seeking a kind of revenge of her own.

Last week when she came into The Bar looking for him, he had taken her by the arm and dragged her outside.

"What the . . ." She'd tried to peel his hand off her bicep, but Mark didn't let go.

"What the hell, Lara. Why didn't you tell me who you were?"

Her face turned ugly with disgust, or maybe it was indignation. "What do you mean?"

"I know who your *daddy* is. John Vaughan the Third. *Prosecutor* Vaughan."

She flicked his hand off her arm and took a step back against the metal outer wall of The Bar. "So? I thought you knew. You're friends with Phillip."

We're not friends, Mark thought. His hand went to his forehead. He took four or five steps, circling, to clear his head.

"What difference does it make anyway?" Lara pulled a pack of cigarettes out of her crocheted bag. "You're a good lay and I think you like me."

Mark huffed and dug his lighter out of his jeans' pocket. He lit her cigarette and said, "Your parents won't like it. I was in prison for the last seven years."

"Phillip told me. Big surprise." Lara coughed on the smoke, covering her mouth with her hand holding the cig. Her fit turned into a laugh, then she couldn't stop. Tickled by something she thought was hilarious, her laughter rose high in the wind.

"What's so funny?" Mark asked.

"Don't you see? It's perfect, me and you. Come on, buy me a drink." Smoke trailed behind her as she ducked back inside The Bar.

Mark's face heated up. His anger at the prosecutor had easily transferred to Lara.

Despite that, Mark had no problem showing up for her after they both knew where they stood. Wherever, whenever she called, he met her in town, at the pizza joint, at the house. It became obvious that she was into trouble—just like Phillip—and Mark wanted to be there. To see what happened. But after that night at the motel, Mark didn't touch her like that again. He drew a clear line in the sand. She could touch him and flirt all she wanted—and she did—but he refused to take her to bed. His revenge became secondary to watching the Vaughan disaster unfold.

Around noon, Mark picked up Lara and drove to the A&W. They sat at a picnic table outside and watched the world go by. Waiting for Tony to bring pot.

Over a cardboard container of fries and a root beer frosty, Tony passed a brown paper bag to Lara. She slid some cash under the table, and the deal was done.

Tony kicked back and lit a cigarette. "I got something stronger if you want it."

Lara's eyes lit up. "Acid?"

"No, man. That shit will mess up your pretty little head. Downers." He leaned forward and lowered his voice. "Quaaludes."

Mark couldn't fight the urge to defend her. "Why are you pushing that on her? She's in high school."

Tony laughed. "She's going to do it someday. We all do, man."

"I'll try some," Lara said.

Tony rifled around in his blue jean jacket pocket, then dropped three pills in Lara's hand. "If you like them, they're two dollars each. I can always get you more."

Just then a police car drove by the root beer stand, for the third time. Mark's cousin Deputy Brandt Simmons, seemed to be itching to arrest someone, and Mark didn't want to be the one he targeted. He'd been warned to stay away from the Vaughans. On top of that, Brandt had been watching him like he was the best new sitcom on NBC TV. Even Jim Strickland, the parole officer, didn't show up that often.

Mark stood and tossed his garbage into a nearby trash can. "I'm leaving. This scene isn't cool anymore."

Lara slung her purse over her shoulder and grabbed the brown bag of weed. "Thanks, Tony." She jogged after Mark. "Where are we going? I'm bored."

"You're always bored."

Mark drove them five miles to a country road near The Bar and parked on the side of the road, where wind rustled the shoulder-high cornstalks that covered most of northern Indiana. Even though it was afternoon, crickets chirped in the tall grass and wildflowers. He sipped the rest of his root beer, biding his time.

"What are we waiting for?" Lara asked.

"That cop was lurking around. I can't get caught."

"My father would fix it if you did." Lara popped one quaalude and washed it down with the rest of her root beer float. "If you even get caught, I mean."

Mark grunted. He still kept it to himself that Prosecutor Vaughan put him in prison. He felt pretty sure that if he told her, she would stop seeing him. His motives weren't exactly moral. After a month together, he couldn't wait to see how this ended. He held his cigarette out the car window and flicked ash into the weeds on the side of the road.

Lara slipped her hand between his thighs and leaned into his chest. With her lips nearly touching his, she said, "I'll vouch for you. I'll tell Father you're one of the good guys. You know I like you."

"You're just using me to make your parents mad." He flicked the cigarette into the cornfield. "When you leave Carlson at the end of the summer, you'll go home to your rich friends and your private school." Mark's lip curled. "You'll forget all about me and the summer of '76."

"I will not."

"Oh? So you're going to drop out of high school? Skip your East Coast college opportunity and move to the boonies with me? That'll never happen, and you know it." The Vaughans had so much going for them—money, education, opportunities that only the privileged get handed to them—yet both Phillip and Lara sought the wrong kind of attention. They would dig their own graves, he predicted.

Lewis seemed all right though. The unfortunate kid got the wrong ideas from Phillip and his sister. And their friend Daphne seemed blind to their charms. He wanted to tell her to stay away from them.

Lara gaped at him.

He kept his gaze locked on the horizon ahead, where the road and the corn stalks merged with the sky. "I can see your future, Lara. Instead of modeling, you'll sit around the trailer home and get fat. Poop out four or five kids and feed them Ho Hos. You'll have to deal pot and downers just to make ends meet. Just to put food on the table. It's the kind of life you always dreamed of, right?"

Lara stuck out her lip in an exaggerated pout. "You think so poorly of me."

Mark only shrugged. He didn't expect Lara to stick around. She was using him too. Somehow, he knew trouble was coming to Vaughan paradise.

"How can I make it up to you?" Lara said. "How can I make you think better of me?" Her hand moved to his crotch. She unbuckled his belt and lowered her face.

Mark groaned and pushed her head down.

CHAPTER 30

AN ACCOMPLICE

Daphne

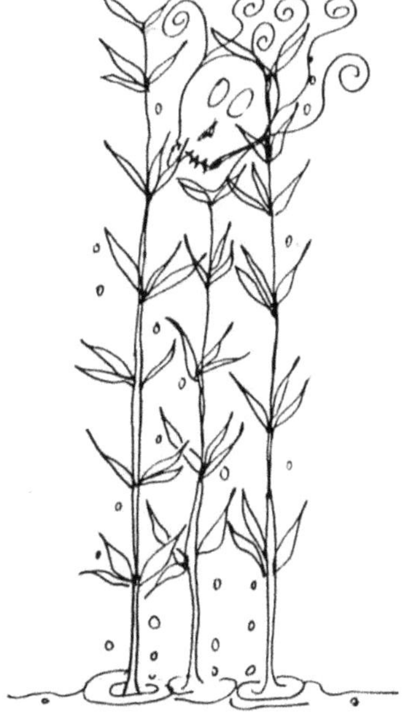

Dad and Uncle Chuck went home after the Fourth of July. Marianne told me to watch the boys while they swam and asked me not to go next door for a few days. Within a week, Marianne forgot about the talk with Dad. I was off the hook. I already knew I'd be able to slip out after dinner once the adults started drinking.

I took a drag of the Winston Light cigarette that Lara gave me and blew it out the bedroom window. I sat with my back to the creepy closet and my arm hanging out the window, so the smoke didn't come into the house.

Margot came into our bedroom and stopped in the doorway. "What are you doing?"

"What's it look like I'm doing?"

Margot stood up tall. "Being stupid. Put that out. I don't want smoke in here."

"Grow up, Margot. Everyone smokes. You're such a loser." It was out of my mouth before I could stop it. Heat rose to my cheeks. "I'm sorry . . ."

Behind her thick glasses, Margot's eyes grew small.

"I didn't mean it, Margot."

She turned on her heel and walked out of the room in a flurry.

I stubbed the cigarette out in a purple clam shell I'd found in the lake. Making sure it wasn't still smoldering, I buried it in the waste basket as fast as I could. I took the steps two at a time, looked into the stag head's eyes and followed the sound of Margot's voice to the kitchen.

"She's smoking in our room."

"What?" Auntie Beth didn't sound amused.

Hours later, I lay on my back in my bikini and sunglasses, listening to watery sounds and letting the sweltering summer sun darken my skin. Motorboats trundled past, and wind blew through the trees.

"Marco," Sammy shouted. He walked through hip-deep water inside the L of our dock.

"Polo," Brandon answered. I couldn't see him, but Duke could hear him beneath the dock. Growing excited, the big dog paced and panted, sniffing the dock.

"Marco," Sammy said.

Lara waved at me from her dock. "Come over!" In her bathing suit and sarong, she looked like a model from *Teen* magazine.

"I can't. I'm watching the boys."

"Watch them from here." Lara rolled over on her belly and rested her head in her hands.

Sitting on the bow of the Hydrodyne, Margot closed her book and placed her index finger between the pages. "I still don't get what you see in her."

"Marco." Brandon walked in waist-deep water between the docks.

A commotion on the patio drew my attention. Tony hustled out onto the dock with Auntie Beth trailing behind and her arms waving in the air. "You can't, Tony. I won't let you."

"Come on, Beth. Have an adventurous spirit," Tony said.

"I said no! Chuck will never forgive me if you do this."

"How will he find out?" Tony was heading straight for Uncle Chuck's precious Chris-Craft.

By the time Auntie Beth made the boys get out of the water and herded everyone back into the house, Tony had untied the cover of the special boat.

I wrapped a towel around my hips and sat on a folding chair while Tony stepped down the ladder into the water. Though Lara had confirmed what I believed—that Tony was dealing drugs—I'd stopped following him after he shoved me to the floor. This act of defiance—against Auntie Beth, Uncle Chuck, and the rules—made him interesting again.

"Are you stealing it?" I said.

Tony stayed focused on rolling the cover back. "Like someone stole joints from the dresser in my bedroom?"

I wasn't scared of him. If he were mad about it, he would have said something. "So?"

"You're too young for smoking pot. Mary doesn't like it."

"What? Am I in trouble?" Tony Baloney had no authority.

"Nah. I like you, kid." He climbed out of the water and folded back the canvas cover.

"You never answered my question," I repeated.

"Not stealing it. Borrowing." Tony dried off before climbing into the Chris-Craft. "Old Chuck won't find out we took it for a drive. He'll never know the difference. We just have to treat his boat nicely and put it away when we're done."

He pulled a screwdriver out of the back pocket of his blue jean cut-offs and waved it at me. "Want to learn something? This is a life skill that may come in handy one day, young apprentice."

I tossed the towel aside and climbed into the Chris-Craft. I'd never ridden in Uncle Chuck's boat before. Careful not to touch anything, I kept my arms crossed. "Why do I need to learn how to steal a boat?"

"Now, you've got it all wrong. This is pretty much the same as a car ignition. Someday you may lose your car keys. You never know. Trust me. It's practical knowledge." Tony lay down with his knees bent on the long bench seat and his head beneath the steering wheel. From there he unscrewed three small screws from somewhere beneath the dashboard. The ignition plate loosened, and Tony sat up, his face turned red from lying upside down.

I kept a nervous eye on the house—as if Uncle Chuck would come running out to punish us both.

Tony didn't seem worried at all. He pulled the thing apart and showed me a box with three colorful wires. "This is the ignition lock cylinder. This sends the electrical signal to the engine. All we need to do is bypass the cylinder using these wires here."

I put my elbows on the back of the bench seat and peered over Tony's shoulder. A question burned the tip of my tongue. "Why are you still here?"

"What do you mean?"

"I can tell you and my mom aren't getting along."

"How can you tell?"

"She's always mad at you."

"She's my old lady. I expect nothing different." He pulled another tool from his pocket and held it up. "Wire stripper. Never leave home without it."

"So? Why are you still here?"

"I've got business here. An opportunity to make some cash. That's why. Now stop asking questions." He disconnected two wires from the cylinder and let it hang. Then he stripped the ends of the two remaining wires. "White is the ground wire. We don't need that one. But these two—"

"Does Marianne know you're selling pot?" I surprised myself by asking that question. It came out of nowhere. And then I worried that he'd shove me again.

Tony shot me a look over his shoulder. "What are you talking about?"

"Have you told her?"

"Don't just stand there. You're already considered an accomplice. Lower the boat into the water."

Was that a confirmation? I leapt out of the boat and began to turn the lift crank. But I wanted to find out the truth. Maybe I wanted him to get in trouble. "Do you deal drugs?"

Tony almost dropped his tools. "What do you think? That stuff will mess with your mind."

"So you don't?" I had to know.

"Hell, no. Don't you ever do it either, you hear?"

His answer didn't satisfy my curiosity.

"Here's the end of your lesson for today," Tony said. "Touch the two wires together and—" The engine rumbled to life. "Presto, magic-o!"

"Cool!"

Marianne and Auntie Beth came running outside with the boys and Duke following. My aunt declared, "Chuck is not to find out about this, boys. Do you understand? We are not saying a word."

"Got it!" Brandon ran to the end of the dock.

Sammy's eyes lit with delight. "I'm not telling."

Tony got an A plus from me for showing me how to hotwire Uncle Chuck's boat. He wasn't mad about the joints I'd taken, and he'd treated me like an adult. It was a gift no one could take away from me. But he'd lied. And the lingering sense that he was dangerous—from that look in his eyes when he shoved me out of the bedroom—worried me.

ASPIRIN

Daphne

By mid-July, my family settled into a slow vacation pace at Aubenaubee Lodge. Marianne and Tony slept late, and she worked at her easel while the boys swam with Duke. Margot waded in the shallow end, built stalls for her horses, and read books. Auntie Beth cooked or put together puzzles.

I wanted to practice, but the new piano hadn't arrived. I didn't feel comfortable asking to use the Vaughans' Baldwin. And yet the music of the lake's rhythm thrummed like a symphony in the back of my mind. An orchestra played an edgy minor melody while jittery violins pulsed a single high note of tension that saturated my days. Beneath it all, constant whispers from waves slapping the shore brushed the hairs on the back of my neck.

One morning, I clomped through the kitchen in my Dr. Scholl's, carrying a towel and a sweater. The sun had just crested the trees east of the golf course.

Auntie Beth sat alone at the dining room table with a newspaper and a cup of coffee. "What are you doing up so early?"

"I'm going water-skiing with Lewis and Lara."

"This early?"

"The water is smooth as a mirror," I said.

"Have fun." My aunt shook out her newspaper and folded it in half.

Still wondering if it had been my imagination, I recalled the white face in the lakeweeds with a sense of dread. The only thing that relieved my worry was smoking pot with Lewis and Lara.

I shuffled in my sandals through dewy grass to meet Lewis on his dock. The sun hadn't yet warmed the air, and I pulled my sweater on. "Where's Lara? We need a third."

He wiped condensation off the vinyl seats and windshield. "I don't know. Making sure her makeup is perfect, or something. Can you help me with this?" He tossed me the tangled ski rope.

I looped it around my elbow and thumb while Lewis lowered the boat into the water. He hadn't brought up the kiss or even acted like anything happened. But I didn't want to lose his friendship over one stupid kiss. "Is everything okay?" I asked.

"It's fine. Why?"

"Hey," Lara said. She came out on the dock wearing fashionable elephant ear pants over her bikini. She had a towel draped over her arm and a flask in the other hand. "Nothing wakes you up faster than a hit of peppermint schnapps."

"Seriously, Lara?" Lewis asked. "You're drinking already?" Something in his tone reminded me of the vision I had when he kissed me. For some reason, I blushed.

"Why not?" Lara said.

"None for me, thanks," I said. Lara had been drinking more during the day and it worried me. I didn't tell her why.

Lewis climbed aboard the Mastercraft. "It's like drinking mouthwash."

"Sensible Lewis," Lara said. "He never drinks before happy hour." She took the wheel and Lewis slalom-skied first.

A natural water-skier, he showed off with hard cuts across the wake. His ski threw big rooster tails—ten-to-twelve-foot fans of water spray. His rooster tails sailed up to the sky. I couldn't help noticing his muscular shoulders glistening in the rising sun.

When it was her turn, Lara declined. "It's too early for physical activity."

I was pretty sure she had other reasons for not skiing. And she was moving a little slower than usual. I quietly kept an eye on her, looking for—what? Signs that she was pregnant? *Did she know?*

I skied next and tried to put the *Jaws* movie images out of my mind. Those images combined with the pale face I saw in the lakeweeds still frightened me. I tried not to show it. I wanted to be brave in front of my new friends. I slid into the water slowly, so I didn't go in too deep, and let the life vest buoy me up. I kept my feet up near the surface where I could see them.

Because the water was so smooth, I had a great run. I couldn't cut across the wake like Lewis did, but I was satisfied with my performance. When I tired, I dropped the handle and glided toward our docks. I climbed out of the water as fast as I could and met them back at their pier.

"Aren't you going to ski?" Lewis asked Lara.

"No, thanks." Lara parked the Mastercraft in their boat lift. "I have a headache. Besides, I need to work on my tan."

While Lewis swam laps to and from the buoy, Lara and I spread out our towels. She opened a zippered pouch she'd brought with her and dropped two round pills into her palm.

I looked closer. "That doesn't look like aspirin."

Lara grinned. "It's not. But it will take away the pain. Want one? I can always get more."

I had a feeling this wasn't a good idea and shook my head. Alcohol and weed were enough for me. When Lara moved to pop one in her mouth, I tried to stop her.

"What?" she said.

Touching Lara's arm gave me all kinds of dark thoughts. She was angry at her parents. She was drinking a lot more than any of us knew. Her plans to go to California would happen sooner than she realized.

I pulled away.

"Are you sure you don't want one? It's cool. They're quaaludes. I got them from Tony. You know, Marianne's boyfriend?"

"You mean *my mom's* boyfriend?" It was probably the first time all summer that I'd referred to Marianne as "my mom."

"Yes, of course. Who else?"

I didn't know what to say. Though the rug burns on my knees from Tony's push had healed, the emotional wound had not. "I don't trust him," was all I said.

"Don't worry about it," Lara said.

It was still important to hide my emotions from Lara—as well as my feeling that she was pregnant. *Ruth had turned everyone against me.* But I didn't know how to tell Lara not to take it without totally losing her friendship.

I lay on the dock and closed my eyes. "I can't believe it's halfway through the summer already. I wish my dad was coming back."

"What's it like, anyway? Do you have two houses, two bedrooms, and two birthdays?"

"Yeah," I chuckled. "But we usually spend weekends with him. This summer, we've hardly seen him at all."

"Sounds like you miss him."

"I do."

Lara sat up. "Let's go to Indianapolis to see your dad's deli."

"How? Will your mom give you the car?"

"No, but I can borrow Phillip's. Or . . ." Lara swallowed the last sip from her flask. "Mark could drive us!"

Mark. The twenty-five-year-old father of Lara's baby. Mark the criminal. "I'll ask my mom."

"Absolutely not." Marianne puffed up with more conviction than I'd ever seen.

I crossed my arms. "Why not? You won't take us home to see Dad and he can't take a day off work."

Brandon collapsed on the floor. "I wanna see dad too!"

"See what you started? You are not driving back to Indianapolis, Daphne. Margot told us about your trip to A&W. Your friend got a speeding ticket, didn't she?"

"No, she didn't," I said. "You have to let me go."

"The answer is no."

I stormed off. I'd already planned it with Lara. We were leaving in the morning. I was going to Indy whether Marianne allowed it or not.

e.p.t.

July 18th: Lara

avid Bowie's "Fame" blasted from the car speakers as Lara sped south on North Meridian Street in Indianapolis. Daphne sat in the passenger seat and Lara could tell she was nervous. She'd been chewing her nails since they got past Kokomo, and she'd hardly said a word for the whole two-hour drive.

"I thought Mark was driving us?" Daphne had asked when they left.

"Phillip lets me borrow his car all the time." She'd tricked Phillip into letting her use his car. He didn't know she'd driven to Indianapolis, and Lara didn't care if he got mad. She needed to get out of that house. Escape, seeing her friends, and having a good time—that was what she needed to kill the summer blahs. And a question niggled at the back of her mind. Something she needed an answer to. She'd been waiting a week for her period and feeling all bloated and queasy in the mornings. It made her uneasy.

"I'll be in so much trouble if Marianne finds out," Daphne said. The two-hour car ride hadn't seemed to calm her down. "How long will this take?"

"Apparently it will take all day." Lara hadn't meant to snap at Daphne, but her moods had been swinging all over the place. Her period was late, and it scared her. "It's fine," she added. "Stop worrying about it. You'll get to see your dad and he'll confirm that you're okay. Besides, you're with me. What could go wrong?" She patted Daphne's knee.

Daphne laughed nervously.

Lara turned left on Kessler and right on College Avenue. By now, Phillip would be calling all over town trying to locate her. He'd need Mother's car to get to work and that would get Mother's attention. Lara didn't care. She was desperate. "Listen, before we go to your dad's deli, I'm stopping at my friend Chandi's house. I need to ask her something."

Lara parked on the street near Chandi's driveway. She shut off the Corolla and the radio went silent. "This will only take a minute," she said.

In *Vogue* magazine, Lara read that the FDA had approved early pregnancy tests for home use this year. They were legal, but not widely sold in Indiana. Chandi Shrivastava's mom was an OBGYN at St. Vincent's hospital. Lara wanted to know if Chandi's mom had any early pregnancy tests. If she could just be sure . . .

Daphne gazed at Lara. "Are you okay?"

"I'm fine." *Not really.* Lara was out of her mind with worry. She reached into her purse and pulled out a baggie full of pills. "Take a quaalude. It'll calm you down."

Daphne eyed the round pills suspiciously. "No, thanks."

"Trust me." Lara dumped two into her palm. "I'll take one too." She held them out for Daphne.

"I really don't want it."

"Suit yourself." Lara washed one down with the rest of a warm Coke. "Let's go. I want you to meet my friends." She hopped out of the car and rushed to the door.

Today, Chandi had the house to herself. While Daphne waited in the kitchen, Lara pulled Chandi into the bathroom. Chandi pulled her glossy black hair into a ponytail. In the mirror, Lara's suntanned skin was almost as dark as her friend's natural color.

"Does your mom have any e.p.t.s?"

"What are those?"

"Early pregnancy tests. Haven't you heard of them?"

Chandi stared at Lara. "Wait. Are you . . ." She looked genuinely worried.

"I don't know. I need a test. Can you get one for me?"

Chandi seemed to think for a moment. "I think I saw some in the cabinet." She rifled through drawers and pulled out three cardboard boxes rubber-banded together. The label announced e.p.t. in bold typeface.

"Oh my god, thank you. Thank you so much." Lara snatched one from her and began reading the directions.

"Are you going to use it now?"

"It takes two hours." Lara grabbed Chandi's wrist and looked at her watch.

Chandi took back her arm and slowly backed out of the bathroom. "Make sure you hide the rubbish. I don't want my mom thinking I used it."

CHAPTER 33

BANANA DAQUIRIS

Daphne

I waited forever for Lara in Chandi's kitchen. She stayed in the bathroom for a long time. When she finally came out, she said, "I'll check it in an hour and a half."

"Check what?" I asked.

Chandi looked at the clock. "Mom won't be home until after five."

I wondered why they looked so worried. "What are we waiting for?"

Lara didn't answer me. "In the meantime, let's make daquiris." She pulled a bottle out of her big purse, and now I was at Lara's mercy.

"Wait," I said. "Lara, you told me we'd leave in a few minutes to go visit Dad and then drive back to Carlson." She'd promised

"I know." She seemed nonchalant, but I could tell something bothered her. "Plans changed."

"I'll call Ellen." Chandi picked up the baby-blue wall phone and dialed.

While Lara scooped ice from the freezer and peeled bananas, I went to her side. "What's going on?"

As soon as she looked me in the eye, I knew.

"It's nothing, okay? I missed my period, that's all. I'm taking an e.p.t. to make sure I'm not pregnant."

I felt the blood rush from my face. Should I have told her? I'd already suspected the test would be positive.

"What?" She looked at me like I was an idiot. "It's not that big a deal."

But she didn't know it would change everything for her.

Ellen bicycled over in a matter of minutes, and she brought a bunch of bananas in her backpack. Lara cut up limes, and peeled bananas. She poured a generous amount of rum into the blender and added more ice. She kept looking over her shoulder at the kitchen clock.

"My brother's been getting the best weed, lately," she said. "I swear, two hits and I'm stoned."

Was Marianne looking for me? Was Margot? Did it matter? Despite my nervousness about getting in trouble, I wanted Lara's friends to like me. "My mom smokes pot," I blurted out.

"That's so weird," Chandi said. "I can't imagine lighting up with my parents."

"I'd never smoke with Marianne. Talk about weird!" I laughed, but it wasn't funny.

"My mother's the president of the Women's Social Society," Ellen said. "Can you imagine her smoking pot?" Ellen was shorter than Lara, and wore her blond hair pulled back with barrettes on either side of her head.

The sound of the blender quieted the conversation, and we gazed eagerly at the slushy mixture.

"Have you seen Patrick Jones this summer?" Ellen asked. "I hear he's dating Julie Voortman."

Lara poured and handed us cold glasses filled with banana daiquiri. "Patrick Jones is a little boy. This summer I'm seeing a real man," she said proudly.

"I heard Julie gives Patrick head in the back seat of his car," Chandi said.

What's that mean? I didn't want to admit to not understanding the phrase.

"This is why he's dating Julie." Lara peeled a banana and opened her mouth. Moving the banana in and out, dragging it over her lips and licking it, she mimicked something I could only guess.

Chandi and Ellen roared, but my mouth hung open. I imagined doing that to Lewis and grimaced.

Ellen caught my gaze and said, "I think someone needs a lesson."

"She's blushing!" Lara said.

"Are you a virgin?" Chandi asked.

"She has a crush on Little Lewis," Lara added.

Now the context was clear. But I'd never admit I was a virgin. I peeled the slightly green banana halfway and opened my mouth. Humiliation flooded my veins, but I was determined to overcome it. To fit in. To be liked by these popular girls.

All gazes locked on me as I closed my eyes. My cheeks heated as I moved the banana in and out.

"Oh baby!" Chandi said.

"Oh, that's so good," Ellen moaned.

"Don't stop!" Their cries and moans were supposed to mimic pleasurable sounds that people made during sex, but I thought they had to be crude exaggerations. I opened my eyes and bit the tip off the banana.

The girls roared. Chandi clapped, and I knew I'd passed the test. I was one of them now.

After we emptied one pitcher of daiquiris, an hour and a half had passed. Lara disappeared into the bathroom. When she came running out to the kitchen, she beamed. "It's negative. It's negative, Chandi!"

"Thank goodness. I was so worried."

"The e.p.t. was negative?" I asked. It didn't make any sense.

Lara told Ellen about the test. "Just don't tell anyone," she said. "I'm serious, Ellen. No one at school can know. Especially the rest of the cheerleading squad."

Ellen blanched.

"One word and you're off the squad." Anger streamed from Lara's eyes so briefly that I thought I'd imagined it. And clearly I imagined that Lara was pregnant too. I chuckled at my overactive imagination.

"Next summer I'm going to California," Lara said, changing the subject so fast my head spun. "Father has connections. I'm going to model for *Vogue* magazine and become famous."

Chandi and Ellen and I stared at her.

"So let's celebrate with another pitcher of daquiris!"

I wondered if we would ever make it to the Asparagus Sandwich.

OH BABY

Daphne

After two, or was it three daiquiris, I could care less how the day would play out.

"Take a step to the left," Lara shouted over the music from *Rocky Horror Picture Show.*

Chandi danced on the bed, but she kept falling down on the pillows.

I preferred to keep my feet on the floor and tried to keep step with Lara and Ellen.

"And a step to the right," Ellen and Chandi sang in out-of-tune unison.

Lara's drunken smile flashed her straight white teeth. "Put your hands on your hips."

"Let's do the time warp again!" We all sang.

I laughed so hard I fell on the floor.

"Shh. Someone's here," Ellen said.

Someone was knocking on Chandi's bedroom door.

Lara's eyes grew wide. "Shh. Be quiet, they won't know we're in here."

We hushed instantly. I clamored up onto the bed. I needed to sit, or I'd fall down.

"It's me. Navi."

Lara opened the door and leaned on the frame. Her glass of the remnants of her daiquiri sloshed to the side. Navi, Chandi's sister, peered past her to Ellen and Chandi sitting on either side of me. "You've been drinking, I can smell the rum. Were you smoking cigarettes too?"

Chandi kicked the ash tray under the bed. "You smoke."

"I'm not seventeen." Navi's dark eyes darted around the room. "Mum and Dad will find out, you know. You better clean up the mess in the kitchen. They'll be home in an hour."

I looked around the room for a clock and my smile faded. "What time's it? I haff to go home," I slurred. I hopped off the bed and staggered into Lara, spilling what was left of her drink. "We have to go back to Carlson."

We quickly helped wipe down the kitchen and take out the trash. Ellen said goodbye and walked back home with her bike.

Outside, Lara leaned on the car. "Should we go visit your dad now?"

I squinted. There were two Laras standing beside the car. Wait, two cars. "No! I thing-k I'm drung-k."

"S'okay. Maybe we should go back to Carlson." Lara took her keys out of her purse, and they fell on the pavement.

"You can't drive." I was in no shape to do anything requiring focus either.

"We had a few daiquiris, tha's s'all."

"A few pitchers." Downward momentum took hold of me, and I collapsed at the curb.

Lara sank into the grass beside me.

I held my head. "I'll be in so much trouble."

"I'll be fine to drive in a little bit. Besides, we can't get in trouble if they don't know where we are."

Another hour passed while we sat in the grass near the street. We talked about everything and nothing. Lara picked dandelions and popped their heads off. A half dozen yellow flowers lay shriveling on the hot street.

Lara talked about TV shows and music she liked. "If you could make out with anyone famous, who would it be?"

"I don't know. Maybe Keith Partridge?" I couldn't imagine making out with any boy except Lewis. And yet, I was a little relieved that Lewis didn't come along. Ever since he kissed me, the tension between us had grown like mold on stale bread.

"You mean David Cassidy. Okay, he's cute, but not my style."

"Who do you like?"

Lara popped another head off a dandelion. "I like John Travolta. You know, Vinnie Barbarino in *Welcome Back, Kotter.*"

"Really?"

"He's kind of a bad boy but I like that. I think he'd be rough in bed."

I instantly thought of Mark.

Lara reached for another dandelion behind me.

"But the test was negative?" I asked. It couldn't be. Unless I'd been dead wrong.

"Duh." Lara popped the head off the last dandelion, then reached for me. In an act of real friendship, she patted me on the back. "Are you feeling better? Are you ready to go?" Her hand lingered between my shoulder blades.

And the fear of getting caught ripped through me, and this time it mingled with Lara's anger. I felt it. Her rage. A thunderstorm. And those lakeweeds. Lara was running to get away. All because of a child. A baby.

Stinging nettles wound up and down my spine. The e.p.t. test was wrong.

CHAPTER 35

NANA'S LOST RING

Daphne

Gray clouds raced across the sky while cooler than normal weather held us prisoners inside. I played cards and gazed longingly at the old piano. It was mid -July. Nana told us six weeks ago that the piano was coming. It seemed like the new one would never arrive. I pulled on a sweater and had no desire to swim. So I thought about . . . everything.

The two-hour car trip home from Indy was brutal. Lara and I made it back to Carlson before dinnertime, but I was quiet most of the way. I couldn't risk losing her friendship and bit my tongue all the way home. I didn't tell her about the baby. Why would she believe me when the e.p.t. test had been negative? Lara would find out on her own, wouldn't she?

Freak.

However, I could now get away with so much more than I realized. Marianne wasn't paying attention. She didn't even notice I was gone all day with Lara. I could come and go as I pleased.

The false sense of freedom didn't reassure me that something was horribly wrong. It seemed like a creepy sense of dread fell on everyone.

Tony snuck away whenever he could. Marianne—finally—seemed suspicious of him. Brandon threw playing cards all over the living room and argued with Sammy. Every few minutes, Auntie Beth barked reprimands at the boys. Margot sulked in the corner with her Breyer horses. When I checked on her, she said, "Leave me alone."

Though the e.p.t. test was negative, I couldn't shake the feeling that it was wrong. Lara *was* pregnant. Tony was dealing drugs. Phillip was a thief. And Mark was a killer. Could this summer get any stranger? I had a wicked feeling that it could.

Prickly hives crawled up my arms when I looked out at the lake. So I watched Tony come and go from the house, and from a distance, I kept an eye on the Vaughans. I could see their house as I watched Margot, wearing long shorts and a baggy long-sleeved T-shirt, wading in the calm, shallow water near the retaining wall.

She'd been making snide comments whenever I slipped over to visit Lewis and Lara. She seemed jealous. I wanted so badly to apologize. To ask for her forgiveness. So I crept closer to the retaining wall and looked in. There wasn't any lake weed here, and the water was beautifully clear and sparkling. I recalled all the times Margot and I waded together, searching for treasures and coming up with stones, purple shells and fossils.

I joined her without a word, slowly stepping into the cold twelve-inch-deep water. We pinched stones and pearly shells, then stuffed them into our pockets.

I reached for a black clamshell as big as my fist. Surprising me, the two shells drew together. The clam was alive. I lowered it back into the water near the mossy wall where green strands spread out like watercolor on a wet canvas. Like hair.

Dirt and sand clouded around my toes as I took a step. In the murky water, I saw a pale face looking up at me. The same face I recognized from earlier this summer. The same pale face from the lakeweeds.

Save me.

I backed away as quickly as I could.

Who needed to be saved? Lara? The baby? Certainly not Tony or Phillip.

Or Mark. I held very still, as a school of tiny minnows swam toward me, their shimmery scales flashing. As they passed, a shiny circular object glittered in the sand. Plunging my fingers into the clear water, I dug it out and placed a gold ring in my palm.

I scraped moss off the ring and the elaborate setting. A bright green, square-cut stone was still intact beneath the layer of grime. I peered at it. In the light inside the jewel, I saw my much-younger grandmother hugging a soldier. I recognized his uniform. The soldier's uniform hanging in the closet belonged to my grandfather.

The ring belonged to my Nana.

Emotions washed over me—anxiety, love. Images of the war and women coming and going from a home I didn't recognize. The sense that someone else was taking care of things. A sense of loss and abandonment made me want to cry.

The wind rustled sycamore leaves overhead and I looked up. I had the eerie sense that someone was watching me though no one was there. My heartbeat sped to vivace.

"Look what I found." Margot broke the spell. She waded toward me and showed me a fossil, a small fish etched in a piece of slate. When she saw what was in my hand, she asked, "What's that?"

"Nana's lost ring."

"How do you know it belonged to her?"

I shrugged and slid the ring onto my finger. "I just know. Nana was lovesick and depressed when she threw it in the lake. She missed our grandfather."

Margot scrutinized me behind her dirty glasses. "Are you crying?"

I wiped my cheek on my shoulder. "She missed him. Nana couldn't accept that our grandfather was killed in the war."

"You're kidding, right? I mean, that's a good story."

Weirdo. Freak.

"I didn't make it up," I shot back.

"It's lucky you found it," she said. "It's pretty."

I dug into my damp, sandy pocket and fished out a handful of shiny shells. "I found these too. Do you want them?"

Margot smiled. "You almost seem like yourself again."

I knew what she meant. But I had to ask. "What does that mean?"

"Nothing. I like you better when you're not hanging out with the neighbors. You always come home so—"

I didn't like it. "What are you trying to say?"

"I like you better when you're not with them." Margot waded to the wall and climbed out with her treasures in hand.

Though my feet were cold, I stayed in the water. I knew exactly what Margot meant, and she was right.

I had begun to dread it. All of it. Going out on the lake, water-skiing, and swimming. The weeds scared me. But something drew me to the Vaughans. Like there was a reason we were together. Though Lara lied about everything and twisted the truth to her advantage, I needed to spend the summer with her and Lewis. The pull to be with them—to be liked by them—was stronger than the tide.

When I was with them, those prickly feelings—like stinging, burning nettles—came over me. Why? Why did the Vaughans make me feel that way? I had to find out. I needed to understand.

CHAPTER 36

SOME KIND OF JUSTICE

July 25th: Mark

Customers filled The Bar, mostly local boys with nothing better to do. More than two weeks later, they were still celebrating the Bicentennial. The holiday wasn't a big deal to Mark, who'd grown up in prison. He'd lost faith in this country years ago. The ones who pumped their fists in the air, the ones who hooted and hollered, wearing red, white, and blue and waving their stick-flags, they really just needed a reason to party.

Red tended bar while Mark took a break and shot pool with Randy and Watson, circling the pool table in the back of The Bar. Randy leaned over the table and pointed at the yellow one ball. "Line it up here," he said. "Shoot the cue ball with enough right spin to send the one ball into the six ball. You've done this combo shot before, Watson."

"Are you sure?"

"Go on." Randy stepped back beside his stool and waited with his arms crossed and his gaze glued on his brother's game.

Mark said, "You two are teaming up on me."

Watson widened his stance and lined up his cue. Sliding it back and forth on his thumb, he took a crack at the ball. It sailed into the one ball, sending it toward the corner pocket where it brushed against the purple four ball. The four stopped in front of the side pocket, perfectly blocking the only shot Mark had on the eight ball.

Mark chalked his cue and eyed the table. "Hey Randy, I need some help here."

Randy laughed. "No chance. Watson's my brother, man."

Mark took a long soft shot off the far rail. The cue barely kissed the eight ball, leaving the purple four ball open to Watson. "Shit."

Watson bent over the table and shot his last ball into the side pocket, leaving the cue right in line with the eight ball. He quickly lined up the shot and sank the ball for the win.

A bunch of guys at a nearby table cheered, shook hands and patted each other on their backs. One grimaced and pulled a few bills from his wallet. He slapped them on the table.

Mark didn't mind losing to them. Watson was a pro, and Randy's game had always been to side with his brother. He gave Watson a handshake. "Good game," he said and took his beer glass to the bar.

Deputy Brandt Simmons rested one boot on the rail of a barstool, and one elbow on the bar. "You let them play you." He was wearing his uniform and uncomfortable patrons were eyeballing him.

Mark shrugged as he took his spot behind the bar. "It's just a game."

"Is it?"

Mark let the question go. Two townies from Knox, a nearby one-stop-sign town, looked sideways at Brandt. Scowling, one guy elbowed the other, who nodded. They downed the rest of their beers, slid off their stools. The scowler spat at Brandt on his way past as they made their way out the door.

"I guess you didn't come here to make friends," Mark said to Brandt. "What's up?"

Brandt loosened his Timex watch and rubbed the red skin where it had been on his wrist. "Hear anything about those break ins?"

"I told you I didn't." Mark picked up a rag and wiped down the bar where the two men had sat.

Brandt pulled in the stool and sat down. The foam had gone from his untouched beer. He clicked the Timex back in place on his wrist. "I saw you with that Vaughan girl. Babysitting?"

"Something like that."

A cue ball cracked against a new rack. Two or three balls rumbled into pockets and guys cheered at the back of the room.

"Listen, Mark." Brandt leaned forward. "We both grew up here. Right here in Carlson. We went to Carlson Community High, number seven-oh-one. My uncle still has the farm near Knox. Dad still owns the garage."

"Pops told me. What's your point?"

"You and I are cut from the same cloth."

Mark didn't know if that was true. Perhaps he just wasn't ready to believe it.

Brandt finally took a sip of his beer. "I know what Prosecutor Vaughan did to you."

Mark frowned. Brandt had no idea what it was like in prison. He had no idea how fast you grow up behind bars. He recalled the night when he was still in high school. The night he had beat the shit out of that preppy asshole, Geoffrey Weir. That summer before his senior year, Mark took a job in road construction with the Indiana Department of Transportation. Julio and Enrique had come all the way from Mexico. Mark made friends with them.

Geoffrey Weir and his well-dressed cronies had no business being in that bar on the northside of Indy. Said they were passing through on their way to Chicago. All dressed in their pale yellow and sky blue button-up shirts. Their slacks and shiny leather shoes. They were there to pick a fight, and Geoffrey singled out Mark, who was having beers with Julio and Enrique. He called Mark a spic and a greaser and insulted him.

They said Mark assaulted Geoffrey without provocation.

That was bullshit.

"Let's take this outside," Mark told Geoffrey. He and Geoffrey faced off in the parking lot. Geoffrey still didn't know what hit him. Once that preppy asshole fell to the ground, Mark took hold of his throat and squeezed. He might have punched him a few more times. A few dozen, maybe. Whatever. He'd been angry. Guys like Geoffrey weren't better than anyone. Maybe Mark was trying to prove just that.

Julio and Enrique pulled Mark off Geoffrey and the instigator lay bleeding and unconscious on the pavement. Enrique looked scared when they left. "This is not good," he muttered.

Good or bad, Geoffrey lived. But like cornered dogs Geoffrey and his rich daddy responded with bared fangs. Peter Weir had pressed charges, and Geoffrey's friends testified that Mark tried to kill him. Maybe so. Julio's and Enrique's statements—that Mark was defending them—had counted for nothing. Vaughan had prosecuted Mark to the full extent of the law.

Mark was tried as an adult. Finished high school in prison. If Geoffrey had died—if Mark had killed him—Mark would still be in prison. But Mark would never have gone that far. At least he didn't think so.

"What do you want, Brandt?" Mark said finally.

"John Vaughan used you as a stepping-stone. Peter Weir funded Vaughan all the way to the Marion County prosecutor's seat. Now look. Vaughan's running for state attorney general. He and his family are in a different class than you and I. It doesn't mean they're above the law."

Mark tossed the towel into the sink behind him. Shooting John Vaughan III would be too quick and too kind. The idea of strangling him appealed to Mark. He'd heard it took one of the inmates four minutes to kill his cellmate by strangulation. After twenty seconds, the guy passed out. The prisoner didn't stop choking his cellmate, though, and the guards couldn't get into the cell quick enough to stop him. That man was brain-dead in three minutes. His heart stopped beating after four and a half. The killer squeezed that man's throat for five full minutes after he was unconscious.

When Geoffrey was struggling underneath Mark, something had happened, like a switch flipped in Mark's brain, and he'd loosened his grip. He couldn't kill Geoffrey. Mark was no murderer.

"What are you saying, Brandt? Get to the point."

"His thieving kids can't run amok here in Carlson. I know Phillip has a history. I just want to catch him in the act."

"You want me to turn him in?"

Brandt looked him in the eye. "I'm trying to level the playing field. Carlson is my town. It's yours too."

"You trying to get me sent back to prison?"

"No. But you keep messing with those kids and you're going to end up back there anyway. I guarantee the prosecutor will come after you again." Brandt got up to leave.

"Wait," Mark said. Thinking about the kids reminded him that he'd made a promise to Daphne. She saw a dead body in the lake. Mark said he would ask about it.

Brandt pushed his stool in and looked at Mark.

"Has anyone gone missing lately?" Mark said.

"What do you mean?"

Mark didn't know how to ask without incriminating himself. "A, uh—friend—she thought she saw something in the lake. Thought she saw a body." He'd almost said "kid," but Brandt didn't need verification that Mark was still hanging out with the Vaughans.

Brandt's face scrunched up in disbelief. "What body?"

"It could have been a dead fish. I told her I'd ask. You know. To ease her mind."

"No reports have crossed my desk. You talking about the Vaughans?"

Mark looked down at his shoes. He knew why he kept seeing Lara and Phillip. Revenge. He was taking back what the prosecutor had stolen from him. But now he had a choice to make.

CHAPTER 37

INCURABLE DISEASE

Daphne

I went to sleep with the ring on my finger. I thought for sure it belonged to Nana and that the soldier had given it to her. In the middle of the night, I awoke with the feeling that he was in the closet. A noise at the bedroom door spread chills over my body. I got out of bed and pulled it open.

Duke shook out his fur in the hallway, jangling his tags loudly. He seemed excited, so I looked around. Everyone was sleeping, even Tony, I assumed. So I called Duke into my room and up onto my bed. He slept there with me till morning.

But I didn't sleep for the rest of the night.

All the next day, I kept looking over my shoulder, feeling like someone was watching me. Shadows moved in the corner of my vision, but I never *saw* anything. It made me feel unanchored, and weak-kneed.

For once, that summer, the four of us kids, Auntie Beth, and Marianne all ate dinner together without Tony Baloney. He had business—or something—and would return later.

Between bites, I fingered the green ring in my pocket. I needed to know if it really belonged to Nana and if the uniform belonged to my grandfather. No one ever talked about him. He died when Auntie Beth and Marianne were very young. I wondered if all the images and feelings I had when I picked up the ring were real or imaginary. I wondered if my fear of the closet was completely unfounded. Then I thought about Ruth falling on the ice and Lara's baby. The baby she didn't know she had. Lara's pregnancy test had to be dead wrong.

And now I feared a nonexistent ghost in the closet of the bedroom. *Woo-woo.* But the ghosts in *Scooby Doo* were never real. The only explanation was Extra Sensory Perception.

ESP was something gypsies at carnivals had. Nana put her faith in palm reading and Tarot, but Marianne didn't believe in any of that.

I didn't know what to believe.

Freak! Weirdo! Ruth was right.

But the ring . . . I was sure it belonged to Nana.

At the dinner table, Brandon was telling a story about catching frogs in the little creek. I took a breath, puffed out my chest. When Brandon finished, I asked, "Was our grandfather a soldier?"

Marianne stopped eating and wiped her mouth. "He was. What made you think about him?"

I put my hand into my pocket and stuck a finger through the ring. "Did he ever come here to the lake house with Nana?"

"Nana bought the house after he died," Auntie Beth said. "She needed time. His death was very traumatic for her."

I was confused. Then why were his clothes in the closet? "So he never came here?"

"Why do you ask?" Marianne asked.

"She thinks she found Nana's ring," Margot said.

I dug it out of my pocket and held it up. I'd cleaned it up with an old toothbrush and the green stone glittered under the dim light of the chandelier.

"Let's see it." Marianne leaned across the table.

"That's not your grandmother's ring, it's mine!" Auntie Beth reached for it.

Confused, I reluctantly passed it to her. "Are you sure?"

"Positive," Auntie Beth said. "I lost this emerald ring while swimming with Sammy when he was a toddler."

Sammy leaned toward Auntie Beth. "Lemme see!"

Auntie Beth showed Sammy. "You gripped my finger so tightly that I didn't see the ring fall off. By the time I noticed it missing, there was no way to find it. I thought I'd lost it to the fishes forever." She tried the ring on. It fit perfectly on her finger. "Thank you for finding it, Daphne."

"You're welcome," I muttered, sunk in my chair, feeling so deflated. The information hadn't landed right with me. I'd been so positive. But maybe this proved I didn't have ESP. And anyway, having ESP sounded like having a sickness, or an incurable disease.

Maybe I really was a weirdo.

CHAPTER 38

SINK INTO IT

Daphne

On my way outside, my gaze landed on the piano. It seemed to be mocking me with its broken-key sneer. Like the old console was laughing, and I was the brunt of the joke. The dissonant chords echoed in my ears though I never touched it. I darted past with my hands over my ears. In my mind, the out-of-tune Chopin Étude rewound and played over and over again.

"When will that new piano get here!" I shouted to no one.

I ran next door, the screen door slamming behind me. In the Vaughans' yard, Lewis was hunched over a golf club, shifting his weight between both feet. He focused on the white ball, shrugged, and shook his arms loose. He swung. The ball didn't move, but Lewis's gaze followed the club's arc.

I stood a few feet from him. "Hey."

"Hey. Are you ready to go?"

I hesitated. I hadn't spent time alone with Lewis since he'd kissed me. *Would he do it again? Would he expect more? Would I risk getting pregnant like Lara?*

My fingers itched to play something—to connect with a melody—any melody would do. Preferably a dark and ominous piece like a Beethoven sonata or one of the haunting Chopin *Études*. "Can I play something on your piano first?"

Lewis followed me to the piano. The songs in my head were a jumble of notes and incongruent chords. When I tried, I couldn't remember "Rêverie" or the Chopin *Études*. While Lewis watched, I grew nervous and finally played a simple F minor scale and a couple of C minor arpeggios. The straightforward and predictable sounds comforted me.

"I know one," Lewis said and sat down beside me. He rolled his fist back and forth across the black keys and played a comical tune. I added a bass line and chords. The duet brought a smile to my face.

Out on the golf course, he let me drive the golf cart. I took off from the clubhouse, fast then slow, then fast again, jerking us both back and forth.

"Wait! I'll get the hang of it." I laughed.

"You're doing great!"

I liked Lewis. A lot. Even though we'd be at the same school in the fall, I still couldn't imagine him carrying my books or buying me hot cider from the apple barn. I had no sense of my friends teasing me or their envy—*he's so cute!*—and I couldn't envision him leaning against my locker at the end of the school day and kissing me.

Determined to have fun, I sluffed off my unnerving, overwhelming sense of unfulfilled promises. I swerved to avoid a large boulder half buried in the ground and Lewis almost fell out of the cart. "Where am I going?"

Lewis laughed and pointed. "The first tee box is over there."

I slowed the cart, and let it roll to a stop behind a group of trees. Lewis picked through the golf bag for the right club. He looked out over the fairway and dropped a golf ball in the short grass. A divot of brown dirt marked where many others had hit the ground with their club. He pressed a yellow wooden tee into the grass and lined up his shot. The shoulder muscles beneath his brown T-shirt rippled when he swung.

The ball moved away so fast that I didn't see it until it bounced a hundred yards away. I didn't know much about golf except that the announcers on the *Wide World of Sports* whispered when the pros were about to swing. "Nice," I said. "That was nice, right?"

"Pretty good." He stuck the club in the bag and jumped back into the cart. "Tallyho!"

I laughed and pressed the gas pedal.

After two more swings on the fairway, Lewis lined his putter up to the first hole. As the ball circled and fell into the cup, I clapped my hands lightly. "Bravo."

"I'd like to try out for Orchard Park's varsity golf team next spring. I think I have a pretty good shot at it."

"I think you'll get in. You're the best golfer I've ever seen."

"I'm the only golfer you've ever seen. You said so." His smile was like sun reflecting off the lake.

"Want to teach me how? I'd like to learn," I said as I sped to the second tee box.

Lewis eyed the line from the second tee box to the flag and invited me to his side. He handed me the golf club. The driver had a heavy feel to it, weighted by the big round head at the end of the club. I held it in both hands and lined up a shot. Just as I was about to swing, he stopped me.

"Wait. No, no, no. Your ball's going to end up in the lake."

"No, it won't." I laughed. "Am I that bad?"

"Let me show you." He moved in behind me and wrapped his hands over mine, and around the club. He was about three inches taller, and for the first time since the Fourth of July, I had a good look at his shorter, missing finger. He adjusted his stance, and I quickly turned my focus to his thighs. Pressed against mine, his legs warmed my buttocks like I'd backed into a campfire. The cheeks on my face heated too. I'd never been this close to a guy except my brother and Dad.

"Look at the flag. Now relax your knees. Sink into it. Let the club do all the work." He swiftly guided my arms, swung the club, and the ball went sailing. It landed about fifty feet away, directly in line with the flag.

"Not too bad." His hand lingered on mine. Muffled sounds—the breeze rustling tree leaves, a distant passing car—became as loud as an engine roar. The waves lapping the shore whispered warnings. Choppy, dark water churned with a stormy breeze. I was breathless, but not because of the golf lesson. Just as suddenly, everything went quiet as if I'd gone underwater. Weeds brushed against my face and in the murky water, something white floated toward me. All I could think was, *breathe. I need to breathe!*

I leapt away from him.

Lewis's smile faded. "Are you okay? You look like you saw a ghost."

I ran away from Lewis and didn't look back.

NO, NO, NO!

Lara

"No!" Lara's thighs stuck to the leather driver's seat in her mother's Lincoln Continental. Tears streamed down her cheeks, and she opened the window, letting the wind whip her hair around as she drove fast along the country highway. Sixty. Seventy miles per hour. On either side, the tall corn stalks turned the narrow road into a corridor.

"No. No. No!" Without telling Chandi, Lara took the remaining two e.p.t. tests from their bathroom—just in case. She didn't know why she doubted the first result, but she had a feeling it was wrong. Two weeks later, her period still never came. Her boobs hurt and she was nauseous in the morning. She suddenly couldn't stand the smell of coffee.

Both e.p.t. test results showed the ring in the bottom of the test tube. *Both* indicated she was indeed pregnant.

Back in June, Mark had apologized a half dozen times. Like he'd regretted doing it with her. Like he was sorry when he realized Lara was still in high school. *He'll be sorry now,* she thought. He'll pay for the abortion—he'd have to—because Father could not find out about this. Father would *never* find out about this.

Her head throbbed like she'd been kicked to the dirt and beaten. She barreled into the parking lot of The Bar, spraying gravel in her wake, and parked next to Mark's gold Ford Mustang. She got out of the car and stormed into The Bar.

Lara watched Mark's face freeze in an open-mouthed grimace.

"Did you hear me?" she asked.

"No. I mean, yes. But no. You can't be."

"I took two tests. They both confirmed it." Lara pushed the stool away and stood facing Mark on the other side of the bar. She couldn't sit down. Sweat dripped under her blouse and down her sides. She yelled at him like they were an old married couple. Like her parents. "What are you going to do?"

"What am *I* going to do?"

"That's what I asked you."

Red shuffled next to Mark with his eyes locked on Lara. "Everything okay here?"

"It's fine."

"It's not *fine*. What are you going to do?" Lara needed to know Mark would take care of it. She needed him to take responsibility. The reality—the truth—overwhelmed her. "I'm going to be a model, or an actress. Don't you understand? This can't be happening to me. This ruins everything!"

Mark grabbed a bottle of Jack Daniels and poured a shot.

More than ever, Lara needed a drink. Though lately, it made her feel sick. "What about me?"

Red said, "She's too young, ain't she?"

"It's for me."

Red shuffled away, looked over his shoulder and said, "I meant she's too young for you."

Mark hadn't actually had a drink since that night in the hotel with Lara. It violated his parole. Without a second thought, he downed the shot and placed both hands on the bar. Hunched over, he didn't look at Lara. The silence in the bar—everyone watching them—and the still unspoken anguish between them became overwhelming.

When he finally spoke, it was almost a whisper. "When I was your age, the summer before my senior year, I was working on the interstate near Indianapolis. I was on the highway road construction crew. Pops couldn't hold a job, and I needed money for college. I had big plans. I was one of the best basketball players in Northern Indiana. My coach said I could get a scholarship if I worked hard enough. And man, I *needed* that scholarship. I needed to get out of this town. I needed to go to college. I was seventeen. I was the same age as you."

Lara sat down on the stool.

"One night after work, I went with the guys to a little out-of-the-way bar outside of Indianapolis. This asshole and his friends came in and started making fun of us. Started calling us names. They were picking on me, mostly. I got real mad and took this one kid outside. I'll never forget his name, Geoffrey Weir."

Lara knew that name. Peter Weir was a good friend and supporter of her father. And Geoffrey was his son. She took a deep breath.

"Well," Mark continued, "I beat the shit out of Geoffrey Weir that night. Even though it felt right at the time, it was the stupidest thing I ever did in my life. His daddy was friends with an Indianapolis prosecutor named John Vaughan the Third."

Lara's face went slack. Mark had her undivided attention.

"Weir promised to fund your father's election campaign—for Marion County Prosecutor—if he'd put the kid in jail who beat up his son."

Mark set a second shot glass down on the warped and stained bar. He poured two more.

"I was tried as an adult. Your father convinced the jury that I intended to kill Weir's kid. I was only seventeen." Mark turned the shot glass between his fingers. "I thought about revenge. Oh, I thought about it. After I met you and Phillip, after I realized who your father was, I went along for the ride. I was determined to get even. But Lara, I promise you. I never . . . *never* intended for this to happen."

Lara couldn't believe what she was hearing. Pinned to her seat by his story, she clutched her purse tightly to her chest. "But I thought you liked me. I didn't understand why you never wanted me after that first night." She tried to choke back tears, but the sadness overwhelmed her.

Mark looked her in the eye. "I like you, Lara. I liked you then, and I like you even more now that I've gotten to know you. I don't care who your father is anymore. But you're just a kid. We have to do the right thing."

She sniffed back tears and snot. Something about his gentle approach. About the care and concern in his voice. His kindness.

"We have to do what's right. You have to get an abortion. And I'll help you. I promise I'll help you. I can't let you ruin your life over one mistake, like I did."

Lara put her head in her hands and cried.

CHAPTER 40

MARK AND LARA SITTIN' IN A TREE

Lara

The day after she ran to see Mark at The Bar, Lara's boobs hurt like someone used them for punching bags. And kneeling over the toilet in the morning had reminded her she needed to find a Planned Parenthood center. She had one more year of high school, two years of college, and at least five years before she married some-one. Not Mark, for God's sake.

A baby would ruin everything.

Father was arriving soon, but at least Mother had stocked the liquor cabinet again. A full bottle of vodka, an opened bottle of gin, a fifth of Jack Daniels. Lara opened the refrigerator and searched for mixers. The pitcher of orange juice was nearly empty, and Coke sounded awful this early in the morning. Mixing vodka and milk seemed like an act of des-peration, but she hadn't been able to hold anything down for the last few days. Behind the gin she found a brown bottle of coffee liqueur. After carefully sniffing the sweet, coffee aroma, Lara poured a little over ice with milk. Like creamed coffee, she thought. With a kick. She topped it off with vodka and stirred it.

Glass in one hand and a beach towel draped over her arm, she took the heavy Yellow Pages book and made her way toward the back door. When she got there, she discovered it was still much cooler than usual outside and the wind had picked up again. She closed the door to the three-season porch, tossed the Yellow Pages onto the davenport and set her drink on a table.

Next door, she saw Daphne walking out on the dock with her little brother and cousins. Perfect Daphne. Innocent Daphne. Lara tried to hate her, but Daphne had gotten to her. *If my family were as cool, I might have turned out like her.*

Sipping the iced milk and vodka, Lara thumbed through the Yellow Pages looking for abortion clinics. A quarter-page ad caught her attention. The clinic in Plymouth looked promising. She called Mark first.

"Can you drive me up there?"

"Yes," he said. Dogs barked in the background. "When is your appointment?"

"I didn't make one. The ad says no appointment necessary."

"How about today?"

"No, I . . ." Lara was terrified for Father to find out and didn't know how she'd feel after the procedure.

"Lara?" Mark was still on the line.

"Not today. Father's driving up this weekend. We'll have to do it after he goes back to Indianapolis. I don't want him to suspect anything." As she said it, she wondered how she'd keep the morning sickness from him. She sat on the edge of the couch and cradled her belly. She'd never admit to anyone how sick she felt.

"Do you want me to come over?" Mark asked.

"Sure. I need a distraction."

Lara hung up. The boys next door were running with the dog while Daphne stood by and moderated. She envied Daphne's super-thin, fashion-model body. When she got to Orchard Park in the fall, every guy in the school would want to date her. Envy shot through Lara.

I have to get this abortion.

Lewis came in and joined Lara with a bowl of cereal in his hand. He plopped down on the davenport next to the open Yellow Pages.

Before she had a chance to close it, Lewis spied the quarter-page ad for Planned Parenthood. His eyes went wide. "Are you looking up—"

Lara slammed the heavy book closed and tossed it to the floor.

"You are, aren't you. You were looking up the number for an abortion clinic."

"You don't know anything."

Lewis ate a heaping spoonful of Sugar Pops and noisily chewed. Milk dribbled down his chin, but his gaze locked on Lara. With his mouth full, he said, "Who's—"

"None of your business." Lara held her belly. The milk and coffee liqueur turned sour in her stomach.

Too curious, Lewis scanned her face. "It's you. You're looking up the clinic *for you*. How did you—"

Lara sat back and crossed her arms. "How do you think? Did you flunk sex ed?"

"Of course not." Lewis slurped another bite of Sugar Pops. Listening to him chew nauseated her.

The milk and Kahlua sloshed in her stomach. She closed her eyes. She used to think she could do nothing wrong in the eyes of her Father. Now, she doubted he'd notice if she did a double roundoff kickflip and landed on her head.

"I'm getting an abortion," she said.

"Father will flip out. He'll never allow it. He's against it."

Every cell in her body went rigid. "Father will *never* find out, Lewis."

"How can you keep it a secret? You're going to get fat. He'll notice."

Lewis's statement struck a nerve. She rose up to her feet and turned on him. Her lip curled as she said, "He won't notice. Do you know why? Father doesn't care about me. He's too busy with his campaign and work. Don't you get it?"

Lewis pushed back. "Oh, my god, Lara. He needs to know."

The corny cereal smell turned Lara's stomach. "But you . . . you're Father's pet project. You keep kissing his ass. He'll always love you for that."

"He's going to find out."

She shoved him, and he fell back on the davenport. "I'll kill you if you tell him. I'll break every bone in your body." It was an idle threat. One they used every time they argued with each other. She took her glass and stormed out of the porch.

Lewis sang, "Mark and Lara, sittin' in a tree—"

"What are you, like eight years old?" She yelled over her shoulder.

"K–I–S–S–I–N–G . . . First comes love . . ."

Lara slammed the bathroom door, then fell to her knees in front of the toilet bowl.

STOP BEING A BABY

Daphne

I dreamed of the lake again. In the dream, I floated on my back along the pane-of-glass still water. It was like lying on a soft mattress or the Dead Sea except that beneath the surface, the lakeweeds formed a thick mat of tangled tentacles.

Save me.

I awoke feeling powerless. Like there was something I needed to do. Whatever it was I'd forgotten it. The thing, the task,

the . . . something was just out of reach like a distant memory or a ghost.

When Marianne knocked on the bedroom door later that morning, I held my belly. Painful cramps shot through my lower abdomen and made my legs feel weak. I dashed past her to the bathroom and slammed the door, searching the cabinets for feminine products.

When I joined the rest of the family downstairs, Auntie Beth asked, "Are you ready to go skiing?"

"I'm not going today." In a way, I was relieved to have an excuse. My dream came to mind. And the pale face that looked like it belonged to Lewis.

"Are you feeling alright?" Marianne asked.

"I'm fine."

"Must be something she *drank*," Margot said.

I shot her an angry stare. Though Margot had kept her word—not tattling on me for drinking with Lara—she seemed bitter about it.

Duke sat beside me as we watched the Hydrodyne pull away from the dock. Tony wasn't onboard and it was unusual for him to skip out on a boating excursion.

I went back inside and sat at the piano. Auntie Beth told me one of the piano movers broke his arm playing football, delaying the delivery again. I opened my *Dozen a Day* technique book and ran through exercises. The discordant scales and shrill chords made me want to cry.

I walked away with added tension instead of relief, so went upstairs to lie down. Passing the library, I heard paper shuffling. Tony sat at the table. A skunky smell drifted through the room, and he caught me staring.

"I thought you went skiing," he said. He set a wad of bills as thick as a deck of cards on the table.

I walked into the room. Stacks of money and several baggies of green weed were splayed out. Just like the vision I had when Tony helped me out of the water. "Does Mom know?"

"She doesn't need to know. Am I right?"

I disagreed, but kept my mouth shut.

"Don't you tell her either, you hear?" Tony stepped between me and the table. I backed away. "I know you're smoking with those kids next door. I can turn you in for underaged drinking."

I didn't know if he could do that or not and decided not to find out.

"Get out of here," he said. "Let me get my work done before they get back."

I didn't want to stick around. But I worried about my mom.

That afternoon, I walked along the shore with Margot to the corner store. Duke came along with us, gamboling at my side. My purse with seven dollars for candy banged an even rhythm on my thigh. We were four houses away from home before I spoke in a hushed voice. "I wasn't sick from drinking. I got my period. That's why I didn't go skiing with you."

"So." Reflections off Margot's thick eyeglass lenses hid her eyes. "My mom thinks you should be grounded. I heard them talking on the boat."

"For what?" I veered toward the shore and hopped down on a narrow strip of sandy beach. Beach toys and a dirty towel littered the shore.

"For drinking with the Vaughans."

"How does she know?"

Margot picked up a purple butterfly clamshell that had washed up on the beach near a small feeder stream. "I told her."

"Margot! Why'd you do that?"

"Because you're different when you come home."

I took off my wooden sandals and stepped into the icy-cold stream flowing into the lake. The chilly water momentarily cooled my temper. "Marianne won't ground me. She never keeps her word when she grounds Brandon. He's always off the hook by the next day." I wondered if Tony would be off the hook when Marianne found out he dealt drugs.

"What do you see in the Vaughans anyway?"

I didn't know how to answer. Lara had lied when she took me to Indiana. I forgave her because I knew she needed my support. But the trip almost got me in big trouble. And Lewis seemed like he only wanted one thing—my virginity. Maybe if I wasn't high when I was with them, I'd listen to my intuition better. Or would I?

Regardless, I felt free with them. Free of my depressing life and my stoned mother.

"Seriously. Why are you hanging out with them?" Margot repeated. "Lewis is always staring at you and Lara is a basket case. Their brother Phillip is a troublemaker. He always has beer, and he smokes—"

"So? Marianne smokes. So does your mom. They both drink wine."

"They're adults." Though she was no social butterfly, Margot was a keen observer of people. "You haven't been the same since you met them. You're always high when you come home, and you're not much fun to be around anymore."

Margot's words hurt. I tried not to raise my voice. "Oh, like playing with dolls and ponies is so cool."

Margot stopped staring into the shallow water and turned her gaze on me with an open-mouthed frown. "The Vaughans are losers. Why don't you see that?"

"You're just jealous because you don't have any friends." I dropped my Dr. Scholl's on the grass and slid my wet, sandy feet into them. "Grow up, Margot. Stop being such a baby."

Lara had used the same words when speaking to Lewis. Lara, who was drunk most of the time and pregnant. I called Duke to my side and left Margot standing on the beach with waves lapping her ankles.

I needed to talk to Lara.

CHAPTER 42

"A CANDLE IN THE WIND"

Daphne

The Vaughans' kitchen door was open. I let myself in and took the stairs two at a time. Elton John was singing behind Lara's closed door. After one full chorus of "Goodbye, Norma Jean . . ." I knocked lightly and let myself in. "Hey."

Lara didn't answer. She lay on the bed, curled in a ball facing the window. I sat on the bed and put a hand on her shoulder.

"What do you want?" she said. Her nose was red, and her cheeks tear streaked. She had a box of tissues cradled in one arm and dirty ones wadded up in her hand.

I'd never seen anyone so distraught. "What's wrong?"

"Like a candle in the wind," Elton John sang.

"My period didn't come. The test was positive this time." Lara blew her nose.

She knows. Hearing the truth out loud sent a wave of sensation up to my ears. Hot stinging nettles caused goosebumps on my arms. "Oh my god, Lara. What are you going to do?" What would I do if I were pregnant? The first person I'd tell, I realized, was my mom. Marianne would know exactly what to do. Dad would be next. He'd understand and do anything to help me get through it. "Did you tell your parents?"

"I can't tell Mother. She'd be mortified. All the ladies at the country club would talk about her. Father would be so angry. He'd never speak to me again."

My parents would support any decision I made. I was sure of that. "But they love you."

"You don't know anything." Lara sat up and threw her tissues on the floor. "Father made it clear that he opposes Roe versus Wade. Even though the Supreme Court legalized abortion, Father would like to prevent abortion in the state of Indiana. It's a campaign promise he's making to the voters. He made sure we all knew his opinion." She inhaled a ragged breath.

My parents had talked about the controversial abortion laws. They supported the Supreme Court decision, women's rights, and their right to choose. But more importantly, I couldn't fathom the complications of having a baby while still in high school. "What are you going to do?"

Lara threw her pillow across the room. "I can't have this baby. It ruins everything. I told Mark. He's going to help me get an abortion."

An idea came to me. "Didn't you say Chandi's mother is an obstetrician? Can she do the abortion?"

"You're so smart, Daphne." Lara wiped the tears from her face and grabbed the phone from her bedside table. She dialed a number on the glowing push-button receiver, then cradled it between her shoulder and chin.

Several minutes into the conversation, she asked Chandi. "Will your mom do an abortion?"

Lara held out the receiver so I could hear Chandi's response.

"I think so, but you have to be her patient," Chandi said. "You need to schedule an office visit. My older sister Navi went through it. Did you tell your parents?"

Lara looked into my eyes as she spoke. "My parents *cannot* find out, Chandi. And you have to keep it a secret. Understand? If you don't, I'll tell everyone that you and Lenny Shoemaker had sex this summer."

"What? He's a total nerd!" Chandi sounded hurt.

"But Lenny would want everyone to believe it," Lara said. "He'd never let the truth slip."

Chandi gasped. "You wouldn't."

"Don't tell anyone. Understand?" Lara hung up on her. "You better not say anything either, Daphne."

Lara's mean gaze scared me. I had a strong feeling she was capable of hurting me worse than Ruth ever did. I shrank back. "Who would I tell?"

"*No one* can know. I have to get an abortion. Don't you understand? If Father finds out, I'm dead." Lara squinted back tears and wiped her nose. "I'm sorry. I'm just so upset about this. Lewis found out yesterday. I'm terrified that he's going to tell Father."

"Oh, no." I tried to console her. "He'd never do that." *Would he?*

I put my arms around her and smelled Herbal Essence shampoo in her hair. The images came in disjointed fragments and mismatched sounds. A door slammed shut. Lara's brothers yelling at each other. Lara's angry Father. A storm. A body falling in the lake and the weeds . . . Worst of all, Lara hated the child growing inside her.

I thought of Ruth and a chill traveled through me. Lara had a mean streak. I just didn't know how deep it ran. And I decided not to say anything about it.

CHAPTER 43

DANGEROUS TERRITORY

July 24th: Mark

Mark filled a bucket with ice and water, then plunged his head into it.

What the hell was I thinking? I'm in no position to raise a kid!

The shock of the freezing water momentarily cleared his head. He hadn't slept at all since she told him. Regret, anger, and rage all tied knots around his throat. He'd been used. Again.

Ice water ran down his bare back and chest. He threw a towel

over his hair and dumped the bucket outside the trailer door. It was mid-day, and a thick layer of clouds covered the sky.

He went to the cage where the dogs were sleeping and opened it. His favorite, Jenny, came up to the fence with her tail wagging. She was a sweet old golden retriever with a gray stripe down her boney back. The other three dogs raised their heads but didn't get up as he led her out of the pen and closed the gate.

"How's it going, old girl?" Mark squatted down and scratched her ears. Jenny was a puppy when Mark went to prison. Now she looked as old as he felt.

"Come on."

She followed him across the yard, sniffing at the towel in his hand.

He sat on the bumper of the rusty old Ford, and she sat at his feet looking into his eyes with a sadness that maybe he reflected back. Like she understood what he'd been through. Like she knew what he'd done.

"I'm not proud of it, Jenny." He rubbed his wet hair with the towel. "She came on so hard. I couldn't help myself. I didn't know who she was. At the time, I didn't know she was the prosecutor's daughter."

Jenny cocked her ears. Her eyebrows twitched.

"I sound like such a jerk." He wadded up the towel and threw it toward the door of the trailer. "You think it's my fault?"

The dog tilted her head, keen to hear every word.

"You do, don't you?"

Mark pulled the comb from his back pocket and ran it through his hair. "Okay, sure. I shouldn't have drunk so much Wild Turkey, for one thing. That was my first mistake. Naw. That was about the tenth mistake. Shit, Jenny. I shouldn't have been flirting with her. She acts about twenty but she's just a kid."

Jenny shook a fly off her head.

"All right, I'll stop seeing her. But first I have to help her get an abortion. Where do we even go for that?" He stuffed the comb into his back pocket and stooped to pick up a stone. He chucked the rock at the mailbox. It hit with a metallic thud and dropped in the dirt. "Besides, I think she's addicted to the 'ludes now. She takes them every day! Shit. I gotta tell Tony to lay off. He keeps pushing them on her."

Jenny looked away.

"Her Daddy would be so proud."

The dog had lost interest in his soliloquy. She found a grassy spot on the side of the trailer and lay down.

Earlier this summer, Mark was dead set on revenge. Now his plan folded in on him in a bad, bad way. It seemed like the prosecutor was still ruining his life even now. "Fuck you, Prosecutor John Vaughan the Third!"

His vision blurred on cornfields in the horizon. It was easy to imagine all the things that could go wrong for Lara. None of this was good. Mark wished the summer were finally over.

But John Wesley Vaughan the Third—Prosecutor Vaughan—was coming back to town. Mark thought of running into him at the grocery store and played out variations in his mind.

"Hello Mr. Vaughan. I'm Mark Walters. Remember me?" Or *"Hello, Mr. Prosecutor. I banged your daughter. She's in a real mess, now. Just like I was at seventeen."* He imagined his fingers wrapped around Mr. Vaughan's throat. *"You ruined my fucking life!"* While in prison, Mark studied the *Indianapolis Star* newspaper archives on microfiche. He researched everything he could about Vaughan. He spent hours in the library studying for his high school diploma, so why not learn about the man who seemed determined to put him away?

Mark could see the prosecutor's fat face turning red as he gasped for air. His lips turned blue as Mark cut off his air supply.

Bile rose to the back of Mark's tongue. The level of his own rage scared him. The day he beat up Geoffrey Weir, Mark had flattened the kid so quickly it stunned him. He was angry, yes, but when faced with taking it all the way, he didn't follow through. Mark left Geoffrey crying and bleeding on the pavement. The kid didn't deserve more.

"Fuck!" *I couldn't kill someone. Not even the prosecutor.*

That same afternoon, Mark carried a brown bag full of groceries to his car—a loaf of Wonder Bread, Grape Nuts cereal, a gallon of milk, a pound of hamburger, and a box of Hamburger Helper. He was watching a pregnant lady struggle with her bags and a toddler and didn't see his parole officer Jim Strickland leaning against the car next to his Mustang.

"Been busy, haven't you?"

Mark jumped so far out of his skin that he dropped his keys. "Not really."

Jim picked up the keys for Mark and held onto them. "You're hanging out with Prosecutor Vaughan's kids. I've seen you over there."

"So. It's not a crime to hang out with people."

Jim's eye tracked the pregnant lady and her now-screaming kid. "Why do they keep coming into The Bar? Aren't they underaged?" Strickland picked his teeth with his thumbnail.

Mark wasn't about to play this game. But his legs were shaky. His need for revenge had gotten him in trouble. "I wouldn't know. Why don't you card them?"

Jim toyed with Mark's keys. "Who's getting them pot? It isn't you. I'm pretty sure you're not *that* stupid."

"I didn't know they smoked."

"Or maybe you are—"

"Look. I haven't done anything to break my parole. I'm not even drinking with them." It felt natural to cover for himself. He didn't consider sipping one or two beers drinking. Not compared to Pops' binges. Or Phillip's wasted weekends. Or Lara with her quaaludes.

The pregnant lady stuffed her screaming kid in the back seat of her car and slammed the door. In the deafening silence, Jim said. "My point is, you're in dangerous territory. I'd ride that horse in the other direction if I were you. Get out while you can. Before something happens." He handed Mark his keys. "You're the one who'll take the blame, you know."

Mark stood there and watched his parole officer drive off. A shudder traveled up his spine and landed between his broad shoulders. He looked up at the darkening sky.

Before heading back home, he surprised himself by pulling into the Carlson police station.

Brandt met him outside. "What's come over you? I'd think you'd stay as far from here as you could."

"You asked me to let you know if I heard who broke into the little store on East Lake Shore Drive, right?" Mark said. "Phillip Vaughan did it."

"Petty theft. Is that all you've got?"

"He borrowed a golf cart from someone's garage."

"Borrowed?"

"A farmer, one of Pops' friends, found it a couple days later in the cornfield a half mile away. He was pissed about the damage to his crops."

"That's all?"

Phillip was an idiot, but Mark was damned if he'd turn him in for dealing drugs. He knew Phillip was distributing pot and pills for Tony. He was selling to the councilors at the academy.

Brandt put his hands on his police duty belt and tapped three times with his index finger.

"There's got to be more."

"He's an idiot. That's all I know."

"A lame charge like that will never make it to court," Brandt said. "The security guys at the academy told me there are reports of weed and drugs. How are they getting it?"

Raindrop circles formed in the dusty parking lot. The rumble of thunder in the distance reminded Mark of the dangers of messing with the Vaughans.

"You've gotten in close with those Vaughan kids," Brandt said. "You think they like you? You think they'll invite you to their college graduations? How about those campaign parties with the governor and Indiana state senators? You think you'll be sipping Chivas with them? You're not in the same tennis club. Understand?"

"You think I don't know that?" he said. "I paid my time. What more do you want from me?"

The rain had begun to fall steadily. Brandt shuffled his feet, and his hand went up to shield his slicked-back hair. "I'm on your side, Mark. Those rich kids come up here and walk all over me too. You think I like it when their speeding tickets and drunk-driving charges get erased because of somebody's payoff? The system shouldn't work like that. I'm asking you to do the right thing. I believe you're one of the good guys, Mark Walters."

"Maybe. Maybe not," Mark said and squinted at the darkening sky. Now that Lara was pregnant, the only thing occupying his mind was trying to find a way to help. He was no snitch. He'd learned the dangerous nature of that angle in prison. But he'd come here with one thing in mind. The real culprit—the real villain—was someone else. "I know the guy who's selling to them and he's not from around here."

SEND THEM PACKING

Daphne

Cool wind pushed clouds quickly across the lake. The gloom kept everyone bundled up and sequestered inside and made us argumentative and surly. Auntie Beth had been on the phone with Uncle Chuck a lot lately. She sat in the corner behind the kitchen door and whispered and cried. A few times, she got angry and hung up. After slamming the receiver down, she wiped tears from her eyes.

I banged out terrible melodies on the terrible piano. Sticky keys infuriated me and playing fortissimo made the anger and frustration grow. "This sucks."

"Language, Daphne."

Auntie Beth acted huffy toward everyone. Marianne flashed her indignant looks. Tony stormed out and went on another errand. Brandon demolished Sammy's massive card house and got sent to his room. Sammy pouted while trying to rebuild his card structure. Margot refused to talk to me.

I heard Auntie Beth talking in a low voice with Marianne. She said

Tony's name, and I snuck halfway up the stairs, skipping the creaky one, and stopped to listen. Tony was gone for the day.

"It's easy. Tell him to go home," Auntie Beth said.

Marianne spoke in a near whisper. "It's not that easy. He's putting a good word in for me at Indy Graphics and I want the job."

"He said some things last night that bothered me," Auntie Beth said.

"Like what?"

I wished I could see them, but I remained on the staircase, hidden from their view.

"I think he's after your money," Auntie Beth said.

"What makes you think that? I don't have any money."

"Come on, Marianne. Don't be so dense. He's enamored with something he sees in you and this house. He's been asking about mother, and the family. I can see dollar signs in his eyes, why can't you? He must be a really good lay."

"Excuse me?"

I knew the expression and grimaced at the image in my mind of the twin beds pushed together in their room.

Auntie Beth lowered her voice, so I cupped a hand over my ear to hear them. "You sat through the whole conversation last night—or were you too stoned? He wanted to know how many houses she has, what her yearly income is from the investment capital, and how much she gives you."

"It was casual conversation."

"I thought he was going home after the first weekend, and he's been here for a month. Doesn't he work?"

"He doesn't have to."

Did Marianne know Tony dealt drugs?

"Marianne, you need help sending Mr. Unemployed packing. Because I'm ready for him to go. I found out today that Chuck's having a fling with his twenty-three-year-old secretary. I told him to be out of the house by the time we return in August. I gave him an ultimatum."

Marianne took a big breath. I did too. My mom didn't have it in her to be like the female black widow who killed her mate. She wasn't that strong. I hoped Auntie Beth could help her.

I was listening so intently I didn't hear Brandon and Sammy come inside with the dog. Brandon stood at the foot of the stairs. Behind him, Duke shook his wet fur all over the hallway. "Hey. What are you doing?" he asked me.

I held a finger to my lips, but it was too late. My aunt rounded the corner at the top of the flight.

"Daphne? How long have you been standing there?"

"I was just going downstairs."

"She's spying," Brandon said.

"Shut up, Brandon."

I darted outside and ran next door.

CHAPTER 45

OH GREAT OUIJA

Daphne

"Sergeant Pepper's Lonely Hearts' Club Band" played on Phillip's boom box. Smoke from cigarettes and pot filled the Vaughans' living room. Outside, clouds darkened the sky. The windows were all shut tight against the rain. Sweaty beer cans rested on plastic coasters filled with condensation.

Squeezed between Lewis and Phillip on the yellow couch, I sat with my hands in my lap holding a beer. I smoked pot and cigarettes like the rest of them, but my gaze kept returning to the piano across the room. I longed to play the dark melodies humming in my head but didn't want to perform for my friends. Phillip had already expressed his dislike of classical music. Besides, I hadn't had a chance to practice in seven weeks. It was the last week of July.

Mark sprawled out in a pillowy chair. With a Coke in his hand, he made an O with his lips and popped his jaw, blowing smoke rings. Lara sat at his feet poking her finger through the rings.

When the music finally faded, Lara said, "I want to do something fun. Father's coming tomorrow and we'll be stuck doing what he wants until he goes back to Indy. Let's play a game."

Fuzzy-headed from two beers and smoking pot, I lazily wondered if Lara had scheduled an abortion. She seemed more like herself today as she cleared the coffee table of ashtrays and empty beer cans. "I know some card games," I said.

Phillip groaned and sat back with his hands behind his head.

"I know something better." Lara bounced over to a closet where dozens of board games filled the shelves. As a thunderclap shook the house, she pulled a box from the bottom of the pile. She unfolded the cardboard and placed a teardrop-shaped game piece with circular glass in the center of the board.

"What's this?" Mark asked.

"Ouija," Lara said. "Haven't you ever played?"

Mark said no, and I wondered if they had board games in prison.

The aged image on the board looked like an old map. The alphabet arched prominently across the center in two rows, A-M and N-Z. In the top left corner, a smiling sun, and the word Yes. In the top right corner, a sad crescent moon and the word No. Numbers one to nine, and ending in zero, lined the lower part and the words Good Bye were scrolled across the bottom.

"How do you play?" I asked.

Lara dropped to her knees beside the coffee table. "It's easy. Ask it anything."

Phillip laughed. "What time is it?"

Lara shook her head. "Not like that, you nerd. We have to put our fingers on the planchette."

Mark sidled his chair beside Lara and plunked his fingers onto the teardrop shaped game piece. Lewis did the same.

"Lightly, you idiots. And the rule is, you can't direct the answer. Let it answer."

Lewis looked as skeptical as the rest of us. "What does that mean?"

"You'll find out. Ask it a question," Lara said.

"What time is it?" Mark nodded at Phillip, and the guys laughed.

"Come on, you guys," Lara said. She seemed determined to play the game. "Get serious. Daphne, help me."

Butterflies burst from their cocoons in my belly. A bad feeling had erupted about this game. *It was just a game—wasn't it?* I leaned forward and tentatively placed four fingertips beside Lewis's on the planchette. Immediately, I felt an energy like the refrigerator running. Like the planchette was plugged into the wall and vibrating.

"What's making it do that?" I asked.

"Do what?" Lewis asked.

Thunder shook the house moments before rain began to fall. I glanced out the window at the choppy lake. Wind whipped waves into the shore.

Lara grew serious and closed her eyes. "As above, so below. What time is it, oh great Ouija?"

Lewis smirked. "Oh, great Ouija?"

Phillip laughed. "This is ridiculous."

I barely touched the planchette, but felt it move. "Are you doing that?"

Lewis and Mark shook their heads.

"I'm following the rules," Mark said. "Are you, Lara?"

"It's more fun if you do," she said.

The planchette moved to the number three, backed away, and hovered over the three again, then moved to the number nine.

Lara smiled as Lewis checked his watch. "Whoa. It's twenty till four."

The hairs on my face and back stood on end. "Did you make it do that?"

"It takes directions from spirits in the room," Lara said.

I didn't like this one bit. I thought about Grandpa Mortensen and Ruth. The pale face flashed before me again and the lakeweeds taunted me. And I couldn't remove my fingers from the planchette. I had to see what would happen next.

Lewis took his hand off and sat back against the couch. "This is stupid. Why don't you ask it something important? Ask it if the baby's a boy or a girl."

I gasped because I knew the baby was a girl.

"Shut up, Lewis," Lara said.

"You told him?" Phillip asked her.

"He found out, okay."

Hostility poured off Lewis. "I figured you'd want to know if it's a boy or a girl before you kill it." He scowled at Lara.

The blood drained from Lara's face.

Mark lunged across the table at Lewis. I scrambled to get out of the way as Phillip intercepted Mark but I got pinned beside Lewis and under Phillip. Lewis backed into the couch pillows. His eyes widened with fear. Lewis and Mark stared each other down.

Lara grabbed Mark by the shirt and pulled him back. "Stop it. Just stop it!"

Mark cocked his fists as if to throw a punch.

Lewis held his hands up to protect his face. "It was a joke. I'm just joking. Geez."

"It's not funny!" Lara pulled Mark back to his chair. "Settle down everyone."

Phillip pointed a finger at his brother. "Cut that shit out, Lewis."

"You knew?" Lewis asked him.

"Of course I knew. She can't keep secrets from me." Phillip slid back to his seat, giving me room to move again.

I took a breath and kept staring at Lewis. He shouldn't have said those things.

Lara closed her eyes a moment. "We're playing a game. Put your fingers back on the planchette. Do it now!"

Mark glared at Lewis but settled into his chair. He seemed to work hard at tamping his emotions down. Phillip reached behind me and slapped Lewis in the back of the head.

"Hey!" Lewis scooted to the corner of the couch.

I didn't want to provoke anyone. I leaned forward and placed my fingers on the planchette. Mark joined in, but Phillip and Lewis only watched. The tension from their anger buzzed in my ears, but they all settled down for Lara. They were playing nice for her.

"I have a question," Lara said. "As above, so below. Oh, great Ouija, where is Adelaide Vaughan right now?"

"That's easy," Lewis said. "She's with her tennis instructor."

Lara shushed him, and a moment later the planchette slid to the letter P and eventually spelled out the name Paula.

Lara laughed nervously. "Mother's at Paula Winston's house up the hill. You know the big mansion. They're playing bridge this afternoon. I guarantee they're drinking gin and tonics."

Astounded, I remained quiet.

"You're pushing the thing," Phillip said and finished his beer.

"I'm not!" Lara said. "You ask it something."

"Fine." Phillip put two fingers of his right hand on the planchette. "Will she be home by dinnertime?"

"As above, so below. Oh great Ouija, will Mother be home by dinnertime?" Lara asked.

This time the planchette sped to the word No. They all laughed. I didn't even crack a smile. This was just too creepy. Though it seemed like the tension between them was relieved, my shoulders still felt like they were riding up to my ears.

Lara adjusted her fingertips on the device. "Daphne, you ask it a question."

"I don't know what to ask." My voice was shaky. It terrified me to think there might be a spirit in the room. It scared me even more because I felt like something was in my closet. Ghosts were real, weren't they? Though I'd never seen one, I didn't want to provoke one either. As far as I knew, they were real.

"Ask something that only you know the answer to," Lara suggested.

In a high, mocking voice, Phillip said, "Oh great Ouija, what am I going to do with all my Barbies? Someday . . . someday I hope I have boobies like hers."

Lewis turned away and covered a laugh.

Embarrassed, I shoved Phillip playfully. He fell on the floor like a stunt man and bounced back onto the couch.

"Come on," Lara said. "Get serious."

Mark lit another cigarette. Outside, the rain came down in sheets.

My nervous smile seemed pasted on my face. I concentrated. "There's a creepy closet in our bedroom next door."

"Shh, don't tell it. Ask the question," Lara said.

I closed my eyes. Stinging nettles burned from the planchette up my arm. But all eyes were on me, so I continued. "As above, so below. Oh great Ouija, is the closet in my bedroom haunted?"

Phillip laughed again. "Maybe by the ghost of Christmas past."

Lara whispered, "Shut up!"

The planchette circled slowly at first, then flowed to the word Yes.

Unsure what I was seeing, I opened my eyes wider as it continued to the letters S-O-L-D-I-E-R.

"There's a soldier haunting your closet," Lara said.

"No way," Lewis said. "One of you is pushing it." He didn't have his fingers on the planchette.

Mark looked away and blew out smoke rings. His fingers lightly touched the game piece. Lara's fingers barely grazed the device and Phillip's two fingers didn't quite contact it.

It continued to spell. M-O-R-T-E—.

I pulled my hand away. "Mortensen. It's spelling the family name. Grandpa Mortenson was killed in World War Two."

"That's insane, man. I need a beer," Phillip said. He began to stand up, but Lara sat him back down.

"Wait. One more question," she said.

"This is getting creepy," Mark said. He kept one finger on the device.

I placed my hand next to his, and Lara closed her eyes. "As above, so below. Oh great Ouija, who are you?"

The planchette spelled M-O-R-T-E-M.

"Mortem is Latin for dead, dude," Mark said.

Lewis hugged his knees to his chest. "That's messed up."

I giggled nervously. "The M and the N are next to each other. Maybe it's spelling Mortensen."

Phillip repeated Lara's question. "Who are you, oh great and powerful Oz?—I mean Ouija."

This time the planchette spelled Y-O-U, then spiraled the board two and a half times. It stopped in the corner nearest Phillip, and he said, "I'm not doing this."

"No, wait. Let it finish," Lara said.

A hush fell over them. Outside, the rain thundered on the roof. I held my breath as it spelled K-I-L-L-E-D followed by the letter L.

Mark removed his hand. "This is bogus, man."

"It's just a game, Mark," Lara said. The blood had drained from her face, but she left her fingertips on the planchette. "Oh great Ouija, who is L?"

Lewis nodded and Mark played along.

The planchette moved, but I didn't see it. A thousand knives were stabbing my scalp and thighs. I was swimming in the dark. There were lakeweeds everywhere and the sound of thunder or engines roared in my ears. Deafening noise, whispers, and cries of *save me* filled my head. I tried to make it to the surface. The more I struggled, the more tangled my feet became in the weeds.

I gasped for air.

CHAPTER 46

HELLO, FATHER

Daphne

As I came to, I saw Mark's face hovering above me. I could see the underside of the coffee table and didn't know how I ended up on the floor.

Lara and Lewis argued in the background. "How much did you give her?" Lewis asked. "She's wasted."

"She smoked too much weed, that's all," Lara said.

Mark looked down at me. "You okay?"

"I think so." I rolled over and my head spun with dizziness.

"She's too young to be partying with us." Phillip paced the living room like a caged tiger.

"Careful. You really passed out." Mark took my elbow and helped me sit up.

The last thing I remembered was swimming in the lake. *But that can't be.* Before that . . . "What did the Ouija say?"

Mark's mouth turned down and his eyebrows drew together.

Lewis squatted beside me. "Nothing. It's not real. None of that mumbo jumbo is real. Phillip made it move."

It had been real, though. I felt something.

Freak.

"You sure you're okay?" Mark asked.

Lara sat on the couch in front of me. "Did you take one of my quaaludes?"

"I must have drank too much beer." Going along with Lara's lie made more sense than saying, *By the way, I'm having wild visions.* I tried to laugh it off. Mark and Lewis helped me to my feet. A headrush made me see stars.

"Get her some water, Lara," Lewis said.

Hey guys, I might have Extra Sensory Perception. ESP? *That* was terrifying. If that were the case, it was a curse. These visions, the weird feelings from touching people and the goose flesh . . . It scared me. Now I had a whopper of a headache and wanted to go home.

Mark looked especially worried. He walked with me to the kitchen and sat me in a chair. Lara filled a glass with water, and Mark handed it to me.

Lewis stood by, glowering at Lara. "What did you do to her?"

Lara put her hands on her hips. "Nothing."

"Will you stop fighting in front of her?" Mark cleared them from the kitchen and guarded the door. I could still hear them arguing. I listened as I sipped cold tap water. What if all the weird images and sounds meant something?

Weirdo.

No one at school believed I had warned Ruth. But on the day of the epic ice storm, those familiar burning prickles crawled up my arms. Could it be ESP? That only happened to people in scary movies. Even now, the visions embarrassed me.

Freak.

I couldn't tell them what I'd seen. Someone was going to drown this summer. Lewis? Lara? *Me?* I wasn't sure. And I still had no idea when it would happen.

I shuddered. The Vaughans' arguing didn't let up. Their loud voices caused my headache to throb.

"Are you okay to go home?" Mark asked.

The sound of crunching gravel silenced the Vaughan siblings. A car pulled into the driveway.

Mark looked out the window and his eyes grew as big as moons. "Holy shit. It's your dad!" He ran through the living room, toward the back of the house. He leapt over the coffee table and shoved Phillip out of his way. The porch door slammed behind him.

"Father's home. Quick, hide the bong." Lara and Lewis scrambled to clean up beer cans. Phillip took the bong and pot paraphernalia to a back bedroom just as their father opened the kitchen door.

Holding onto the chair, I stood to greet him. "Hello, Mr. Vaughan."

"Is that your car in the driveway?" He set his keys on the counter and a small suitcase on the floor.

"No. I live next door. I'm Daphne Post." I tried to stall him until they could hide the evidence of our party. "So nice to meet you." I held out my hand.

Mr. Vaughan sniffed the air. "What's that smell? Where's Lara?"

"I'm here, Father." Slightly out of breath, Lara swept into the kitchen.

Lewis appeared at her side. "Hello, Father."

Mr. Vaughan saw the empty beer cans on the counter. "What's going on here? Where's your Mother?" The sound of Mark's car starting up in the driveway turned his attention to the window. "And who was that?"

I decided it was time to leave.

CHAPTER 47

NOW WE'RE EVEN

July 27th: Mark

Mark got in his car and drove the hell out of there. The last thing he needed was a face-off with the prosecutor. The man who put him away.

Putting five miles and fifteen minutes between them, he stopped on a country road near a patch of tall corn and wildflowers. There, he got out of the car and caught his breath. The sky spit on him. He leaned on the tailgate and coughed into the wind. Grey clouds swirled overhead and, though the rain stopped, droplets fell from nearby trees.

The prosecutor had looked older and thicker around the middle. He was gray-haired and clean shaven. He wore a loosened red and blue-striped tie. He looked like a politician.

Echoes of his opponent's campaign speech buzzed through Mark's head: *"He opposed Roe versus Wade. Is that what you really want, Indiana?"* If the prosecutor found out Mark Walters had gotten Lara pregnant, there would be hell to pay.

Because of the prosecutor, Mark never had those opportunities. As soon as the prosecutor went back to Indianapolis, they'd get the procedure done. He had agreed to take Lara to the clinic. She would move on with her life. She'd finish high school and grab up every opportunity she had coming. As he stooped over the trunk of his Mustang, he hoped it would be like that for her. Like this summer never happened.

Not Mark. He'd remember this summer for the rest of his life.

Now we're even.

CHAPTER 48

IT'S JUST A GAME

Daphne

Duke ambled by my side, sniffing and snorting at spots on the ground. The chilling quiet from the house next door made me nervous. I kept an eye on it, on my friends, as I walked along Aubenaubee Creek, zipping my windbreaker to my neck. I picked up a fallen stick, dabbed the stick in the cloudy stream, poking at stones and moss on the bottom. Water bugs skittered away, and the wind whispered, *Save me.*

Out of the corner of my eye, I saw something move, and my heart just about stopped. But when I turned my head, nothing was there. Duke stared across the creek and panted. His nervousness made me tense.

I sat in the grass and struggled to figure out the visions. The Ouija had freaked me out. I'd believed something—Lara said it was a spirit—communicated through that thing. But who? Or what? It frightened me.

The sun went behind a cloud, and I grew intensely cold. Like I was under water. Like I was swimming. I closed my eyes and blurry images flashed out of order, like a barely remembered dream. There were tangling lakeweeds wrapped around my legs. Someone was in danger. The whispers and warnings grew thunderously loud. The sounds of

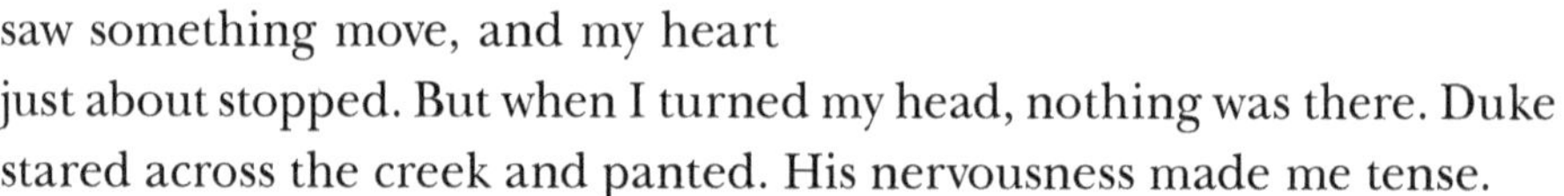

engines—or was it thunder?—roared above, churning the waves and stirring up the weeds. I couldn't get to the surface. Not until I found the person I was looking for.

The Ouija had spelled out a name. The Ouija had said, *"You killed L"* L. The name was on the tip of my tongue—

Duke barked at something across the creek. I didn't see a thing, but he was agitated.

It brought me out of the reverie. I realized I was lying on my side, on the lawn.

"Daphne! Are you all right?" Lewis strode across the lawn.

Duke stuck his dripping wet nose in my hand and ran his tongue along my fingers. The scent of decaying fish rose from his fur.

"What did you roll in, Duke?" I gently pushed Duke's nose away and sat up.

Lewis came to my side and took one look at Duke. "That dog needs a bath."

I wanted to smile but couldn't. The lingering effects of the vision I had made me feel sad and frightened. This thing I had was definitely a curse. I couldn't talk about it. "Is your father mad? There were beer cans everywhere."

"A little. Phillip took the blame for it. He told Father he had the weekend off and he brought the beer. Father's always angry at Phillip anyway."

I pushed myself to my feet and shoved my hands in my pockets. It occurred to me that touching things triggered the visions. When I hugged Ruth, I saw her fall on the ice. When Tony helped me out of the lake, I knew he was involved with drugs. When I embraced Lara, I knew about her baby.

"About that game," Lewis said.

"Hey, I'm sorry about passing out—"

"Don't worry about it. I don't believe in that hokey stuff anyway." Lewis scratched Duke's ears, and the dog sat beside him with pinched, worried eyebrows.

I didn't know whether I believed *that hokey stuff* or not. I wanted to.

But then again, it really frightened me. If it was real, it meant that I was psychic. And that was really scary. "I'm going inside to lay down." I needed an Excedrin.

"Can you come by later? Mother and Father will be out."

"Sure. Yeah." Lewis liked me. I was sure of it. But I sensed a darker side of him. He reminded me of Judas in *Jesus Christ Superstar*. And I didn't trust him.

His eyes remained locked on mine. "See you soon."

I watched him go and thought of the disembodied head—the face— I saw underwater. A cold wind blew the hair out of my face.

While I was hosing down Duke, Tony pulled into the carport in his car. I went inside and heard snippets of a conversation. I was standing in the kitchen with a handful of towels to dry Duke off. Tony and Marianne were in the back hall at the bottom of the stairs.

"Where were you?" Marianne asked.

"You're starting to sound like my old lady," Tony said, his voice sounding like a bulldozer crunching over gravel.

I dried Duke off and gave him some water as quietly as I could.

"You didn't answer the question," Marianne said.

"I've been around," Tony said. "Seeing friends. Look. I need to ask a favor. Can I borrow some money?"

"What for?"

"I'm in a bind," Tony said.

I stood quietly by the kitchen door, listening to their voices carry down the hall.

"How much do you need?"

"Three grand."

"What?" Marianne gasped.

"I'll pay it right back. I just owe my landlord in Indy—I haven't been home—and she's going to kick me out if I don't pay for the last two months. And now she wants the next two in advance."

"I don't have that kind of money, Tony."

"But you can get it, right?"

"No."

"Okay, look. I gotta skedaddle. We'll talk later."

"Wait. You don't get off that easily," Marianne said. "Where have you been going every day?"

"Don't start sounding like my old lady."

They tromped through the back hallway. I grabbed a bag of Doritos and hoped the crinkling sound of the bag covered my steps as I crept closer. I could just see them now.

"I've asked you how you're making money this summer and you said you worked for Indy Graphics. Is that even true?"

"We'll talk later."

"If you go, don't come back here tonight."

This was new. Was Marianne kicking him out? Hope and excitement grew in me.

"Come on. You don't mean that," he said.

Auntie Beth ran through the kitchen and passed me. "She might not mean it, but I do. Once you walk out that door, Tony, don't come back here." They moved toward the kitchen.

"Are you ganging up on me?" The look on his face told me he thought they were joking.

"If that's what it takes." Marianne crossed her arms. Auntie Beth stared him down.

He gave my aunt his winning smile, flashing white teeth beneath his dark mustache. "Look, I'll only be gone a few minutes." He flashed Marianne puppy dog eyes and kissed her on the cheek. Then he ducked out the door.

"He better not come back." Auntie Beth crossed her arms too and watched him go.

I put the Doritos away.

"He's lying about something." Marianne went to the phone.

"Who are you calling?" Auntie Beth asked.

"Indy Graphics." Marianne cocked her head and pressed the receiver between her cheek and shoulder to free her hands. She picked up a pen and paper. "Hello," she said into the receiver. "I'm an artist, and I'm . . . I'm actually looking for work . . ."

Tony would return, just like he said. And Marianne would let him in. As I watched his car drive away, I considered coming clean and telling Marianne what I knew about him. But why would Marianne believe a cursed teenager?

CHAPTER 49

NO, NO, NO! PART TWO

Lara

"It seems like we never talk, Lara. How has your summer been?" For once, her father was paying attention to Lara. Right when she needed him to ignore her.

"Fine. Boring. Nothing to talk about, really." On the porch, she sat on the davenport looking down at her feet. There on the floor, behind the chair leg, the fat Yellow Pages book mocked her as she recalled the last thing she'd looked up. Planned Parenthood.

Father cannot find out. Despite the damp chill in the air, Lara sweated beneath her tank top and poncho.

John looked clean-shaven, like he'd drawn a razor over his afternoon stubble before coming downstairs. He'd changed out of his shirt and tie and put on a short-sleeved zip-neck shirt with a long pointy collar. Sitting in the wicker rocking chair across from her, he had a tobacco pipe in his hand. "Have you made any new friends?"

"One or two. Daphne the neighbor is nice." Lara didn't know what else to say. As much as she still wanted to hate Daphne, she couldn't summon those feelings.

"She's Harriet Mortensen's granddaughter. I could use someone like

Harriet to back my campaign this fall. I'll go over there and talk to her, later. Tell me about your other friend."

"Who?"

"The young man driving the Mustang."

"Oh, Mark? He's nobody. Just a townie."

"How did you meet?"

Lara took a deep breath. "He's Phillip's friend," she said. At least it wasn't a lie. Father always knew when she was lying.

"Does he work at the academy too?" Father scooped tobacco into his pipe and tamped it down with a small pocketknife tool.

"I don't think so." She didn't dare tell him that Mark worked at a bar. That he was twenty-five. Or that Father knew him. Mark had been to prison because Father convicted him. The connection was too strange to be believable. Everything about Mark reminded her about the problem she had. *The problem Father cannot find out about.*

"Hello, John. You're a day early." Mother walked in wearing her tennis skirt, a pale green-and-orange-striped shirt and a pair of white sandals. The cloud of her perfume hit Lara when she sat next to her on the davenport.

"Hello, Addy. We were just talking about Lara's friend, Mark."

Mother put her white leather purse on the couch beside Lara. "Are you still seeing that boy?"

"What? No." Suddenly, Lara felt very hot. She removed her poncho.

Mother turned to face her. "Why are you blushing?"

Lara leaned back and crossed her arms over her aching boobs. "I'm not."

"Yes, you are."

Lewis walked in and Lara pressed her lips together. She gave him the signal, a tiny shake of her head. *Don't say anything!*

Mother asked, "Lewis, what do you know about this fellow, Mark?"

"He's okay, I guess. His last name is Walters."

"How do you know that?" Lara asked.

"I asked him. When he came over last week." The smug look on Lewis's face infuriated Lara.

"How do you know him?" Mother asked.

"He hangs out with us. Lara, didn't you tell them?"

Lara ground her teeth together and shot daggers at Lewis with her gaze.

Lewis grinned. "I'm a little afraid of him. Phillip found out he went to prison. So I decided to do some research. I called one of my friends at home in Indianapolis, you remember Clark, Father."

Their father seemed to have his full attention on Lewis. "I do. He's Judge Sturman's grandson, isn't he?"

"That's right." Lewis smiled, but Lara didn't like where this was going.

Lewis continued. "Clark went to the county to look up records, to see if he could find a Mark Walters in the system. He did. He went to prison in 1969."

Father set the pipe down on a side table. "Mark *Walters*? Is that his name? Why does that sound familiar?"

Lara shook her head. *No, no, no—*

From the way Lewis had raised his eyebrows, he clearly enjoyed seeing Lara in the hotseat. "You might even remember him, Father."

Father's face paled. "I put that boy in prison for nearly killing Peter Weir's son Geoffrey."

He went on, but Lara didn't hear. Acid rose to the back of her mouth. The odor of perfume and this conversation made her empty stomach churn. She lunged out of the couch and pushed Lewis out of the doorway. She made it to the bathroom just in time.

CHAPTER 50

HAPPY HOUR NIGHTLY

Daphne

The aftermath of the Ouija game haunted me well into the next day. Lakeweeds. Thunder. Nothing made sense. I sat at the piano one last time trying to make music out of the cacophony. Nana had promised the piano would arrive this week. She said she'd drive it here herself to get it out of her living room.

I needed it now. The clashing atonal sounds didn't clear my mind. Instead, they mirrored my confusion. If Lara's father hadn't arrived, I could play their piano.

If only.

My gaze swept the empty room. By the sound of it, the boys were upstairs jumping off their beds. Margot played quietly in the library upstairs. Marianne and Tony sequestered themselves in their room. Hopefully, Marianne would kick him out for good.

Lights were off in the galley, the bar between the kitchen and dining room. An old sink, like the one in my bedroom, had dual spouts and rust stains around the drain. On the wall hung a framed old poster of a triangular drink glass with two olives and a triplet of bubbles rising from it. The words, Happy Hour Nightly! sent a cheery invitation.

I was ready to put my curse to rest.

While Auntie Beth cooked dinner in the kitchen, I stepped out of my sandals and moved quickly, quietly to the bar. I surveyed the options. Vodka, Jack Daniels, and a dark-green bottle of something called Vermouth. Beneath the counter, a small refrigerator was filled with green wine bottles, tonic and seltzer waters. I poured vodka, filling half a 16-ounce plastic Solo cup, then twisted the cap open on the tonic water.

Pfitz.

I stopped to listen. Auntie Beth didn't come around the corner, so I topped off the vodka with the bubbling tonic and put everything away.

The boys ran downstairs and dumped a basket full of Hot Wheels cars on the floor. The noise they made covered my steps. With the cup in my hand, I went to the piano and sat down. The drink went down with a cough. So I drank more.

I played out of tune scales and an awful version of Debussy's "Rêverie." By the time I finished my drink, the piano didn't sound so bad. And by then, I made too many mistakes—although, how would anyone hear the difference?

Frustrated, I took my empty cup to the bar for a refill. I'd just closed up the vodka bottle when Auntie Beth blazed through the bar on her way to the dining room carrying a basket of warm sliced garlic bread.

She stopped to look at me. "What are you looking for?"

"Nothing," I lied. My tongue felt thick. "I wanted a glass of soda."

"You know the kids' sodas are in the fridge on the back porch." Auntie Beth stumbled over my Dr. Scholl's, nearly launching the basket of bread across the room. "Ouch! Are those your sandals? Why on earth did you leave them in the middle of the doorway?"

I couldn't suppress a giggle.

Auntie Beth frowned and said, "Help me set the table."

I slipped the sandals back over my toes and took stainless steel silverware from the buffet drawer at the end of the dining room.

"Are you feeling okay?"

"I'm fine." I was better than fine, I was invincible. The vodka had given me a strong buzz, softened my tongue, and numbed the whispers and wild songs, the images of murky water and lakeweed.

Auntie Beth laid woven straw placemats on the dining room table. "You and I haven't gotten a chance to talk."

"Oh?" I suspected she was talking about the Vaughans. I was wrong.

"Your mom's going through an important time in her life. The divorce was hard for her. She may not seem available, but that's because she's juggling a lot. She's trying to figure out how to make ends meet. She wants to support you and Brandon, and she'll have to work very hard to make enough money."

The divorce was hard for Marianne? She'd caused it. She'd kicked Dad out and asked for a divorce. I didn't have anything to say. I let the silence grow until the room was filled with it like cotton pillow stuffing.

Auntie Beth completed her circle around the table. "You can talk to me. I wanted you to know I'm here for you. I can be a good listener."

I nodded and kept my head down, carefully setting the forks and knives on each placemat.

"You can even talk to your mom. She wants to hear your point of view. She's just as scared as you are."

"Mom's not scared." *She's dating a drug dealer.*

"She loves you deeply."

I snapped. "All she cares about is herself."

"That's not true, honey."

"Then why did she leave Dad?" I slammed the rest of the silverware down on the table.

"What's going on here?" Marianne and Tony stood in the doorway of the dining room.

"Auntie Beth said the divorce was hard on you," I let my emotions loose. "If it was so hard, then why are you with him? If it was so hard, why don't you go back to Dad? And why did you screw around in the first place?"

"Daphne!" Auntie Beth said. "Language."

The astonished looks on Mom's and Tony's faces fueled my rage. Behind them, Brandon and Sammy had gotten up from their Hot Wheels to see what was going on.

"So what," I said. "Marianne fucked him and made Dad move out."

Brandon punched Sammy in the arm. "She's in so much trouble."

"Tony deals drugs," I continued. "He's selling pot and, I don't know, pills. Downers. Quaaludes. Lara told me. But you knew that, right, Mom? I saw the joints in your dresser. You're doing them too."

"It's not true! I don't do . . ." Marianne looked at Tony. "You're dealing?"

The whites of Tony's eyes showed, and his lips disappeared in his beard. "Where are you getting that information, Daph?"

"Daphne, this is not the time or the place," Auntie Beth said.

"You're not my mom."

"Boys! Go to upstairs!" My aunt herded Brandon and Sammy out of the room.

I looked at Marianne. "And you're too afraid to say anything. Aren't you?"

"I want to talk to you. I've tried—"

"I don't want to talk with him here!"

Marianne shot a glance at Tony.

"Fine. I have errands to run anyway. I'll be back." He tried to kiss Marianne on the cheek, but she pushed him away. "Just go."

He disappeared through the kitchen.

Auntie Beth returned from sending the boys away. "Lara Vaughan is just like her mother. She'll say anything to get you on her side."

"Lara's my friend! And you have no idea what she's going through."

"Tell me!" Marianne opened her arms wide.

I bit my lip. Lara's secret was not one I could share. "God! You don't get it, do you? Just leave me alone!" I reeled past them and let the door slam.

CHAPTER 51

PARANOID DELUSIONS?

July 28th: Mark

Tony blew into The Bar like a tornado, knocking over chairs and stools in his path. "You mother—"

Backing away, Mark held his hands up. "Tony."

Tony's hands gripped the edge of the bar. Fury sparked his dark beady brown eyes. "Did you turn me in?"

Mark would never admit it. A week ago, he'd given Tony's name to Brandt Simmons. "What are you talking about?"

Tony reached across the bar, nearly knocking the old man off the nearest stool. Glasses went flying and bottles broke on the floor as Mark backed into Red.

Mark grabbed Tony's shoulders. "Tony, what the hell!"

Droplets of sweat beaded on Tony's forehead. "They're watching me, man. They're everywhere!" He swung his legs over the bar and landed with a crash beside Mark. "Did you tell them? Did you narc on me?"

Another bottle fell off the shelf and shattered on the floor. Red shoved them both toward the door. "Get him outta here before he causes anymore damage!"

Mark pushed Tony outside and released him. "Cool off, man."

Tony paced the parking lot. "They're after me, man. The cops are everywhere."

"Cool off. You sound paranoid."

Tony ran a hand through slick, wet-looking hair. "I *am* paranoid, man. My old lady wants me to move out. Her freaky daughter spies on me. She knows. The kid knows I'm dealing. You know what? Maybe it was her. Maybe Daphne turned me in. Am I right?"

"Settle down. Daphne's just a kid. She'd never do that."

"How do *you* know her?"

Mark didn't want to answer that question. "We'll figure this out, okay? We'll work it out." He didn't like this though. He was caught in the middle again.

Tony pulled a small bottle out of his pocket and popped a pill. "I'm freaking, man. My old lady's the best thing I've got right now. If I lose her, I'll have to go back to work. Like, real work."

"She's loaded?"

"You said it. She's sitting on a big inheritance from her family. I can't lose her. I can't let the cops catch me."

Mark didn't know what to say. He'd never met anyone with that kind of cash. He took the pack of cigarettes from the rolled-up sleeve of his T-shirt and tapped the tobacco down. Tony didn't fit in with the townies, and he was nothing like the rich vacationers who had money to burn.

"Look. I gotta be very careful here," Mark said finally. "The local deputy knows I did time."

"You did? I'm not cut out for that, man. I can't get arrested."

Tony reminded Mark of some men he'd met in prison. But Mark knew what it was like on the inside. The hard-timers would beat the crap out of him. "You sound worried."

"I owe my supplier a pile of money. If I don't pay it off by the end of the month, he's coming after me."

Mark lit his cigarette. "I don't know how to help you."

"But you know this town. You know people. You're in with the locals and the rich kids. You gotta help me."

Mark shook his head. Seven years was long enough. He wouldn't mess up his parole for this dude. Tony was desperate and losing his mind. "Sorry, man. I can't."

A slow burble came from Tony's chest, then he laughed. His eyes crinkled, and he slapped his thigh. "You're right. You're right, man. I won't bother you anymore."

Suddenly, Tony's demeanor changed, and he lunged at Mark and his thick fingers clenched around Mark's throat.

Mark clawed at Tony's fingers. He should have seen it coming.

With a desperate look in his eye, Tony stared him down. "Find buyers for me! I need to sell this shit! I need the money!"

Mark nodded and choked the word, "Okay." He gasped for air once more, then Tony released him, and he fell onto the dirt drive.

Tony slammed the door to his car and sped away, his tires spewing gravel.

Mark got to his feet and swiped dirt off his palms. He had no attachment to Tony. He didn't give a shit what happened to him. But then he remembered: When he'd told Brandt Simmons about Tony, Brandt had said he had to catch Tony in the act, making an actual deal before he could arrest him.

What if Mark could make that happen?

CHAPTER 52

MONTANA

Daphne

Marianne didn't follow me outside, but that made me angrier. Why didn't she care? Why didn't she do something about Tony Baloney? Tony the loser.

Thick cloud cover brought dusk earlier than normal. Under the car port and out of the rain, I swiped tears away from my eyes and pounded my fists on the side of the VW bus.

Music soothed the raw emotions better than drinking or smoking pot. Playing piano was the one

thing that worked. Without it, I felt lost, argumentative, and unfocused. When Dad left—when Marianne kicked him out—I played piano every day. I practiced in the morning before the school bus and after I got home. If I didn't have homework, I battled the television volume in the next room, and played my repertoire until bedtime.

I went over to the Vaughans and knocked on their kitchen door, but no one answered. Both their parents' cars were gone, but the door was open. I let myself in and went straight to the piano. I tried to play the introductory arpeggios of the Chopin étude, and my fingers fumbled. I was still drunk. The precision and control were gone.

"Argh!" I slammed my hands onto the keys and held down the pedal, letting the strings ring.

When the sound died completely, I let up my foot. In the silence, I heard a whimper. Someone in the next room sniffled. I went to the patio, where Lara huddled on the davenport with her knees tucked in.

"What's wrong?" I said. It was a stupid question. Lara had some big decisions to make. Her future and the future of her unborn child were both at stake.

Lara sniffed. "Father is sending me to Montana to have the baby."

I gasped and sat down. "What about high school?"

"He wants me to complete it there." Lara wiped her nose with a wadded-up tissue. "Fucking Lewis. He told them! He ruined my life."

"Lewis told them?" I didn't know what to say. Maybe Lewis really wasn't the person I thought he was.

Lara put her elbows on her knees and her hands on her head. She fell silent for a while. When she finally sat up, she smoothed out her hair and looked me in the eye.

"You know what?"

I shook my head.

"I'm going to have a party."

It was the last thing I expected her to say.

A PINBALL WIZARD

Daphne

Lara sat on the side of her bed with the phone pressed to her ear. "Invite everyone, Chandi. It's going to be the biggest party anyone has ever been to."

While Lara talked with friends and made plans, I went back to the piano. The Baldwin had stiff action, and the lower register had gone sharp with the humidity, but it was a zillion times better than the one at Aubenaubee Lodge. I connected arpeggios and melodies awakened in me. I was on the verge of knowing

the meaning of those whispers—*save me*—when Lewis came to my side.

"Hey." His messy hair looked like he'd been sleeping on it. He wiped his eyes.

"I didn't mean to wake you up," I said. After hearing Lewis told their father about Lara's situation, my feelings toward him were conflicted. I stood to go back into Lara's room.

"I was just resting," he said. "Want to come upstairs?"

Despite reservations, I followed him into his room, where Roger Daltrey sang in the background, "Welcome to the camp . . ." The worn vinyl skipped on a small scratch every few measures. His room had two twin beds with matching brown comforters printed with flying ducks. The pillows looked like no one ever slept on them.

"Come on in." He went to the turntable in the corner and turned the music down.

I stood by the closed door with my hands folded at my waist.

"What's up?" he asked.

"I heard you told your parents about Lara. Why would you do that to her?"

Lewis sat on one of the twin beds, causing wrinkles on the bedspread. He smoothed them with the hand missing the finger. "They figured it out. She's been really sick."

"But now she won't finish high school."

"Yes, she will." Lewis looked up at me like I was out of my mind. "Come on, Daphne. What's the right thing to do? Lara's not going to be a good mom. I thought they should know. They'll take care of her and the baby."

Lewis sounded older. Like he'd made some decisions about life this summer. Like he'd grown the confidence of a kid whose parents fully supported him.

"She had plans for next year," I said. "Doesn't that mean anything to you? She wants to be an actress. She was going to get an abortion. Now they're sending her to Montana."

"And I'm going to boarding school in New York."

That made no difference to me. I shrugged.

"It's a preparatory school that I've wanted to go to since middle school," he continued. "They finally agreed to let me go."

"When?"

"Monday. That's okay, though. I need to get out of this dump." He moved to a wooden chair by a desk where a cold Coke made a sweaty puddle. "I don't regret it. Telling them." He finished the Coke. "Want one?"

"Sure." I didn't really. But I hoped it would make my headache go away.

"Make yourself at home. I'll be right back." Lewis left the room.

I sat on one of the beds. Not a single personal item lay on the dresser or the desk. The bedroom seemed too neat—an empty laundry basket in the corner, closed closet doors—like Lewis hadn't lived here all summer.

Like he never existed.

Lewis returned with the Coke and handed it to me. I followed his gaze out the closed window where the sky had turned black. Rain poured from an overhead gutter.

Music drowned out the watery sounds. Daltrey sang, "Gazing at you, I get the heat . . ."

"Do you know what this album is about?" he asked.

I shook my head, and my short hair brushed my neck and shoulders.

Lewis swiped the condensation puddle off the desk with his arm. "Tommy is deaf, dumb, and blind because he was traumatized by witnessing his father kill his mother's lover. He becomes a legend—a pinball wizard and a spiritual leader—after getting tortured by his uncle and a perverted babysitter."

"I wouldn't be traumatized if my dad killed my mom's boyfriend," I said.

Lewis moved from the chair to the bed beside me. "You kidding? You couldn't handle it."

"Yes I could. Tony is stupid."

"Wait, that's right." Lewis nodded like it just dawned on him. "Your mom is dating a drug dealer. That's the kind of gossip that gains traction in Indianapolis. If Mother found out, the women's society would have a henpecking party."

I imagined chickens dressed in tennis dresses and wanted to laugh until I cried. "I wish Marianne would dump him."

Lewis put an arm around me. "Parents can be the worst."

I set my drink on the desk and leaned back with him. I smelled his sweet, minty breath.

Lewis's gaze was upon me, soothing and stroking me. He reached up and touched my cheek. His fingers combed through my hair.

I gazed into his amber eyes as he pulled me closer. His thighs rubbed mine as he rolled me back on the bed. He pressed his lips against mine and his tongue snaked into my mouth.

I stiffened. *This is wrong.*

"Relax. You want this." His hand felt for the bottom of my tucked-in shirt.

I tried to stop him. His palm lay against my belly now, feeling for my boobs. Wishing I wore a bra, I gripped his wrist and followed his hand as it covered my nipples.

With his free hand, he unzipped his fly. "You want me." He pressed me down on the bed and forced his mouth upon mine.

I thought of Lara—now pregnant—and tried to move my legs out from under him. Through the clouds in my foggy, still-drunk mind, I saw something else. A party. Dozens of people drinking and smoking. Singing, dancing and yelling. A boat motor. A getaway. I heard people arguing, thunder booming and waves trashing the shore. Lakeweeds waved their gross slimy limbs.

I pushed Lewis off me and rolled out from under him.

"What the . . ." He wiped his bottom lip with the back of his hand. His shorts were open but at least his man parts were still put away.

I sat up. "I don't want this."

"Then why'd you come here?" He gripped my arm.

My ears seemed filled with water. The boat engine moved farther away. I sensed I should go after it. And then I was swimming. Gasping for air. Tendrils of lakeweed tangled around me.

Lewis shook me. "Daphne?"

Sadness came in waves, and I choked it back. Someone was dead. Now, I knew who was going to drown.

I bolted and took the stairs two at a time and ran outside through the wet grass to the golf course. I crossed Aubenaubee Creek and kept running all the way to the tree line on the far side of the fairway.

CHAPTER 54

THIS PARTY WILL BE LEGENDARY

Lara

In forty-eight hours, Lara's life had turned upside down. She felt sick. And not just because she was pregnant. She was trapped in a situation she couldn't control and furious at Lewis for telling her parents. Father had bought the plane ticket to Montana and sealed her fate.

Montana? This was not happening!

During the day she'd called her mother's obstetrician—a doctor she visited a handful of times. He assured her that as long as the procedure was performed in the first trimester, it wouldn't damage her body. He even said the procedure wouldn't be painful. More like the cramps during a menstrual cycle. She didn't schedule an appointment. Not yet.

Lara took a quaalude and swallowed it with a Coke, hoping it would stay down. She needed a distraction. She needed to escape. She needed this party to be the biggest blowout of her life.

Father and Mother drove back to Indianapolis to meet with his important friends. They took both the cars, leaving Lara alone with Lewis, and stuck in the house. Father's campaign meant more to him than Lara's life, apparently.

As she stared out the kitchen window, Phillip parked in the driveway. He carried three hockey sticks in one hand and slung his black duffle bag over one shoulder.

"Is summer camp over with?" Lara asked. The zipper didn't close on the hockey pads. His gear smelled like feet and sweat.

"No, something came up. I have to split."

Phillip was the only one she could talk to. Her favorite brother leaving felt like a final blow. "Where are you going?"

"I was selected from a dozen finalists to join the Junior Hockey League in Minnesota. I'm dropping out of college to do this." Phillip looked at his hockey sticks leaning against the corner and laughed. "I can't believe I got in. The cutoff is age twenty. I'll be twenty-one in January. I'm almost too old. So I can't throw this opportunity away. Olympic players are selected from this group. They are the very best hockey players in the world."

"Wow, Phillip. I'm so happy for you." Lara embraced her brother. It had been a long time since she'd heard any good news.

Phillip's mouth scrunched up and he looked at the ceiling. "I wish I could share it with Father. That would show him."

"He doesn't know?"

Phillip shook his head. "I've been happy, you know? I don't want to ruin it by telling him. I haven't told Mother, either."

Lara's throat closed with rising emotions. She was intensely proud of him for working so hard, following his dream, and succeeding. She stuffed the emotions back down and cleared her throat. "When do you leave?"

"I'm driving to Minnesota on Monday."

"So you'll be here for my party?" Lara opened the fridge, looking for something to nibble on.

"What party?"

"I invited everyone from Indy. I figure, if I have to go to Montana, then I'm going out in style."

"Montana?"

She closed the fridge because it smelled bad. "Haven't you heard?

Lewis told Father about my situation. They're shipping me to Aunt Stephanie's."

"No shit." Phillip lit a cigarette. "I guess Lewis wins."

"Lewis is Father's little puppet. He can die for all I care."

"When do you leave?"

The surreal truth took the wind out of Lara. If she let it, it would make her cry. "Mother will return Sunday night and drive me to Chicago. I fly out Monday."

Phillip took her by the shoulders and looked her in the eye. "Let's go out in style, Lara. You and me. This party will be legendary."

MOM

Daphne

"What's wrong, honey?" Dad's voice through the phone receiver felt like a calming salve.

"I don't know," I said. My throat closed. I hugged my knees to my chest and took another tissue from the box next to me on the couch.

"Are you crying?"

My chest heaved a few times before I could get the word out. "Yes."

"Hey, I'm here for you. Let's talk this through. What's going on?"

I sniffed. "I don't know. I'm really scared."

"Of what?"

"I'm worried something is going to happen to my friends." I left out the part where I knew one of them was going to drown. Maybe I shouldn't have.

"Like what?"

The tears streamed down my face. I tried to dry them, but they kept coming. I wanted to share with him. I wanted him to know what I was going through. The visions scared me. No. They terrified me. "Remember that Christmas at Grandma and Grandpa's?"

"That was a long time ago."

"I know. I was five."

"You wouldn't sit on Grandpa's lap."

"That's because I knew he was going to die."

Dad was silent for a few beats. "I'd forgotten about that. We found out Dad had pancreatic cancer a few months later."

"It's happening again."

"What is?"

"Daddy . . ."

Brandon and Sammy came tearing down the stairs with Duke. I was supposed to be watching them while Marianne and Auntie Beth went to the laundromat. I thought Margot was entertaining them with a card game upstairs.

Brandon sat on the couch next to me and Sammy dropped to his knees on the floor where their Hot Wheels cars were piled up like an accident on the highway. "Who are you talking to?"

"What are you scared of, Daph?" Dad asked.

Brandon touched my face. "Are you crying?"

I pushed my brother away and got off the couch. A half dozen dirty tissues fell on the floor. I told Dad, "The neighbors . . ."

"Your friends? Are you scared of them?"

"Not *of* them."

"You're worried something's going to happen to them?"

"Yes." I stretched the phone cord and walked through the kitchen doorway.

"Who are you talking to?" Brandon asked.

"My friends don't know, and I'm so worried. I don't know how to tell them."

Brandon followed me. He tugged on the cord. "Is that Dad?"

I covered the receiver. "Yes. Leave me alone."

"What do you think will happen?" Dad asked. "Can you just tell them the truth? Can you warn them to be careful?"

"Dad, Dad, Dad!" Brandon wouldn't get out of my face, and I didn't feel comfortable sharing anymore.

"Brandon really wants to talk to you," I said.

Dad said, "Daphne wait—" But I handed the phone to Brandon, and he took it to the couch.

I returned home after a long walk down the shore. I never got to tell my dad what was really going on. That I thought I was cursed. Because while walking, it hit me how off-axis, how out of balance and weird this summer had gotten. I thought of Phillip stealing from the little store. Of Tony dealing drugs and Lara trying to give me quaaludes. That Lara was pregnant. That Lewis tried to get in my pants.

You want this.

No. I hadn't wanted any of it.

Poor Lara. I couldn't imagine what she was going through. And she wants to have a party?

But the party was tops on my mind. I'd seen it unfold like a bad magic trick.

Freak.

I wanted to cry again.

Marianne and Auntie Beth were waiting for me when I got home. They sent Sammy and Brandon upstairs and sat me down in the big wingback chair in the living room.

I looked around for Margot. I needed an ally.

"Where were you?" Marianne asked. "You were supposed to be watching Brandon and Sammy. They made a huge mess in the kitchen. Cereal is everywhere. They spilled milk on the floor and Duke tracked it all over the house."

"Where was Margot?"

"Margot wasn't the responsible one. You were supposed to be."

"Sorry. I just went for a walk. That's all."

"With your friends?" Auntie Beth asked.

"No." I scowled. If I were them, would I believe me?

My aunt took a stance with her hand on her hip. "I found the Solo cup with vodka and melted ice, Daphne. I did some detective work and figured out that it didn't belong to any of us."

"Why were you drinking?" Marianne asked.

I shrugged.

Marianne sat in the chair opposite me. "It's those neighbor kids, isn't it?"

Auntie Beth crossed her arms. "It has nothing to do with them, Marianne. This is all on Daphne."

"Do you mind, Beth? I'll deal with this."

"Okay. I'm going to put the laundry away." Auntie Beth puttered around, picking up empty glasses and stacking cards. When she finally crept away, Marianne's shoulders dropped.

"What's going on, Daph?"

I dropped my head into my hands and started sobbing. I never told Dad about the premonition. I couldn't tell my mom.

Marianne slid into the big wingback with me, and I curled into her. I cried all over her shirt, soaking the sleeve. For the first time since the divorce I really, really needed her.

And Mom was there for me.

CHAPTER 56

SEARCH WARRANT

July 30th: Mark

Dew drops in the grass glistened in the early morning sun's rays. Before dawn, the cops arrived with a search warrant and started tearing apart the inside of Mark's trailer. The dogs didn't stop barking. Three officers and a K-9 unit with a German Shepherd ransacked the trailer, upturned the couch and mattresses. They dug through cabinets and piles of clothing. Pots and pans strewn out the door lay in a pile.

Mark bent over the side of the patrol car with his hands spread wide. Deputy Brandt Simmons kicked Mark's feet wider as he patted him down.

"What the hell are you looking for?" Mark asked.

"Anything." Brandt released Mark. "Someone said you broke parole."

"Who? I haven't done anything!" Mark turned around and raised a fist at his cousin.

Jim Strickland pulled Mark off and held his arms behind his back. "Don't go doin' something you'll regret."

"Are you dealing?" Brandt asked. "Making a little extra cash on the side?"

"No!"

An officer with a German Shepherd walked around the yard and the dog. *Goddam dogs!* "Shut up!" Mark yelled at them.

A laundry basket full of clothes flew out the trailer door and landed on the pile.

"Hey, do you mind? We live here!" Pops said. The dogs started up again. He held Jenny's leash taut.

Brandt stood two feet from Mark. "The school's full of drugs. Before the end of this camp session, they busted a half dozen kids for smoking on campus. Some had narcotics."

"I told you where the drugs came from. Tony Gennaro. He's pushing it. Why don't you go after him?"

Brandt placed his hands on his gun belt. "The order came from Marion County. From the prosecutor's office. It's not even their jurisdiction."

Mark stiffened, his mouth hanging open. "Prosecutor Vaughan?"

Brandt spit in the grass to confirm it: The search warrant came from none other than John Vaughan the Third. This was revenge. He knew Lara was pregnant. And he knew Mark had something to do with it.

"There's nothing in here, chief. The place is clean." The female officer, Gretchen Olsen, stepped off the trailer and picked up an old Revere Ware pot. She set it on the pile—as if that helped clean up the mess—and signaled the others. "We're through here."

The officer with the K-9 led the dog to the car. The German Shepherd hopped in. The other cops congregated and quietly stole incriminating gazes at Mark.

Jim Strickland finally let go of Mark. "So, you've covered your bases, Walters. You think you're off the hook?"

"No, sir, I don't." Mark spun to face him. "But I got a feeling Vaughan's not gonna stop until he puts me back in prison."

"I'm on your side, Mark." Brandt's sunglasses tan made racoon eyes. "I never believed you hurt that kid on purpose. It was politics. I know that."

"This isn't about politics."

"Then what?" Jim asked.

Pops put Jenny back in the pen with the other dogs, then struggled with the gate. He muttered to himself and stooped over to pick up a frying pan. Eventually, someone had to take care of the old man. Though he hoped that day didn't come anytime soon, Mark still hoped he could be around for his Pops one day.

Mark looked out over the horizon. In a near whisper, he admitted the truth. "Vaughan's daughter is pregnant. He thinks I'm the dad."

Jim let out a grunt. "Jesus."

Brandt only shook his head. "What are you going to do?"

"She's too young to have a kid," Mark said. "She wants an abortion. I suspect her family will take care of it the way they see fit."

"Well, believe it or not, I'm on your side, Mark," Brandt said. "I don't want the prosecutor to win. I never did."

"Summer will be over soon," Jim said." You need to behave until they all go back to Indy."

No one spoke for a moment. Finally, Brandt said, "So, are you ready to help us?"

"There's something else you need to know," Mark said. "There's a party tonight at the Vaughans' house. The kids invited everyone they know. People are coming up from Indy. Summer stock from all around the lake will be there. I think Tony Gennaro's staying on the lake with renters. He's been here all summer, and like I said, he's selling pot, pills, you name it. He'll be at the party too."

Brandt and Jim exchanged glances. "Thanks, Mark," Brandt said.

Mark crossed his arms and kicked a stone near his feet. An inner voice told him not to go to the party. The problem was, he'd gotten too close not to see this through.

CHAPTER 57

DÉJÀ VU

Daphne

Something felt off. The gloomy and windy weather churned the lake, lashing the boats in their lifts and tossing sailboats around like tub toys.

Mom was there for me, but she also grounded me again. Which made me miserable. I wanted to go next door. I wanted to see Lara and hear about her party, whenever that was. Though I couldn't face Lewis after what he did, I needed to be sure Lara was okay. That she was getting her problem taken care of.

And I didn't know what to do about the vision. I wanted so badly to tell Lara, but I couldn't risk pushing her away.

It felt like everything hung on a precarious perch.

I sat at the piano wishing I could play Chopin's "Revolutionary Étude," or the first movement of Beethoven's *Pathétique*. I was hurt and angry and needed to express it.

Raindrops hammered at the lake, but I went out to the end of the dock anyway. I pulled my hood over my hair and sat on a towel. A lost, hopeless feeling fell on me like the rain on my shoulders.

Water lapped against the pilings and slapped the bottom of the

Hydrodyne. The random rhythm had voices behind it. Shouts like someone calling. Their urgency flooded me with panic. Despite the cool temperature, my skin was on fire. I swam through a forest of lakeweeds searching for something.

No, someone.

Longing for the vision to stop, I put my fingers in my ears and hugged my knees to my chest.

That night, Tony grilled hamburgers for us. Right when we were all eating, Lara stopped by.

"Hi, wanna hang out?" she asked me. Lara wore bell bottoms and a silky bright yellow top. She looked happy and radiant. "I'm having a little party tonight."

A strong sense of déjà vu prickled my skin. I dropped my fork. "Tonight?"

Tony looked up from his burger. Crumbs and catsup stuck in his beard, and he stopped chewing.

Lara looked long and hard at Tony too. The exchange didn't go unnoticed.

"Do you two know each other?" Marianne asked.

Tony shook his head and looked down at his burger. "I don't know her."

"No." Lara's cheeks were pink. I knew she bought pot and quaaludes from Tony, but I wouldn't give that away at the dinner table.

She came over to my side. "It's going to be really radical. I mean, radical-ly normal," she said, slowly covering her mistake. "It's going to be cool. My friends are coming from Indy."

"She can't go next door, she's grounded," Brandon said with his mouth full.

"What kind of party is it?" Marianne asked.

Auntie Beth shook her head. "Marianne—"

"I'll handle this," Marianne said. She looked from Lara to me, to Tony, and I saw a decisive shift come over her. "Can you promise there won't be any booze?"

"Absolutely. Father won't allow it. We're playing board games. Mother made lemonade." Lara sank into her hip and gave Marianne her *Charlie's Angels* smile.

I knew it was a lie—which was fine—her parents were back in Indy. This was *the* party. The prickles marched up my elbows all the way to my scalp. I needed to be there for Lara. I needed to know that she'd be okay.

With both elbows on the table, Tony held his dripping hamburger with two hands. His eyes narrowed. "You should go, Daphne. You've been hanging around like a recluse."

Talk about hanging around. I glowered back at him across the table.

"So, can you come, Daphne? Chandi and Ellen will be there. They'd really like to see you."

"Your friends from Orchard Park? I'd like to *meet them* too." Blood drained from my face. I didn't want to get caught in a lie, not at this point.

"Marianne," Auntie Beth began to say—

"It's not up to you, Beth. I decide," Marianne said, sounding like she'd made up her mind.

"Mrs. Post, I'll make sure Daphne doesn't get in any trouble." Lara flipped her hair over her shoulder. She looked like a good church-going girl, a member of a key club or honor society. "I'll send her home right at eleven."

Silence filled the room, apart from Duke chewing on Brandon's handouts.

"All right," Marianne said.

"May I be excused?" I asked.

Lara and I were out the back door seconds later. Across the lake, the sky burned orange under a smear of dark clouds.

THE FRAME-UP

August 1st: Mark

This time when Tony called, Mark was ready. All the engine parts were greased and oiled. The only gear missing was Tony. Mark was done with him.

Tony asked, "Any new buyers?"

"Yeah," Mark said. "There's a big party tonight and rich kids from the academy will be there. They want to get high, and I told them you'd bring the goods."

"Is it—"

"At Lara's," Mark said. "I hear it's going to be huge. A bunch of

kids are driving up from Indy. I'm sending over three kegs."

"I can't really talk here," Tony said. "My old lady . . ."

"Sure. I understand." Mark was dead serious. This was a set up. "Come out to my place, we'll go together."

Tony pulled up twenty minutes later. "See you later, Pops," Mark said, looking around the trailer. Pops had cleaned up after the cops tore their place apart. For the first time since Mark got out of prison, the trailer looked nice with everything put away.

"Working tonight?" Pops asked.

"I got the night off." Mark stuffed his wallet into the back pocket of his jeans.

"Don't do anything I wouldn't do."

"Sure, Pops."

Outside, Tony sat on the hood of his 280Z. He lit a cigarette with his hands cupped to his face and blew smoke into the evening air. "Did you know I live right next door to that party? I could have walked there."

Mark never knew where Tony lived—he didn't care. But something dawned on him. "Daphne, the kid who hangs out with Lara, lives there too. Doesn't she?"

"My old lady's daughter."

"That's crazy."

"Guess where she's hanging out tonight."

Mark knew Lara invited her. She and Phillip invited everyone they knew. He suddenly worried Tony might change his mind. "So we're on? You're coming with me, right?"

Tony looked up at the dark sky. Neither the stars nor moon shone through the thick cloudy tarp. "Summer's almost over and my old lady is going all Serpico on me. I'm worried my days are numbered. As I said, I owe my Chicago supplier. He sent down a kilo of ripe bud. I needed to move it yesterday." He chuckled. "I could make bank at this party. I want to come out ahead, you catch my drift? I like you, Mark. If this works out, I know a guy in Plymouth who needs a mechanic. If you want a better job, I can hook you up."

Tony was such a weasel, Mark thought. He probably had no intention of helping Mark get a job. All the more reason to set him up.

"That's cool, man, but no thanks," Mark said. "So you'll go with me?"

"Damn right. Can you drive? I can't let my old lady see my car parked next door."

FOREWARNED

Daphne

As Lara and I passed lilies in the garden, I caught sight of a spiderweb between the long leaves. On top of it, a black widow waited patiently for prey. I shuddered as I jogged past.

"Mother's gone to Indianapolis with Father," Lara said. "We have the house to ourselves. Chandi and Ellen are here and some of my friends from Orchard Park. Come on, I'll introduce you."

Cars lined the street outside the Vaughans'. The party had started long before I got there. Lara hurried to the door. Rock music and laughter came from inside the kitchen while another car with the radio blaring unloaded kids in the Vaughan's driveway.

Lara waved and shouted hello. "Park on the street, okay?"

The driver waved and backed out. Lara held the door open for the new arrivals. "Make yourselves at home. Phillip got three kegs."

"You seem better," I said. "Did you, you know . . ." I didn't want to say the word abortion.

"Not yet. I'm supposed to fly out Monday. Father bought the plane tickets. I'm still trying to get out of it."

"Your parents didn't change their minds?"

"No." Lara lowered her brow and moved in close to me. "So stop asking. And don't tell anyone, either. Got it?"

I backed away. "Sure."

Lara took a deep breath and straightened her yellow top. "Phillip's leaving too. This is our last big blowout of the summer." She looked me in the eyes. "Listen, I'm sorry. I just don't want to think about it right now."

I understood. "I still can't believe your parents are sending you away."

"Yeah, well. This is my little revenge party, if you know what I mean." She reached into her pocket and then took my hand. As she pressed a quaalude into my palm, I felt a storm coming. Lara was angry. She was bitter about the pregnancy, and rage was building like a tornado inside her.

I pulled away and the pill fell onto the ground.

"What's wrong with you?" she asked.

I stooped to pick it up. I couldn't ignore the images. For days I'd thought about the Ouija board. That night with Lewis. The disembodied head floating under water. I took a chance. "Remember that day we played Ouija?"

Lara made a face. "You don't believe in that nonsense, do you?"

I was gob smacked. "I thought you did."

"It's just a silly game." Lara looked at the pill in my hand. "Do you want it or not?"

I handed it back to her. I wanted to stay straight tonight. "No. You shouldn't take it, either. Lara, I'm worried about you."

"Why?"

"Because I'm your friend."

"That's so sweet, Daphne. But I can't drink. These days, quaaludes are the only thing that stays down. So, let's go in there and pretend nothing's wrong. What am I saying? Everything's fine! Come on."

Something was off with her, but I couldn't pinpoint it. I massaged my hand, my wrist, and my arm. But I couldn't shake the stinging nettles. I decided not to say another word to her about my intuition.

Lara and I entered the populated kitchen, and a new wave of partiers followed us inside. Phillip's boom box blared Jimi Hendrix. Booze bottles lined the counter beside stacks of Solo cups and bottles of pop and juice. Three kegs lined the dinette, where Phillip filled cups and passed them out.

Lewis was leaning against the counter with his arms crossed. When Lara walked by him, their eyes locked. Whatever passed between them, it wasn't just sibling rivalry. Something deeper festered there.

It gave me a bad sense that all the pieces were falling into place. I needed to tell Lewis. Nervous, I stopped beside him and opened with casual conversation. "You haven't called. I thought we were going to hang out this weekend."

"After what you did?"

I searched his face for his meaning. He was angry that I'd turned away his sexual advances. "I wasn't ready," I shouted over the rising noise.

"Look, it's a party. Go party."

"I'm the one who should be angry after what you did to Lara. Do you have any idea what she's going through?"

"What do I care? Father finally sees me. He sees me! Don't you get it?"

"Is that all you care about?"

Lewis spun to face me. "You don't know anything, Daphne. Someday, I'll be a powerful politician like Father. And you, you'll always be just some girl I met the summer of seventy-six."

His words stung. Unexpected tears welled up in my eyes. I sniffed and looked away.

"Go get drunk with Lara. She likes you."

I didn't want him to know how much that hurt, so I stood taller. "Make me a drink first."

Glowering, he took two Solo cups and scooped ice from the cooler at his feet. Someone bumped into me, and I fell into Lewis. When we touched, goose bumps climbed up my arms and legs. The room momentarily darkened. Warning bells—like sirens—rang in the music. In the conversations around me, I heard people shouting and looking for someone. Beams of light streaked across the black sky and the oily surface of the lake. I gasped for breath and saw myself from far away, reaching for Lewis.

I had to stop what was coming or Lewis wouldn't see the sunrise tomorrow.

"Take it. Will you just take it?" He was handing me the drink.

I took the cup. "Lewis, you have to be careful tonight."

He didn't make eye contact. "I should have known my sister and brother would poison you." It didn't seem like he heard me. "You changed, Daphne. And to think I liked you. I really liked you."

A group of academy girls crowded nearby and asked what he was pouring. He put on a smile for them. Just like that, Lewis became the bartender for the next wave of partiers congregating in the claustrophobic room.

I felt like a freak. But I had to make him understand. I had to warn him.

CHAPTER 60

SAVE THEM

After Dark, August 1ˢᵗ: Mark

Heat lightning lit up heavy clouds over the lake. The hair on Mark's arms stood at attention. Parked cars lined the road on both sides of the house. He parked on the street five houses away from the Vaughans and he and Tony walked the rest of the way.

With his pockets loaded full of dime bags and pills, Tony shielded his face from oncoming cars. "You could have dropped me off at the house."

Mark only nodded. He couldn't wait to ditch Tony. The smell of weed coming off him could get someone high. He wouldn't be standing next to Tony when the cops arrived.

As soon as they walked inside, Tony pumped his fists into the air. "The party favors have arrived!"

Mark left him there and went looking for Lara. He had to warn her the cops were coming to crash the party.

Daphne

In one big lightning flash, it all made sense. That nagging feeling–the tingly prickles and the strange visions—had everything to do with to-night. The lightning and the churning lake. Those weeds.

Lewis . . .

After Ruth, I vowed to never tell anyone about my curse ever again. Tonight, I had to break my vow.

I sucked in air and bravery and put it on like armor. I chased Lewis through the living room, where thick pot and cigarette smoke clouded the air. Three kids at the piano banged out a horrible version of chopsticks. Sweaty drink glasses and ashtrays lined the lid. My heart fell when someone sloshed their beer over the keys. I didn't have time to stop.

I caught up with Lewis as he slipped out the back door. "Lewis, I need to tell you something!"

Outside, the air smelled of rain and electricity. Silent heat lightning streaked across the clouds. He ignored me.

"Lewis!"

"What?"

When I opened my mouth to talk, Mark brushed past. He turned as he recognized me. "Daphne. You need to go home."

I froze for a moment. The frightened look in his coffee-colored eyes scared me. *Did he know what I did?*

"I said go home." Mark looked from me to Lewis. "The shit's going down here tonight, and you don't want to be caught up in it."

A cold blast of wind blew my hair back.

He must have seen the look on my face. "Just get out of here, okay? I'll tell you later. Lewis, come with me."

Lewis crossed his arms. "I wouldn't follow you if the world was coming to an end."

The comment seemed to stun Mark. Lewis pushed him out of the way and beelined out toward the dock.

Phillip came outside with a drink in one hand and a dozen people following him. He was wired and high-strung, Phillip the Pied Piper. Near the back patio, Lara frowned at Ellen and Chandi doing cheerleading routines in the side yard.

Dangerous warning voices whispered in the wind. The party grew suddenly louder and a crowd of about twenty danced in the living room to "Play That Funky Music." The smell of pot followed two girls out the door.

A thread came unraveled, and water gushed and gurgled out of the seam, soaking everything. The ringing in my ears echoed, *Save me!*

CHAPTER 61

"FLY ROBIN FLY"

Lara

L ara was the star of the party. Just like she wanted. Like it was meant to be. Though her pants were tight, and her boobs ached, she pasted on a smile as big and bright as the sun. And with a drink in her hand, she was invincible.

She and her friends stood in the grass and watched all the cute academy guys parading like peacocks for giggling girls. A few played frisbee on the lawn. Another group out on the dock watched swimmers.

Idiots, Lara thought, *there's lightning in the sky.* She wrapped her poncho tightly around her arms to ward off the cool wind.

Chandi finished her beer and started to sway her shoulders to the music. "Fly Robin Fly" by Silver Convention vibrated the windows of the house. "Did you figure out how to deal with your situation?"

Lara elbowed Chandi. "Not here."

"Seriously." Chandi pulled Lara's elbow. The music stopped, but Chandi's voice carried. "What are you going to do about the baby?"

Everyone nearby looked at Lara.

The moment stretched out like the elastic of a paddle ball. Lara's breath went ragged. She didn't want anyone else to know. She'd already decided how to fix this and didn't need anyone's help.

"What baby?" Ellen said, clueless as ever.

Tears of embarrassment only made Lara angrier. "Shut up!"

As she stumbled away, Mark came to her side.

CHAPTER 62

THE CURTAIN OPENS AND OZ SPEAKS

Daphne

I watched Mark jog to Lara and whisper in her ear. *What does he know?*

Inside the house, the music thrummed. Tony—*Tony?*—leaned against the piano. People sloshed drinks and smoked weed openly. Flashing lights on the hill stole my attention. I watched in horror from the side yard as one, two, three sets of headlights passed Aubenaubee Lodge. They slowed in front of  the Vaughans' house and pulled into the driveway. The headlights like spotlights on a stage illuminated the yard.

The curtain drew open. As if I'd never seen the Vaughans before—seen them clearly—the light exposed them. Phillip the instigator and ringleader, in charge of nothing. Lara using her good looks to her advantage. She was cruel and given the opportunity, she'd use her friends and drag them down with her. And Lewis, the youngest, competing with his two older siblings for their father's attention.

"Come with me," Mark urged Lara to go with him.

A siren chirped and I shielded my eyes from the blinding headlights.

Police sprung from their cars. Flashing red and blue strobes sent people scurrying past me, scattering into the darkness.

The music stopped and a wave of panic spread through the partygoers. Tension wound through my body, and it sounded like the rumbling tremolo baseline of Beethoven's *Pathétique.*

"This is a bust!" someone cried.

I backed up toward the house. People rushed out the back door and ran past me.

Lara seemed to realize what was going down and pushed Mark away. "Phillip!" She searched the crowd for her brother. Out on the dock, people scrambled out of the water and gathered their clothes. I caught Lewis's gaze and ran against the exodus toward him. I ran to warn him.

Tonight, unless I could stop it, Lewis was going to die.

Activity blurred around me. Blue and red lights whirled on the side of the house. Inside, two police officers talked to Tony while others checked IDs. I pushed through the crowd of underaged drinkers still exploding out the porch door. I had to get to Lewis.

Thunder rumbled above.

Chandi caught my arm. "I can't get busted. My parents will flip out!"

Close behind her, Ellen dumped a drink in the grass and tossed the cup in the bushes.

Mark found Lara again and swept her away from the rest. "Come on!"

Lara stumbled along with Mark with her arm through his. "Where are we going?"

"Out on the boat. The cops don't want us. They're after Tony."

Mark kept Lara, Lewis, and Phillip moving out toward the dock and I followed.

I couldn't let them go out there. This was my moment to stop them. I ran after them. Mark grabbed the handle of the lift crank and began to lower the boat.

Phillip jumped in and prepared to start the engine. "Father's going to be pissed!"

"They're not here to arrest you," Mark said.

"You can't go out on the water," I told them.

"What are you, the hall monitor?" Lewis said.

"Have you seen what's happening?" Lara asked.

"It's too dangerous," I said. Heat lightning accented my words.

Lara stood between me and the boat. "Go home, Daphne."

Phillip said, "You're not in Kansas anymore, Dorothy."

"No, seriously. You have to believe me." I shouted above a thunder crack, "You can't go out there!"

Lara put her hands on her hips. "What's wrong with you? The cops are here. Father's going to have a shit fit. He's already upset with me. This is going to make it so much worse."

"I have a really bad feeling about this." I could hear the plea in my voice. "I can't explain it—well, I can. You just have to listen to me." I grabbed Lara's arm as if it were a life preserver.

"Daphne can't come with us," Lewis said.

"I know!" Lara shot back.

"Just get in!" Phillip started the engine.

Mark spun the boat lift to its lowest position. "Get in the boat, Lara!"

"Go home." Lewis shoved me out of the way.

The ticking sound of the lift, like a countdown clock or a time bomb, disappeared into the howling wind. *Was this really happening?*

"What's wrong with you, anyway?" Lara slurred at me.

Lewis and Mark jumped in the boat. Mark reached out a hand to help Lara climb in. "Let's go!"

"Please, don't go!" I tried to climb on board, but Mark stopped me with a hand on my shoulder.

"This isn't your fight, Daphne," he said. "The cops don't want you. You'll be okay if you just go home and pretend you were never here."

I looked him in the eye and saw something kind and redemptive. "Mark, something horrible will happen out there. You have to stop it."

He stared at me for a moment, then pushed the boat away from the dock.

Lara looked me in the eyes as they drifted off. "You were never one of us, anyway Daphne. Just go home."

Lightning lit the sky, punctuating her hurtful words. I stumbled backward. Ruth had said the very same thing to me when she came back to school. Tears filled my eyes.

Phillip revved the engine of the Mastercraft and took off, speeding into the oncoming storm.

CHAPTER 63

DO IT

Mark

The smattering of lightning intensified, and now bigger arcs punctuated consistent flashes. Phillip hunched over and held onto the steering wheel, ignoring the "no wake after dark" speed limit, and sped across the lake. To Mark it seemed like an hour before they reached the middle of the lake, and he finally shut off the engine.

"Who gave the cops the tip?" Phillip asked.

Mark looked out over the dark water. On shore, red and blue flashing lights from the police cars lit the house like one of those discotheques he'd seen on TV.

Lewis sat in the rear-facing passenger seat. "You think someone told them about the party? Mark's a criminal. Maybe they're after him." He smirked at Mark. "Who'd you beat up this time?"

His smug tone triggered Mark, he couldn't help it. He lunged at Lewis. He gripped Lewis's shirt and lifted him out of the seat. Looking him squarely in the eye, Mark cocked his fist and tensed every muscle in his arm.

Lewis's eyes glistened with fear. Just like Geoffrey Weir's.

Mark hesitated.

"Do it," Lara said.

A cold chill ran down Mark's spine. This night had turned into some kind of hell.

HOTWIRE

Daphne

Things spiraled out of control again, just like that winter when ice coated the world. I thought of Ruth lying on the ice. In the hospital, the back of her head was shaved and stitched. She'd changed after her fall. She turned everyone against me.

I didn't want to live through that nightmare again. I refused to do it. I could still see the Mastercraft's red and green bow

lights as it sped toward the middle of the lake. I had to follow them out there.

Ignoring the bright headlights and the cops rounding everyone up, I ran toward home.

The windows were all lit in the cottage, and Auntie Beth and Marianne stood on the patio watching the activity next door. I stayed in the shadows. Auntie Beth kept the yard lights turned off since they attracted so many bugs at night. I used the dark to my advantage and ran as quickly and quietly as I could out onto the dock.

Auntie Beth kept the key to the Hydrodyne locked up in her room. So Tony Baloney had been good for one thing—he'd shown me how to hotwire Uncle Chuck's Chris-Craft.

Lightning roiled across the sky followed by a chorus of thunderclaps.

I scrambled to untie the cover of Uncle Chuck's precious speedboat, yanked the cover off and heaved it onto the dock. I spun the lift wheel and lowered the boat into the water as the Mastercraft's lights disappeared into the night.

Waves from the approaching storm bashed against the Chris-Craft and it drifted out of the lift toward shore. In the dark, I couldn't see the dashboard. I felt along the smooth, glossy wood for the glovebox. Within seconds, I dug out a screwdriver and got to work.

Ducking down low in the driver's seat, I felt for the screws around the ignition plate and used the screwdriver to loosen them. Once removed, the plate dangled from the ignition wires. Tony had shown me one red wire and one yellow wire, but in the dark, I couldn't see the colors. A third ground wire wouldn't spark the starter.

"Daphne! What are you doing?"

I heard Marianne calling me and looked up. She and Auntie Beth waved from the dock. They wanted me to stop. But the Chris-Craft floated forward out of the lift into the shallower water, headed toward the shallow rocky shore.

This was the moment of no return.

Fumbling with the wires Tony had conveniently stripped, I touched two together. Nothing. I tried another pair and still nothing.

"Daphne!"

I dropped one wire and picked up the third.

"Daphne, stop!" Auntie Beth this time. I felt bad ignoring her.

A spark. Suddenly the engine choked to life. The dashboard lit up. I put the boat in gear and backed out.

The family had gathered on the dock. Brandon and Sammy were laughing and cheering me on. Marianne waved for me to stop, and Auntie Beth crossed her arms in fury. Margot strode to the end, matching my pace as Duke ran past her wagging his tail.

Ignoring them, I turned toward the middle of the lake and sped towards the dark spot where I last saw the Mastercraft.

SAVE ME

Daphne

Lake Carlson looked like black oil. Like it would suck you under and kill you if you let it. With one hand on the steering wheel and one hand blocking the spray of rain drops, I approached the Mastercraft slowly. I only saw three people on board.

Mark waved his hands in the air. "Cut your engine! Man overboard!"

My worst fears had materialized. I cut the engine and searched the choppy black water. I saw nothing but angry waves.

"What have you done, Lara?" I heard Phillip say despite the wind. "What have you done?"

"Lewis, stop messing around!" Lara leaned over the side. "Oh my god, Lewis, I'm sorry."

The Chris-Craft drifted closer to their boat, and I shouted, "What happened?" But I knew. One of them had killed Lewis.

Mark and Phillip leaned over the side of the Mastercraft. "I don't see him."

"There. There he is!" Lara stripped her poncho over her head and dove into the water.

"Lara! What are you doing?" Mark said, his light-colored shirt was splattered with something dark.

I felt helpless. It was all happening too fast. Not like what I imagined at all. "Where's Lewis?" I said, watching in horror as Lara swam toward something bobbing in the waves.

"I found him," Lara yelled. "I can't get his head above water."

Phillip paced on the boat like a caged animal. "This is messed up." He took a wide stance in front of the steering wheel. "Oh, God. I need to get out of here." He started the engine.

"Phillip, stop!" Mark said. "You can't leave them."

I was already perched on the side of my boat. I dove in to help Lara.

The cold hit me like a shock. Waves tossed me around and rolled over me. Ahead, Lara struggled to keep Lewis's head above water. She choked on a wave, and gulped air. "Help me get him out of the water."

I swam toward them and hit a thick mat of weeds floating on the surface. They tangled around my arms and weighed me down. I fought to stay above water, but they clung to me.

"I'm coming." I swam as fast as I could, kicking at the long strands. The more I moved, the more tangled I became. I panicked. *Save me!*

The weeds pulled me down. Something was wrong. All the images and visions this summer made no sense. I didn't have time to get my breath before the weeds dragged me under.

CHAPTER 66

HANG ON

Lara

Lewis was too heavy for Lara. She spun him onto his back and saw what she'd done. She'd swung an oar at Lewis' face. She'd expected him to catch it or something. Instead, it hit him square in the face and he went overboard.

She let go of him. *What have I done?*

Tears choked her as she struggled to stay afloat. Fucking Lewis. He'd done this to himself. He wouldn't shut up. He provoked her. *He provoked us all.*

Lara couldn't have helped it, she was so angry.

The Master Craft engine came to life.

"Hang on," Mark said. "I'm coming, Lara." He dove into the lake and swam toward her.

Lara treaded water. High waves washed Lewis down and away from her and she watched him sink. She sputtered and coughed. "He's tangled in the weeds."

Mark took one look at Lewis and said, "I'm taking you back to the boat first, then I'll get Lewis." He pulled leafy strands off her shoulders.

Lara didn't argue. Mark helped her swim to the closest boat, Daphne's

Chris-Craft. The older boat sat high on the water, but he helped Lara up, boosted her over the side and she safely flopped into it.

"You have to save Lewis," she said. "I didn't mean to—"

"It's okay. I'm going back for him." Mark dove under and vanished into the gloomy depths. He came up and took a breath. "Did you see where Daphne went?"

"No." Lara frantically searched the roiling surface with each lightning flash. She couldn't lose Daphne too. Then she saw her under the surface. "There," she shouted. "Over there!"

Mark took another breath and dove down.

CHAPTER 67

AN ANGEL

Daphne

The water bubbled and whispered, lulling me into a feeling of safety. Nestled in the forest of lakeweeds, I stopped fighting. The twisty weeds snagging my legs. It was all just like my premonitions. I heard music in the watery sounds. Like the bubbling, burbling *Sonatine* by Ravel. Piano notes fluttered and trilled a minor melody.

As darkness enveloped me, I opened my eyes one last time.

There. In the leafy depths.

Lewis's white shirt made him look like an angel. His eyes were closed, and albino lashes feathered his lids.

I wanted to call out but I had no strength left to shout, *Save me!* Could Lewis hear?

Lewis's blond hair surrounded his head like a halo. He swam to me and smiled like the day we lay on the golf course looking up at clouds.

What happened to you? I wanted to ask.

He reached for the lakeweeds tangled around my ankles and gracefully, swiftly released me. By then, I had no strength left. My body sank to the silty bottom of the lake.

The truth came as a whisper. Lewis told me what happened on the boat. He told me he betrayed their trust. He confessed everything. And now too late, he was sorry.

I felt someone pulling me to the surface.

And then, Lewis was gone.

REPLAY

Before Sunrise, August 2nd: Daphne

" . . . four, five, six, seven, eight."

The pressure on my chest woke me. I rolled to my side, coughed, and puked water. Chills wracked my body, and violent shivers shook me from the inside out. My lungs burned as I drank in air. Cool, nourishing air.

I slowly became aware that I was on the Lake Patrol boat. Someone cradled my head in their hands. "She's breathing!"

Lara.

I opened my eyes. Makeup streaked down Lara's face. She caressed my shoulders. "I'm right here, Daphne. I've got you."

I saw Lewis sitting right beside her. His hair dripping wet and his face so pale. They wouldn't find him alive.

I'm sorry. I mouthed the words.

It wasn't your fault, he said.

Lara pinched her mouth closed and shook her head. She'd been crying.

I tried to sit up.

"Careful." As a uniformed officer kneeled down beside me, Lewis vanished. The officer pressed two fingers against the soft side of my wrist, timing my pulse.

Mark huddled nearby with wet hair. A heavy blanket was draped over his shoulders. "Is she okay?"

"She's going to be fine," an EMT said.

Lara helped me up and someone laid something heavy across my back. I coughed. "Did you find Lewis?" I meant to ask, did you find Lewis's body, but I couldn't form the words.

"We're searching for him," the officer said.

Lara shivered, but it didn't seem to be from the cold. Mark slid to her side and shared his blanket with her.

The Lake Patrol officers called out over the water. It was a replay of the voices and images I'd heard all summer. Spotlight beams crisscrossed like lines from a spirograph. Thunder rumbled farther away, and the wind and rain stopped. The whole world seemed to have changed into a ghostly dream.

CHAPTER 69

THE TRUTH?

Daphne

Lewis's body was pulled from the lake around sunup. The police didn't say the cause of death. I knew there was more to it than drowning. Lewis had told me.

The EMTs listened to my breathing and checked my heart rate. I'd been lucky, they said. No water in my lungs.

I didn't feel lucky. I lost a friend.

I sat in a hard wooden chair across from Deputy Marshal Brandt Simmons. Outside the window, the black sky faded to red on the horizon. To me it still felt like the middle of the night. My short hair and clothes were still damp. Though it was the height of summer, a scratchy woolen police-issue blanket wrapped around my shoulders couldn't stave off the chills.

The sparsely furnished police station smelled like burnt coffee. The putrid pastel-green concrete-block walls glowed like a ghost possessed them. From the flickering fluorescent bulb to the mole on Simmons' forehead, it was all familiar. Until this moment, I had chosen to ignore each and every sign.

My mom stood beside me. Though I was glad she was there, I didn't really need her support.

The female officer I recognized entered the room and reached out her hand. "I'm Deputy Gretchen Olsen. So nice to meet you, Daphne. Can you tell us what you saw last night?"

Deputy Olsen's handshake was firm and warm. Her watery green eyes were filled with concern.

"I wasn't there when it happened." I tensed at the memory. This summer I wanted more than anything to be friends with Lara and Lewis. They were beautiful, fallen angels.

"Take your time," Simmons said. His tan uniform sleeves were rolled twice, exposing a few inches of black hair on his arms and a Timex watch with green radium dashes where the numbers would be.

"We were all hanging out at the Vaughans," I said.

The officer's pen made staccato sounds on the paper as he wrote notes. "How well did you know them?"

How well, indeed? I thought about each time I grazed Lara's hand and saw images of her home life. Of her baby girl. I thought about Lewis and all the promise of his talent, upbringing, and youth. Phillip's unknown future lay ahead, and still I wondered if I really knew who any of them were.

The Vaughans had offered a way to escape the depressing reality of my life. Just as I was taken in by their fashionable clothes and good looks, they took me under their broken wings and offered something I needed as much as air. They became my friends. "I guess I knew them pretty well."

"Did you know Mark Walters was once convicted of assault?" Deputy Marshal Simmons said. "If he had something to do with last night's events, I need you to tell me."

My eyes darted from Mom to Simmons to the paper pad on the table. What I knew about Mark and Lara wasn't my business to share. "He didn't hurt anyone. He tried to stop it. Like I did."

"Stop what?"

"Something bad was going to happen. I just . . . I just knew."

Deputy Olsen had smooth rosy cheeks. Those green eyes had turned warm and bright, like a campfire. "How did you know?"

I was so tired. I shrugged off the blanket and Mom folded it. "I get these feelings. Prickles on my skin. Like bug bites, stings or tiny thorns tearing at my skin. It usually comes with an image."

"Tell me about that."

I briefly described the day we played the Ouija game. Of all the times I received impressions, playing a game seemed like the most relatable experience. I didn't give details, but I did share my unreasonable fear of the weeds.

"Daphne's grandmother is psychic," Mom said.

It was another secret that Mom kept from me. I stared at her. "No one ever told me that."

"She has dreams that come true. Nothing like that has ever happened to me, but maybe you inherited the gift from her."

I half smiled at her. Mom was the last person I expected to believe me.

"I fully believe in those gut feelings," Deputy Olsen said. "I always tell my officers if it smells bad, or it feels off, it probably is. It's your body telling you what your brain cannot. It's a little like ESP. But ESP isn't exactly the right term," Deputy Olsen added. "What you're describing is clairvoyance. I've been reading about it in the library."

"The Carlson Public Library?" Simmons asked.

"The Academy Library. My point is, I fully believe in psychic experiences. What you're telling us is that you were forewarned about Lewis's death."

The validation from Deputy Olsen was enough to bring tears to my eyes.

Simmons looked skeptical. "Daphne, I don't know anything about ESP. I'm not sure I believe that. So I'm going to have you write out these events as you know them to be true. Tell me only the facts without any speculation or woowoo." He pushed a piece of paper and pen toward me, and I began writing.

Without woowoo. No Problem. I wasn't ready to commit to paper the truth about my *ESP.*

Not a freak? I wasn't convinced.

A GOOD MAN

August 2nd: Mark

After the police questioned Mark, he arrived home around lunchtime. He inhaled deeply, savoring the smell of the lake mixed with cut grass. Despite all that happened, things could be worse.

Brandt thanked Mark and told him that he arrested Tony and confiscated several pounds of weed along with several bottles of the narcotics Tony intended to sell. They also arrested a handful of teenagers for underage drinking, and a number of kids for possession—a mild charge compared to what Tony faced. Simmons considered charging John Vaughan and his wife Adelaide for hosting a party for minors but knew Vaughan would slip out from under those charges.

Mark surmised that when they found Lewis, there would be evidence of severe head injuries. The Medical Examiner would perform an autopsy to determine the  cause of Lewis's death before an investigation could get underway. For once in his life, Mark hoped John Vaughan would perform his magic and help his children escape the hell of prison.

At the trailer, Mark pulled open the screen door, full of holes, and it fell off the hinges into the yard. It didn't matter. The flies found ways to get in anyway. He wanted to fix things up, but he wasn't making enough money at The Bar. His income only supported him and Pops with barely enough left over to care for the dogs.

Jenny retrieved a ball and dropped it at his feet. He stooped to pick it up and when he rose to throw it again, Pops stood in the doorway of the trailer. He slicked a hand through his hair and hiked his loose jeans up around his waist. "You working last night? You didn't come home."

"I was at the police station."

"Oh." Pops went back inside.

Jenny jogged back with the ball and lay it down at Mark's feet. The old golden retriever didn't have the energy she used to. Right now, neither did Mark.

Pops came back outside with two cups of black coffee. He handed one to Mark. "Want to talk about it?"

Mark sipped his coffee and shook his head. "Why are some folks born evil, Pops?" It was an absurd question. And evil wasn't the right word. He wondered why some people did bad things. Like some of the guys in prison. He heard their stories. Some of them were there simply because they reacted to a situation. Some were irresponsible or reckless. Some just never managed to get a break. Like Mark.

As if waiting for more. Pops didn't answer.

"I saw a kid die last night," Mark said.

Pops sipped his coffee and listened.

"But I saved another kid's life."

"Your mother and I always knew you'd turn out to be a good man." Pops looked at him as if seeing his son for the first time.

They leaned on the rusty old Cadillac and looked wistfully out in the distance.

There, he saw someone moving through the trees.

CHAPTER 71

GOODBYE

Lara

Needing air, Lara had walked from the police station in Carlson. She wasn't ready to face her father and mother, so she didn't go back to the rental house. Mark seemed surprised to see her approaching from the trees, but he'd met her with open arms. Outside his trailer, Mark tapped down a soft pack of Camel cigarettes and held it out to Lara, sitting cross-legged in the grass beside him. She declined. "No thanks. They make me sick."

"That's a first." Mark was kidding around, but Lara was not.

She brushed the soft dandelion flower against her lips. "Father and Mother are on their way back from Indianapolis. They have to identify Lewis's body."

"Did you tell them what happened?"

"The police called them while I was at the station."

Mark lit his cigarette. "What about Phillip? Did he go back to the house?"

"I haven't been back. But I bet he went to Minnesota." She looked at the white Indiana sky.

Cicadas purred in distant trees.

Out of habit, Mark popped his jaw and blew smoke rings.

"I hope someday when I'm watching the Olympics, I'll see my brother out there skating like his life depends on it," Lara said. "I hope he is happy to be doing something he loves."

"How are you doing, Lara?"

She didn't know how to answer. She had behaved shamefully. Regretfully. She'd treated Mark with indifference. She'd said something to Daphne that made her face heat with embarrassment. *You were never one of us.* Lara didn't mean to hurt Daphne's feelings. After all, Daphne was the only one she could confide in this summer. She tried to forget the look of utter horror on her friend's face and hoped Daphne would forgive her.

But her relationship with Lewis had been different.

And now it was over.

Lara held her belly. Heavy cramps started when she got to the police station. They hadn't stopped. It looked like she would get what she wanted. But she wouldn't tell Mark about it.

She stretched her legs out in the green grass and picked another dandelion. "Well," she answered Mark's question, "I'm angry at Phillip for leaving me. Besides that, I'm nauseous all the time. I have a headache, and I want a drink."

"I meant about Lewis."

Lara didn't answer. Her tangled hair fell into her lap. She rolled the flower between her fingers.

"I'm sorry he died, Lara. That doesn't mean much, I know. But you're too young to go through this. Is there anything I can do?"

"No." Lara beheaded the dandelion. "I just came to say goodbye."

CHAPTER 72

A NEW PIANO

Daphne

When I returned to Aubenaubee Lodge, the Vaughans' yard next door looked like a battlefield. Trash was strewn in bushes and bottles were broken on the rock wall. Yellow tape blocked off the dock, as if anyone wanted to go out there. The Mastercraft was not in the lift. The Chris-Craft was gone too. Probably considered part of a crime scene. What would Uncle Chuck have to say about that?

I'd had enough of boats and the lake to last a lifetime.

I collapsed into my bed and sadness enveloped me. Grief about Lewis's death, and sorrow for Lara and Phillip shuddered through my body. I cried myself to sleep.

Hours later, I woke to the smells of bacon and coffee. Margot had made her bed and the sun's reflection off the water shone on the ceiling. The steady rhythm of waves lapping the shore reminded me there were only two weeks left in the summer.

It was almost over.

I dressed in shorts, and found Lewis's polo shirt, the one he lent me earlier this summer. It still smelled like him. Like faded Polo cologne and suntan oil. When I pulled it over my head, the closet door popped open.

A gust of wind whistled through the screen in the open window.

I wasn't scared of it anymore. I pulled the closet door open wide and

peered inside. No one was there. Just the ancient curtain rods and zippered clothing bags. But a clear thought formed in my mind. I recalled Lewis pulling me out of the weeds and pushing me to the surface.

Lewis saved my life. *Save me.* Perhaps the voice in my premonition had been my own.

Dad's voice floated up the stairs. "Help me move that couch out of the way." He must have arrived while I slept.

"Not there. Here." Nana's voice followed. *Nana's here too?*

I rushed down the steps past the stag head and its all-knowing eyes. Today, the taxidermized stag seemed to be smiling.

In the living room, two big men wheeled a brand-new upright piano into the room. Nana directed the movers with her scarves and floor-length muumuu flowing behind her. "Put it here. And be sure to take that old piano with you."

A man's voice said, "Where should we deliver it?"

"I don't know," Nana replied. "Drop it in the lake for all I care. Just get that thing out of here."

They hoisted the piano onto the furniture dolly and moved it out of the way. Brandon and Sammy peered over the back of the couch and Dad held Duke's collar.

When they cleared the room, I approached the new upright with tears in my eyes. My fingers tingled in anticipation at the sight of the shiny new ivories.

"Go on." Dad released Duke. "Sit down and play something."

I sank onto the piano bench. "I haven't really practiced this summer." My hands hovered above the keys.

"That's okay," Mom said. "I'm sure it will come back to you." She handed me the piano books.

I spread them out on the music stand but didn't need them. This piano was already singing to me. I began the second movement of Beethoven's *Pathétique* No. 8. The peaceful cantabile melody flowed from my fingertips, and from the kitchen, Nana's singing voice drifted through the air. Mom joined in harmony, and both hummed along with the soothing song.

Emotion choked me as I reached the end of the movement. I put my hands over my face and cried.

Dad sat down at the bench and put an arm around me. Soon, I felt another hand on my arm, and another stroking my back. Brandon slid into my lap and Duke licked my bare knee. My family gathered all around.

Nana rubbed my shoulder. "I've been trying to get this piano here all summer, you know."

"She doesn't suck," Brandon said.

"Brandon, language!" Auntie Beth said.

Sammy giggled.

"No, she doesn't suck." Margot said. "She's really good."

I hugged Nana. "Thank you, so much. I really missed playing. I had to go to the neighbor's house and . . ." I could no longer speak. My heart filled with melancholy, where sorrow, tranquility, and relief tied me in knots.

CHAPTER 73

AN UNFORTUNATE ACCIDENT

Daphne

Several days passed quietly as the summer of 76 entered its final act. Classes at the academy would resume in a few short weeks. Crime scene tape remained at the Vaughan cottage, but no cars came or went. I stood at the window wondering what happened to Lara and Phillip. Though Lara was sometimes hard to please, I longed to find out if she was okay. I missed them all.

While practicing the Chopin étude, I listened to Auntie Beth, Mom, and Dad talking on the patio. I heard Tony's name.

"I heard he's in prison awaiting a hearing," Dad said.

Mom said, "How could I be so blind?"

Perhaps Mom only saw what she wanted to. I realized how much alike we were.

Margot came inside with wet feet and pockets full of treasures from the lake. She slid into the chair beside me with a new look of respect for me. I'd earned it the hard way.

I swallowed the lump in my throat. "Can you show me how to make a halter for the horses again?"

"I'm getting tired of playing with dolls. Want to go for a walk?"

I took Margot's hand. As we started down to the shore, Duke loped after us, followed by Brandon and Sammy.

The sky was clear of clouds and the hum of motorboats and jet skis filled the hot August air. Swarms of no-see-ums hung over the water gently lapping the shore. We explored the shore along the way, collecting purple shells and wading in the shallows near larger, newer mansions. None, I believed, had the character or warmth of Aubenaubee Lodge.

At the corner store, Brandon bought Bottle Caps and Wax Candy Bottles full of colorful sweet liquid. Margot's favorite was Necco wafers. Sammy liked M&M's. I waited in the parking lot with Duke until Margot came out. When it was my turn, I opted for the newest rage, Bubble Yum.

They stuffed their treats into my purse, and we walked home along the road. The golf course was devoid of golfers, so I allowed Brandon to run in the grass with Duke. Halfway home, we stopped at a bubbling, natural spring well. Cold water smelling of minerals poured from a three-foot-long pipe sticking out of the ground. A square metal grate coated with orange residue from the iron-heavy water surrounded the pipe. Beneath it, water dripped and splashed into a dark hole in the ground. I never tasted water so rejuvenating. So refreshing.

Duke and the kids took turns sipping from the ancient pipe while I gazed out at the public pier. There, under the trees, stood someone wearing a familiar orange poncho.

"Margot, will you make sure the boys get home safely?" I asked. "I need to go talk to someone."

Margot saw her too, and for once, she didn't complain. "No problem, Daph."

Lara gazed out at the lake. "I hoped you'd stop by. When I saw you all go for a walk, I followed you."

I followed her gaze out to the choppy, gray water. The strong wind blew my longer hair out of my eyes. "I didn't know you were still next door. Where are your parents? I haven't seen any cars."

"They're in Indy. They drove me home after . . . you know."

I never had a chance to talk to her after that night. My heart went out to her now. "I'm so sorry, Lara."

Lara kept her sights on a single sailboat fluttering in the wind.

"Phillip hasn't been in contact with anyone. He didn't tell the police what actually happened. Neither did Mark."

"Mark's a good friend."

"You are too."

"My grandmother sent Mark a check for saving my life. She was very, very grateful, I guess. I heard it was enough to help him buy a house if he wants."

"I heard," she said. "He said he wants to go to law school."

"So you're in touch with him?"

"I stopped by The Bar."

I watched a sailboat speed across the water. I wished I'd been able to warn Lara. I still carried guilt about it. "I'm sorry I wasn't there when it happened."

"Did you know, Father refused the autopsy? Called it an unfortunate accident. A tragedy—which it was. He's using the story to boost his campaign. He tells reporters, 'We're all suffering.' Channel Six News was at the funeral." A tear rolled down Lara's cheek. She didn't wipe it away. "I left Indy this morning."

"You did?" I admired her strength and determination.

Lara nodded. "I'm dropping out of high school. I'm going to California—to Hollywood. I hitchhiked to Carlson and for now I'm staying in the empty house. I know where they keep the key."

"The cows in Montana will miss you," I said, hoping to get a smile from her.

She chuckled. "I won't miss them. But hey. Good luck at Orchard Park this fall. There's this guy, Spencer Thorne, in the junior class. You'd like him. Tell Chandi I said thanks for helping out. And let Ellen know, I think she'll make a great head cheerleader." Lara's gaze hadn't wavered from the middle of the lake.

I didn't know what to say. "What about the—"

"I miscarried."

"Oh, Lara, I'm so sorry."

"I suppose it was inevitable. I was drinking a lot this summer." Lara turned away from the lake and wiped her tears. She pulled me in for a hug and I tried to ignore the images of Lara's future. There were smiles and happy times ahead, but not for many years to come.

At the base of the dock, where wooden planks were half buried under sand, I saw her brother Lewis' ghost wandering the shoreline. His gaze followed Lara's, looking out at the spot where he drowned. Then he walked right into the lake—without making a ripple—and he disappeared.

EPILOGUE

I kept it secret from Lara. I didn't tell her about Lewis's ghost. I tucked away all the stories I'd never tell about this summer and packed my suitcase. The last week of August approached, with breezes carrying the scents of marigolds, leaves, and autumn. I thought about the new school and making new friends. Tomorrow, we'd close up the house and drive back to Indianapolis.

In the bedroom at the top of the stairs, I lay between cool sheets with a heavy comforter tucked under my chin. In the bed next to mine, Margot slept with her head gear on and her mouth open. Somehow, the closet on the other side of the room had become less scary.

In the dark, I lay awake listening to the lake lick the retaining wall under the sycamore tree. Over those soft soothing sounds, I heard the closet door pop open. I heard someone or something drift past my bed and pass through the door.

A few minutes later, I heard talking downstairs. At first it was unintelligible whispers. Then a single syllable or word stuck out. I grew curious and slid my feet to the floor. The bedroom door popped open before I touched it.

Duke lay at the top of the stairs. He looked up with a soft jingle of his tags. The stuffed deer gazed at us. A low light glowed in the living room, and Nana spoke softly. "I've missed you this summer. But it's important for me to stay busy. You understand."

"Yes," said the whisper of a man's voice.

I crept down the stairs, skipping the creaky ones. When I arrived at the bottom, I peeked around the corner. Nana, with her back to the stairs, faced the soldier I imagined living in the closet. Grandpa Mortensen wore a pressed military uniform and cap. Though he flickered like bad television reception, he gleamed in the yellow lamplight.

"This one's so much like you, Harriet," he said and then he faded away, leaving nothing but a wisp of smoke.

A moth landed on the lampshade and fluttered his wings.

Nana turned in her chair. "Daphne. What are you doing up?"

"I heard you talking to Grandpa." I stepped into the room.

"You can see him too?"

"I couldn't always. But a few weeks ago—"

"You almost drowned."

I nodded. *Not a freak,* I thought.

"He told me he was watching you this summer," Nana continued. "He was trying to help you."

I plopped down in the chair next to her. "What else did Grandpa say?"

Duke lumbered down the stairs and swished past us, sniffing the floor where Grandpa had been.

"When I'm here at the lake, he tells me everything. That's why I kept his uniform in the closet upstairs. I'm afraid if I get rid of it, he won't return. I don't know if that's true or not." Nana turned a ring on her finger.

"Nana, that ring . . ."

"Beth told me you found it in the lake. I let her borrow it many years ago. I asked for it back last night."

"He gave it to you," I said.

She nodded. "He did."

"When I was little, I was afraid of the closet in our bedroom. I was scared of ghosts, though I didn't ever see one."

Nana's bright eyes sparkled. "Nothing to be afraid of. He was killed in the war. He can't hurt you." She took one of my hands in her knobby fingers. "He *won't* hurt you."

"Do you have prickly feelings when something bad is going to happen?"

"All the time, Daphne. Do you?"

"This summer, I had lots of them."

"Oh, dear. I'm so sorry about your friends. It must have been really scary for you."

My nose grew stuffy. I cleared my throat. "I wish I'd said something sooner. I could have stopped it from happening."

Nana gazed past my shoulder. "I knew when Ed was going to die. But there was a war going on. Your grandpa was determined to help. And they needed him. I couldn't stop him from going. What I'm trying to say is, sometimes, there's nothing you can do. Sometimes, people make their own choices."

I sniffed away tears.

"Come. Walk with me to my bedroom and I'll tell you a story."

We talked until the sky brightened in the east. Nana let me in on secrets she'd kept from Mom and Auntie Beth. I told her about Ruth and the Vaughans. As the sun rose, I came to terms with Lewis's death. I stopped feeling guilty about knowing what would eventually happen. None of it was my fault. I couldn't have changed a thing.

The End

ACKNOWLEDGEMENTS

It has taken five years and countless revisions to finally publish this book. I couldn't have done it without you. You readers and reviewers make this writing life so worthwhile.

Special gratitude goes out to numerous editors. Kim Taylor Blakemore helped with the first draft. Christine DeSmet was key to developing Daphne's musical scenes and the piano as a secondary character in the book. Jess Taylor brought Mark Walters out of the shadows and into the light. And finally Steve Anderson's clear copy edits saved this book from permanent residence in a drawer. I'm also grateful for the Dark and Stormy critique group. Sharon Michalove, Sharon Boehlefeld, Amanda Marbais, and Sara Brass, your continued support and encouragement means the world.

So many readers have helped me along this journey. Hugs to you, Margaret, Sharon Lynn, Val, John DeDakis, Nick, Sheila, Judy, Vicki and Dave. I'm lucky to have you in my supportive community which includes, Sisters in Crime, Wisconsin Writers, Chicagoland Siblings, and the Blackbirds.

But most of all, husband, you've been at the heart of this. Your support and encouragement keeps me going.

Watch the video on Tracey's
YouTube Channel
@traceys.phillips-author9669

FOREWARNED SOUNDTRACK

Born to be Wild – Steppenwolf
Piano Man – Billy Joel
Dirty Work – Steely Dan
Purple Haze – Jimi Hendrix
Fame – David Bowie
Sara Smile – Daryl Hall and John Oats
Seargent Pepper's Lonely Hearts Club Band – The Beatles
Candle in the Wind – Elton John
Pinball Wizard – The Who
Play that Funky Music – Wild Cherry
Fly Robin Fly – Silver Convention
Moonlight Sonata – Beethoven
Sonata no. 2, *The Pathetique*, First movement – Beethoven
Sonata no. 2, *The Pathetique*, Second movement – Beethoven
Trois Etude no. 1 – Chopin

Link to Playlist on Amazon Music

Tracey S. Phillips: Tracey has played the piano since age three. She considers herself a serial artist who is an avid gardener, musician, piano teacher, artist, and author. She writes psychological thrillers and romantic suspense. Her debut, BEST KEPT SECRETS (Crooked Lane Books, 2019) won a Hugh Holton Award in 2018. She is a two-time finalist for the Claymore Award for best unpublished novel in '22, and '23. She has published 3 short stories, and one was a finalist for Writers' Digest Genre Fiction awards. In 2020 she created Blackbird Writers, a community of like-minded authors willing to help promote each other and share their love of stories with readers. She is an empty nester living in Wisconsin with her husband and like her character Daphne, she occasionally speaks with spirits on the other side.

Start Reading *Best Kept Secrets* here.